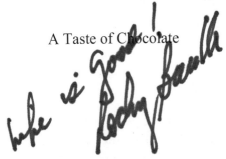

A Taste of Chocolate

by

ROCKY BARILLA

D1616032

ROSQUETE PRESS

ii   Rocky Barilla

Copyright © 2023 Rosquete Press

All rights reserved. No part of this book may be used or
reproduced in any manner without the written permission of
the copyright owner, rosquetepress@gmail.com, except in the
case of brief quotations in critical articles and reviews. This is
a work of fiction. Names, characters, places, and events are
either the product of the author's imagination or are used
fictitiously, and any resemblance to actual persons, living or
dead, events, or locales is entirely coincidental.

Cover and book design by Rocky Barilla © 2023

Library of Congress Control Number: 2021919096
ISBN: 978-0-9904851-9-3

OTHER WORKS BY ROCKY BARILLA

LA PERLA NEGRA – The Black Pearl
First Place Winner of the 2023 International Latino Book Awards for Best Novel - Historical Fiction

SHATTERED DREAMS
Award Winner of the 2023 Latino Literary Now's Latino Books into Movies Awards for Latino-Themed Novel
Honorable Mention Winner of the 2022 International Latino Book Awards for the Rodolfo Anaya Best Latino-Focused Fiction Book

SANCTUARY
Award Winner of the 2023 Latino Literary Now's Latino Books into Movies Awards - Drama
Honorable Mention Winner of the 2021 International Latino Book Awards for the Rodolfo Anaya Best Latino-Focused Fiction Book

STARS
Honorable Mention Winner of the 2020 International Latino Book Awards for Best Novel - Romance

Esmeralda
First Place Winner of the 2019 International Latino Book Awards for Best Novel - Fantasy Fiction

Harmony of Colors
Second Place Winner of the 2018 International Latino Book Awards for Best Novel - Latino-Focused Fiction

Ay to Zi
Award Winner of the 2018 Latino Literary Now's Latino Books into Movies Awards - Romance
Second Place Winner of the 2017 International Latino Book Awards for Best Novel – Romance

The Devil's Disciple
Award Winner of the 2018 Latino Literary Now's Latino Books
into Movies Awards - Suspense/Mystery
Second Place Winner of the 2016 International Latino Book
Awards for Best Novel – Mystery

A Taste of Honey
First Place Winner of the 2015 Latino Literary Now's Latino
Books into Movies Awards - Fantasy Fiction
Second Place Winner of the 2015 International Latino Book
Awards for Best Novel - Fantasy Fiction

*All works are published by Rosquete Press. All works are or
will be available as Kindle or CreateSpace editions on
Amazon.com*

DEDICATION

This book is dedicated to three strong women in my family: my mother, Lucera; my grandmother, Herculana; and my great grandmother, Norberta.

In this story, the real heroes are my bisabuela Norberta Pérez and my nana Herculana Campos. Both my nana and bisabuela were very resilient and independent personalities. Family lore claims that my bisabuela Norberta was unique in her village of Teocaltiche, Mexico. She was one of the few women in the pueblo who was able to read and write, and thereby became the town escribana. In addition to being a scribe, she made and sold chocolate bars for making hot beverages.

Then there was my nana. Herculana was a kick in the pants. She was born in the State of Jalisco and lived in Arizona and California. She raised six children plus a few orphans here and there. She was tiny but wore tall block heels that made her at least 4'10". She was a hard worker and was tough as nails.

And then there was my mother, Lucero. She used to read to us children every night. It was better than television, as I saw in my mind's eye the places and adventures that tumbled off the pages of the books. Perhaps my desire to be a writer began as I sat listening to my mother's words.

NORBERTA PERÉZ TORRES

TABLE OF CONTENTS

ACKNOWLEDGEMENTS

I would like to thank the indigenous Mesoamericans for making chocolate and spreading their celestial ambrosia throughout the universe.

Life is about love and chocolate. Who hasn't inhaled a Baci or licked a Dove Bar and felt the rush into an ethereal state?

Historically, the harvesting and processing of cacao beans has been traced as far back as the Olmecs, predecessors to the Aztecs and Mayans. Originally, cacao beans were made into a bitter beverage, sometimes with chile added. In Nahuatl it was called "xocolatl." Cacao beans were used by the Aztecs not only to brew chocolate as a beverage, but also as a tribute to their gods and as their monetary currency.

The Spaniards discovered chocolate when they conquered Mesoamerica. They called it something like "sacred excrement." They transported it back to Europe where sugar was added and chocolate became the rage.

Theobromine (Latin for food of the gods) is a chemical derived from the cacao tree that has medicinal properties. We all knew that. Furthermore, chocolate can be used to treat asthma, high blood pressure, and muscle tension.

But what about the love part. Chocolate is rumored to be an aphrodisiac. It causes the brain to release dopamine, which is the body's pleasure chemical. That sounds to me like the recipe for love.

Most importantly, I want to thank my wife and partner, Dolores, for her encouragement, support, and love. She deserves lots of chocolate.

Dear Diamond,

We all know who a girl's best friend really is.

Love,

Chocolate

Life is like a box of chocolates. You never know
what you're gonna get.
Forrest Gump

Chocolate comes from cocoa, which is a tree and
that makes it a plant. Therefore, chocolate is salad.
Anonymous

All you need is love (and more chocolate).
The Beatles, edited

PROLOGUE

This story unfolds during the early days of The Mexican Revolution. The Mexican Revolution started in 1910, when liberals and intellectuals began to challenge the regime of dictator Porfirio Díaz, who had been in power since 1877, a term of 34 years that was called *El Porfiriato*, violating the principles and ideals of the Mexican Constitution of 1857.

The motives for waging the Mexican Revolution grew out of the belief that a few wealthy landowners could no longer continue the old ways of Spanish colonial rule, a feudal-like system called *la encomienda*. That system needed to be replaced by a modern structure in which those who actually worked the land, should extract its wealth through their labor.

Two great figures, Francisco "Pancho" Villa from the north of Mexico and Emiliano Zapata from the south, led the revolution and remain key cultural and historical symbols in this fight for social reform. The *agrarista* (supporter of land reform) ideals of Zapata and his followers, the *Zapatistas*, are summarized in their mottos: *"Tierra y Libertad"* ("Land and Freedom") and *"La tierra es para el que la trabaja"* ("The land is for those who work it"). These slogans have not ceased to resonate in Mexican society.

In late 1910, Francisco I. Madero, in exile for his political activism, drafted the *Plan de San Luis Potosí*, which was widely distributed and embraced by rebel movements across the nation. In this plan, Madero called for an uprising starting on November 20, 1910, to restore the Constitution of 1857 and replace dictator Díaz with a provisional government. Its main purpose was to establish a democratic republic and to abolish unlimited presidential terms. By early 1911, a large armed struggle was underway in the northern state of Chihuahua led by a local merchant Pascual Orozco and Francisco "Pancho" Villa. The success of the northern troops, or *La División del Norte*, sparked uprisings against *terratenientes* (landowners)across the country.

In the southern state of Morelos, as early as 1909, Emiliano Zapata had started recruiting thousands of peasants to fight for land reform in support of *El Plan de Ayala*, approved by Zapata's supporters in 1911. Paramount to plan was land reform to help *campesinos* (landless peasants) by re-distributing the land back to the peasants and away from powerful landowners.

On May 25, 1911, Mexican President Porfirio Díaz resigned and left the country. Francisco I. Madero, author of the Plan de San Luis Potosí became president after the elections in 1911. He was assassinated in early 1913 by a commander of the federal forces, Victoriano Huerta, who joined the counterrevolutionaries led by Porfirio Díaz's nephew in order to seize power. Huerta dissolved the congress after the assassination of Madero and assumed power but faced heavy opposition. In 1914, U.S. President Woodrow Wilson sent U.S. Marines to Vera Cruz, Mexico in retaliation to an incident involving the U.S. Navy in Tampico. Losing key battles to revolutionary troops, Huerta resigned in the same year and left the country. At the end of Huerta's presidency, Venustiano Carranza, a wealthy landowner and chief of the Northern Coalition, gathered revolutionary and military leaders to a conference to determine the future of Mexico. Villa, Zapata, and their followers supported the *Plan de Ayala* for land reform, in opposition to Carranza and his supporters, all of whom supported the *Plan de San Luis Potosí*.

Eventually, Carranza (now supported by the United States) and his followers, called for a constitutional convention to draft a supreme law of Mexico, which was later presented to Congress. The final version was approved in 1917, enshrining agrarian reform and unprecedented economic rights for the Mexican people. After approval of this constitution, in 1917, Carranza, as the president of Mexico, proceeded to ignore its promises. As a consequence, the revolution continued until 1920. Carranza was assassinated and General Álvaro Obregón rose to power.

These were times of great turmoil and confusion. Mexico was still embroiled in a war of ideals and deeply-felt beliefs. However, many small towns were fortunately spared from any direct contact with battles, so life appeared tranquil. The setting for this story, Teocaltiche, is one such town, where life moves at a slow pace, as if inside a bubble that can burst at any time.

CHAPTER 1 – THE WHISTLER

Sunday, May 8, 1910
Teocaltiche, Jalisco, Mexico

Sixteen-year-old Pedro and his cousin Ricardo were
carefully driving a two-horse, four-wheel wagon down the
bumpy, rocky path from the tin mining town of Atepoca that
was situated at an altitude of six thousand feet. They carefully
minded the potholes, zigzags, and frequently eroded gravel
road. Neither dared to look over the edge to the dry gorge far
beneath them. The pair continued inhaling dust and tasting grit
on their journey toward the valley floor that eventually leveled
out and led to the little municipality of Teocaltiche in the
heights of the State of Jalisco. The young dark-skinned mestizo
rider, Pedro, adjusted his sombrero under the midday sun. Next
to him, his cousin, Ricardo, was half asleep. The path became
flanked by Joshua trees, prickly pear cacti, and palo verde
trees. The pungent smell of wild sage brush permeated the air,
a murder of crows cawing on its branches.

"What do you want to do in town, Pito?" Ricardo had awakened and called his cousin by his nickname. Ricardo gave a big yawn as he stretched out his arms.

"I don't know," Pedro replied to his cousin Rico. "I've never been there before."

"I'm just bored. I need some fun."

"Hey, primo, at least we have jobs," Pito countered. "I need to earn money for my family. I can't afford to be without work."

Pedro "Pito" Campos was born in the state of Durango, Mexico, in 1894. When he turned fifteen, six months earlier, his cousin Ricardo had recruited him to work in a tin mining company camp in Atepoca, a freckle of a town with 76 inhabitants. As the surface tin ores declined, tinners began to dig deeper following the vertical sheet lodes. Due to rock falls, blasts, and accidents, tin mining was considered very hazardous. Nonetheless, there was an overabundance of itinerant diggers.

At the Atepoca Tin Mining Company, Pedro was put in charge of twenty mules and eight horses because he had worked on ranches back home. He also was responsible for a multitude of odd jobs around the mining camp and the adjoining ranch. Sunday afternoons were the camp's only day off. His compatriots called him by his nickname "Pito," because he whistled all of the time.

As part of their routine Saturday duties, the Campos cousins were charged with picking up the mining camp's supplies at La Compañia Los Olivos in Teocaltiche that was about six miles down the mountain side and through the valley.

The cousins finally arrived into town, covered from head to toe in dust from the drive down the mountain. After loading the wagon and securely covering it, they decided to make a day of it. Their foreman was lax with them as long as they came back before dark. Obtaining the supplier's permission, they were allowed to store the wagon and the two horses in a warehouse barn out of sight of unwanted eyes.

"We need to have some fun, Pito," Ricardo pleaded. Pedro didn't respond. We have too much to do and not enough time to do it. We can't be playing silly games and wasting money.

The pair hadn't eaten since morning. Their stomachs were growling. They had a few centavos from their *domingo*, their weekly allowance. They ambled over to the main town plaza. The park was flush with colorful flowers and tall palm trees. The primos bought some *elote*, corn on the cob, to munch on as they sat on the grass.

"Pito, it's great being away from the pinche ranch!" Rico laughed.

They laid back and closed their eyes. A while later, they sat up. They were about to return to the supply wagon when the church of Our Lady of the Sorrows' bell struck five. The plaza had come alive. Parents were walking their children, vendors were selling aguas frescas and candies, and some locals were drinking tequila. The level of conversation intensified. The smell of flowers mixed with cigarette smoke filled the air.

A group of musicians dressed in chocolate brown charro jackets and ties started to make their way to the octagonal roman arched pavilion in the middle of the plaza. They started to tune their instruments. The boys knew that the tuba was off key and laughed as they pointed fingers at each other.

At the end of the promenade that radiated from the walkways that surrounded the plaza, groups of two and three young ladies started strolling toward the kiosk followed by their adult female chaperones.

The sound of a waltz melodiously emanated from the bandstand. Now cliques of young men made their way to the pavilion. One-two-three. One-two-three.

"Rico," Pedro curiously asked his cousin. "What is happening?"

"Don't know," Ricardo answered back. "But we gotta be going. We still have to unload all the supplies before night fall."

But temptation caught the better of them. The cousins decided to stay a while at the plaza. Pedro got up from the lawn and went over to a diminutive wizened old man with a wispy moustache and missing teeth who had sold them the elote.

"What is going on, señor?" Pedro inquired.

The elfish man spit to his right and began to explain the tradition of "El Paseo." This was a traditional stroll around the zócalo (the central plaza) by young girls and boys, usually at least fifteen years of age. In Teocaltiche, groups of girls would walk counterclockwise around the promenade followed by their chaperones. The escorts were nannies or relatives who wore frozen smiles. The boys at the same time would walk around the pavilion clockwise. There was very little overt interaction. There was the tipping of sombreros by the young boys and fluttering of fans by the young ladies.

If a boy was bold and wanted to show a girl that he was interested in her, he would dash over, give her a fresh flower, and then immediately retreat. If a girl wanted to reciprocate the interest, she would nod her head and then welcome the boy to converse with her under the supervision of her chaperone.

However, if the girl was not interested in the boy, she would return the flower to the boy on the next go around, to the embarrassment of the potential suitor.

Pito and Rico emerged from behind a poplar tree. The waltz was followed by another waltz. The oom-pah-pah sound from the tuba was still off key.

The girls usually walked in pairs or trios twirling their parasols or waving their fans. The first threesome, wearing long white dresses with red, green, and white lace, was giggling as they passed the boys opposite them and Pedro and his cousin.

"These girls are spoiled brats," remarked Ricardo. "Who would ever want to talk to them?"

"Those boys?" Pedro pointed to a group of rambunctious boys clad in trousers that looked too short.

"What do you know about girls?' Rico asked forcefully. Pedro remained silent.

A moment later a pair of girls wearing pink dresses with their black hair plaited with colorful ribbons strolled by. They stopped their tittering and one of them gave the cousins a big smile.

"You see, Rico, they really like us."

"You're crazy," his cousin sighed. "They're like little children."

"Come on, primo," Pedro was excited. "What do we do now?"

A moment later another 14-year-old girl with her long reddish-brown hair in curls gave a cursive glance toward the two boys with her hazel eyes as she and her girlfriend walked by. She was wearing a royal blue dress with a pink bow tied in front and her companion had on a lacey pink one. She raised her fan to her face.

"Rico," Pedro's mouth was agape. "I'm in love!"

"With whom?" his cousin inquired skeptically. "Not that white girl, I hope!"

"She is like an angel," Pedro's heart was beating like a drum. He had never really been in love or even had a real girlfriend. Of course, he had experienced his rite of passage in some brothels in Durango. But this was different.

Pedro let out a loud two-note wolf whistle. The girl turned around trying to discover the source.

All of sudden, Pedro took off leaving his cousin behind. Ricardo was surprised but stayed where he was. Pedro reappeared with some small palm fronds that he had found on the ground a short distance away. He studied the leaves and then began to bend and twist and fold them into a pattern. In the end he produced a flower made from the fronds.

"Pito," his cousin pointed at the object. "What in the heck is that?"

"I don't have enough money to buy a flower. So, I made this."

"You are crazy, primo."

"I'm in love."

"Ay, pendejo, who could love you? You smell like horse shit," pointing to Pedro's soiled pants.

Pedro tried to wipe the muck away but was unsuccessful. Now the two cousins were waiting patiently under the shade of the poplar. About ten minutes later the same two girls appeared followed by two matronly chaperones wearing long black dresses.

As quick as a jackrabbit, Pedro made a dash toward the feminine foursome. Ricardo was in shock. At first the girls did not see Pedro. He was trying to intersect them. They casually paused for a split second. The two chaperones behind the girls were deep in conversation with one another and were not paying attention to Pedro's frontal encounter.

Faster and faster, he ran. He thrust out his hand and shoved the palm flower into his fair-skinned love interest almost causing her to drop her lacquered fan. He kept on running past without stopping

The girls were stunned and said nothing. They looked behind them and saw that their escorts had not observed the strange occurrence.

"María Antonia," remarked Araceli, the girl in the pink dress. "It looks like you have an admirer."

"It was probably just a rude boy from one of the villages," the love interest stated. "I can't believe how presumptuous these peasants are, especially the natives."

"How do you know he was a native?" inquired her companion.

"What difference does it make?" María Antonia said smugly. "He is beneath our station."

"What are you going to do with his flower?"

"Flower? Do you call this a flower?"

"Actually, I like it. I think it's very thoughtful," her friend said in a soft tone.

"Well," María Antonia gave the palm flower a second glance. "I am going to give it back to him when we pass him. That will show him. He will never dare show his face around here again." She laughed.

About ten minutes later they arrived at the part of the paseo where Pedro had given her a token of his affection. There was no one there except an elote vendor.

"Where did that desconocido go?" said the girl in royal blue as she huffed disappointedly.

CHAPTER 2 – LA ESCRIBANA

Sunday, May 15, 1910

The following Sunday, Pedro returned to Teocatliche. This time he came by himself. He was taking his time as he rode the roan-colored Azteca steed named "El Brujo." Now, since he was in charge of the stables at the mining site, he was allowed to use the company's horses. Most of his real work was caring for the mules that transported the mined ore down from the hills.

All week his cousin Ricardo teased him incessantly or berated him.

"Pito, you are pendejo!" Rico reproached him. "You have never even kissed a girl!"

"Yes, I have," Pito said weakly.

"The putas don't count," his cousin ranted. "Who?

Pito hemmed and hawed for a long moment. "Natalia," he responded.

"She's our cousin, pendejo!" blurted out Rico. "She doesn't count. Don't let Tio José hear you say that. He'll beat your ass!"

Pedro's enthusiasm was slowly eroding. *Maybe this is a stupid idea. I have no money. I smell like a barn. Who could love me?*

Every night the miners would come back to camp and grab chili or something else to eat. Half of them didn't even wash the dirt and grime off their faces and clothes. Why should they? They were going to get filthier the next day anyway. A few of the workers would gather around the fire and sing songs. Songs of lying, crying, and dying. They were far away from their loved ones, if they even had any.

Pito looked up into the heavens and saw a million stars. *Does one have my name on it?* At that instant, Pedro made up his mind to take a chance of finding someone to love. *Screw everyone! ¡Si se puede!*

Earlier that morning Pedro had washed his mestizo brown face and hands after doing his morning chores which included feeding the animals and cleaning out the stalls. He used strong lye soap in an attempt to remove the pungent smells that stuck to him like pine tar from the work on the ranch. His hands were inflamed. He found a clean blue work shirt and put it on. Next came his faded blue jeans and worn leather boots. Now with his right hand and spit, he slicked his black hair and parted it down the middle. His face showed no signs of growing hair. He tied a multicolored sash around his waist. Pedro was trying to look his best.

He heard the finches singing and began whistling. The guapo sixteen-year-old Pedro "Pito" Campos was always whistling. His favorites were corridos that he learned in the mining camp. These days he was practicing the "Corrido de Rosita Alvirez." When he was growing up, his mother used to wake up and sing songs to begin each day. Pito couldn't remember to feed the chickens, but he remembered each tune and could whistle them in perfect pitch. *"¡Ay, mijo!"* she would sigh.

After about an hour of riding, Pedro finally reached the bottom of the incline of the mountain and stopped. He took a swig of water from his canteen. The sun was beating fiercely on him from overhead. There was no breeze. He kicked the sides of El Brujo and they proceeded another mile until they reached a main road. This was one of the main arterials that led into Teocaltiche. He turned left and followed the dozens of wagon wheel tracks. Pedro knew that he had another hour before reaching the center of the pueblo. He spotted some activity in front of him.

Two older men had pulled their black horses off to the side of the road and stood under a willow tree. The pair wore big sombreros and bade Pedro good afternoon as he approached. The tall, slender one wore a red bandanna around his neck; the short, chubby one a yellow one. The pair were eating bruised bananas and throwing the peels toward the pine trees. They were going to take a siesta before entering the town.

Pedro returned the greeting. He decided to stop and ask the two men a question.

"Señores, do you where there is a scribe in town?"

Cisco and Pancho looked at the young man and then each other. Broad grins beamed across their faces. Pancho had a yellow bandanna tied around his neck and wore a black sombrero. His round face, that was like leather parchment, puffed up and asked, "What kind of scribe are you looking for, *mocoso*?" Pancho good naturedly called Pedro a snot-nosed kid.

"I need to write a letter to a girl that I'm in love with," Pedro naively responded. "She's the most beautiful girl that I've ever seen."

"Well, my little friend," the moustached man pressed on. "How many girls have you known?"

***

Teocaltiche, or as it was called in Nahuatl "Teocaltillitzin," was a sacred site and economic hub for the Aztec tribe of the Cuyuteco peoples. It literally meant the "place near the temple." After the invasion and conquest by the Spanish it slowly grew into a colonial town. It was located in the northeastern foothills of the State of Jalisco, Mexico. Over the decades, the population grew first with Spanish and then after Spanish Independence mainly with Mexicans. There were always influxes of Yanquis, French, and Chinese. Agriculture and livestock became the main industries, with occasional endeavors in mining, textiles, and artisan goods.

This pretty, little colonial town was centered around Our Lady of Sorrows Church and the pavilion in the municipal plaza. While there were shops and businesses in the commercial district, the major portion of economic activity emanated from the marketplace booths surrounding the square. The town plaza was a park filled with gardens and walking paths.

In a little wooden stall in the marketplace was a boney but muscular, brown-skinned arm stirring a chocolatey liquid in the terra cotta jar. The mestiza wore a green indigenous apron over her white cotton dress. She ladled out two Mexican hot chocolate drinks for the two churchgoers. Norberta Pérez instructed her youngest daughter, Herculana, to wash out some more earthenware cups.

The six o'clock mass at the rose-colored Our Lady of Sorrows Church was just letting out. Per the local custom, some of the faithful would wander over to the marketplace at the southern end of the plaza. It was here that Norberta Peréz and her full-figured comadre Guadalupe "Lupe" Nava shared a makeshift booth selling chocolate and churros. Norberta was also the most popular *escribana* in Teocaltiche.

A few more parishioners came by and ordered the chocolate drink. They were mostly older ladies, especially compared to Norberta whose long braids were dark black. One "viejita" with silver-capped teeth bought six churros from Guadalupe to share with her lady friends as they gossiped.

As part of their daily routine, Norberta and her three daughters would wake up at four in the morning on Sundays in El Pueblito del Valle and load up their chocolate products for the market. Francisca, the oldest daughter, would make a simple breakfast for everyone. Usually, it was tortillas and beans. The middle daughter, Julia, was in charge of clean-up. Francisca and Julia rarely went to the market but stayed home doing chores and preparing the chocolate bars for sale.

Norberta's fifteen-year-old godson, Ramón would load his little wooden cart with the goods along with his mother's fresh churros. He always had a big smile on his face. Norberta's youngest daughter, Herculana, was Lupe's goddaughter. And so, together the comadres and two youngsters would make the fifty-minute journey to the plaza to set up.

Norberta and Herculana would attend the six o'clock service but leave about ten minutes early in order to make final preparations for the after-mass crowd. Guadalupe and Ramón tended the booth during their absence. At seven o'clock the process was reversed, and Guadalupe and Ramón went to mass while Norberta and her daughter staffed the stall.

When the church clock showed seven-fifteen, one could always find Norberta's most loyal customer buying hot chocolate from her and a few churros to dip in it. Alberto Nuñez was a very heavyset man with a barrel for a stomach. His head was spotted with tufts of black hair, and he had a short, grey lock beard and drooping moustache. He waddled over to a park bench on the plaza. Today, Alberto pulled out his thin glasses and, with his tired, sagging eyes, read the newspaper. On other days, he smoked stale cigarettes and sat with his breakfast companions. If he found something of note in the newspaper, he would lean over to his friends Noe Medina and Mauricio Laronda and report the news.

"Madero is causing trouble again," he would state with authority about Mexican presidential politics. "Díaz won't show him any mercy."

Alberto had been a legal scholar at the Royal and Pontifical University of Mexico City (which would later become UNAM - Universidad Nacional Autónoma de México). Thereafter, he was a history professor at the University Interregnum in Guadalajara. He was an outspoken advocate for academic freedom and antidisestablishmentarianism, and eventually was terminated for his beliefs. He moved to Teocaltiche to be close to his brother's family.

***

The Mexican Revolution began in 1910, a century after the Grito de Dolores declared Mexico's independence from Spain after three hundred years of conquest. Mexico struggled to maintain a viable government with limited finances but with ample territory and natural resources. The country was ripe for international intervention by the U.S. and countries like France and Germany. One invasion resulted in the U.S. Mexican War where half of Mexico's territory was stolen by the United States; and another intrusion created a Mexican empire under Maximiliano I.

Then came the 30-year dictatorship of Porfirio Díaz who favored foreign enterprises and wealthy landowners over native Mexicans. Political repression and keeping the masses uneducated were his tactics. Everything for him was political. One day he would attack the Catholic Church and then the next day make exceptions. His goal was to make Mexico "anglicized."

When the people opposed him, they would suffer the consequences. Finally, during his bid for his seventh re-election in 1908, Díaz stated that he was in favor of the democratization of Mexican society. His opponent, Francisco Madero, was a wealthy liberal who opposed Díaz's reelection. Months later, on the eve of the farcical election, Madero was arrested on charges of sedition. He escaped to Texas, where in October 1910 he would publish the *Plan de San Luis Potosí*, declaring himself the president of Mexico, and calling for an armed insurrection to begin on November 20.

***

"Our economy is growing," coughed Mauricio Laronda, Alberto's colleague who had to retire his medical practice because of cataracts. His spectacles were thicker than a church window. He stroked his long white beard. "We're safe here. The mayor protects us."

"Protects us, no!" Alberto began to get angry. "Extorts us, yes! His pinche police won't even let us express our opinions."

Ever the compromiser, the middle-aged Noe Medina, an accountant by profession, would always end the debate with, "It really doesn't matter. They're all the same."

***

Norberta was within ear shot of the conversation. She just nodded her head. She didn't want to get involved. The politicians were all the same, she thought. And the poor always suffered.

However, Norberta was also the scribe for the town. There were a few others, but they were not very good or were scam artists. Although she paid the same municipal licensing fees as her male counterparts, she was not permitted to use wax to seal her letters. Instead, she used a homemade water and solution glue solution that was inexpensive and more affordable for her clients. It was a blessing in disguise since she rarely did official documents that required wax seals.

Many years before, Alberto had asked her how she became a scribe. Most men could not read or write, and women not at all. He blamed President Díaz' repressive political agenda toward native Mexicans. *How is it that Norberta is literate?* Alberto wondered.

Norberta explained to him that she did not remember much about her early childhood. Her parents or someone had sent her to an orphanage. She knew that she was born around 1879. The nuns at La Virgen de Tepeyac Convent took in young girls and taught them how to read, write, and sometimes even learn a trade. The orphans were also rigorously trained in the Catholic religion. Those who showed promise were trained to be lay proselytizers.

Mexico and the Catholic Church had always had a love-hate relationship. After the 1860 Revolution, President Benito Juárez nationalized Catholic Church property and suppressed religious orders. This anti-clerical sentiment was continued by President Porfirio Díaz, which was ironic since his mother had enrolled him in a seminary as a boy.

The Catholic Church devised a strategy to protect its priests and nuns. They educated lay-persons, usually orphans, to go out into the villages to preach and convert the citizens. Thus, the priests were safe from any political repercussions from the anti-Catholic sentiment.

In Norberta's case, she became an excellent student, but her heart was not in moralizing. Her heart had been in a young seminarian's hands. It was her first love, and it would be her last. She was expelled from the orphanage when she was sixteen and pregnant. The boy was not punished but was allowed to continue his training. Norberta was heartbroken when her lover was ordained and subsequently sent to Manila in the Philippines.

At the abbey she had learned how to make Mexican chocolate from the nuns. This was how she was able to survive when she had to move to Teocaltiche.

Then it became known in Teocaltiche that she could read and write. The prior scribe had become senile, and his handwriting was incomprehensible, not to mention that he charged outrageous fees. After Norberta sent out a few letters on behalf of some friends, she became the new de facto scribe.

***

Herculana, wearing her older sister's hand-me-down white dress that was too big for her, asked in a demanding voice, "Mamá, Fernanda wants to purchase one and a half packets of the chocolate. Can we do that?"

"Sure, mija," Norberta knew Fernanda well. Fernanda was the cook for the family of a notario publico in town. She was a regular customer. Norberta knew that her economic survival depended on her being flexible and attentive to the consumer's needs. "I'll cut the second packet. Give me some wrapping paper."

The packets of the solid Mexican chocolate contained two tablets each. She removed one tablet and wrapped it up.

Norberta gave the one and half packets to Fernanda who smiled and paid her.

"Thank you, Señora Norberta."

"You're welcome, mija. *¡Que le vaya bien!*"

The early church services were now over. The last one was still going on.

"*Oye, comadre,*" hailed Guadalupe. "Would you and Herculana like some churros? I think I have a few left over."

Guadalupe had silver streaks in her black hair. She had beautiful cinnamon colored skin. She was always nosy about everyone's business.

"Herculana, do you want one of your madrina's churros?" Norberta asked her daughter.

"Yes, mamá."

"Well, then, ask her politely."

Herculana gave Guadalupe a sad puppy-dog look and meekly said, "Sí, por favor."

Guadalupe had a soft spot for the young, brown-eyed girl. "Here, mijita."

Herculana slowly bit into the sugar-covered fried dough pastry.

"Here, mijita," her mother gave her a half cup of Mexican chocolate. "Dip it in this."

Herculana did so slowly, but with a satisfied smile in place.

The morning had been good for both Norberta and Herculana. Their earnings would have to last them until market day on Wednesday when all the vendors from the neighboring villages came to town to sell their wares.

Norberta and Guadalupe had a natural advantage since they had a permanent stall on the plaza in front of the church. However, the government had begun repressing the poorer people and times were getting hard and more desperate for everyone.

"Oye, comadre," bellowed Guadalupe. "Will you be ready to leave when the 12 o'clock mass crowd is gone?"

CHAPTER 3 – THE MYSTERY GIRL

Sunday, May 15, 1910

Pedro tethered El Brujo to a wooden post after allowing his horse to inhale gallons of water. The plaza, where he had been the week before with his cousin, was right in front of him. From the south side of the city plaza, Pedro could see the beautiful rose-colored church of Our Lady of Sorrows with its twin towers and clock that he had first espied the week before while observing the paseo. This was very close to where he and his cousin had loaded up the supply wagon. It was all coming back to him. What he hadn't remembered was the market booths just to his left. He walked past a couple of trees. A brownish-grey squirrel with a bushy tail was skittering between one tree and another. Doves were cooing as people threw them pieces of tortillas or old bread. Families were eating mangos dipped in chili powder and impaled on sticks. His mouth began to salivate.

There was a leather goods booth with dozens of black and brown tooled belts, billfolds, and saddles. An older gentleman customer was haggling with the owner.

Then Pedro came upon a used clothes stall that sold children's attire. Indigenous mothers with their tots picked through the piles and piles of secondhand garb.

The church bell rang once. He could see that the hands of the clock on its front façade indicated that it was one o'clock.

He was having second thoughts about why he had come. This time Ricardo was not with him. He had to figure out what he had to do by himself.

A week earlier the two boys had received an earful from their irate foreman when they had arrived back late at the mining ranch. Ricardo had tried to blame it on the slowness of the supply store, but the boss would not have any part of it. Finally, Pedro confessed that had fallen in love with a girl in town.

The derision and teasing that Pedro suffered from the miners during the week was insufferable.

"Hey, Pito, does she have more than four teeth?"

"Have you ever been with a girl, macho man?"

"She must be blind if she likes you."

His cousin Rico had already admonished him for trying to socialize with the white-skinned Spanish upper class.

"I think it's against the law. Don't be so stupid"

Pedro worked extra hard during the week and ignored his work companions.

The foreman finally relented.

"Pito," the boss said sternly. "You may go to town today. But, by yourself. You have to be back by five. If you screw up, you'll never leave the ranch again. Do you understand?"

"Yes, sir."

"I am not joking. ¡No la cagues!"

The boss had given him five centavos for his weekly domingo.

As he prepared to leave camp, he ran into his cousin.

"Sorry, Rico," Pedro put on his sombrero. "The boss man is only letting me go."

"No problem, primo," his cousin slapped him on the back. "I didn't want to go anyway. Just be careful, and like I said before, don't be stupid."

Pedro nodded his head.

"We'll be going into town next week anyway," Ricardo paused. "If you don't mess up."

***

Norberta's business hours for that Sunday were over and she was starting to pack up her things. The two customers from the twelve o'clock mass were finishing up their chocolate drinks. Guadalupe and her son, Ramón, had already loaded up the peasant cart that he pulled every day to and from their casita fifty minutes away.

The dark-skinned youth approached the women's stand.

"Perdón, señoras" he took off his sombrero. "I'm looking for the town scribe. La escribana."

Guadalupe shot her comadre a glance. She wanted to get home as soon as possible. Her feet were hurting. She didn't have time to waste.

"I am Norberta Pérez," the escribana wiped her hands on her green apron. "I'm at your service. What can I do for you?"

"I need you to write a letter for me."

"What kind of letter?" Over the years Norberta had written almost every kind of missive possible. Long or short. Kind or angry. Sincere or playful. She was now thirty-one years old and believed that she had seen just about everything.

"A letter of love," Pedro said meekly.

"Oh, my God," groaned Guadalupe who was standing nearby. "Another enamorado!"

"I will have to charge you," Norberta informed him. "You have to pay in advance."

Norberta went over the fees with him for one page, more than one page, a folded letter, a letter in an envelope, and delivery of the letter.

Pedro reached into his pants' pocket and pulled out the five centavos he had. He extended his hand toward Norberta. She took the coins.

"Okay, let's get started," she opened up a leather satchel where she kept her writing supplies. She took out one of her quill pens and dipped it into a little bottle of Indian ink that she used only for love letters. "What is your name?"

"Pedro. Pedro Campos." He shared where he lived and where he worked.

"What is the young lady's name?"

"I don't know."

"What a shame!" interjected Guadalupe.

"I don't understand. You don't know?" Norberta frowned.

Pedro explained about the paseo from the prior week and how he had seen this girl.

"What did she look like?"

He described her as being fair-skinned with long reddish-brown curls.

"Oh, great!" interrupted Guadalupe again. She could never hold her tongue. "This lover boy wants to get involved with the gachupines! Don't be such a fool, boy! You can't mix with those pinche Spaniards!"

Norberta tried to calm the situation down.

"Well, Pedro, I can't write the letter if I don't know the girl's name. Can you find out who she is?"

"I don't know how," his face looked dejected. "I can't stay much longer. I have to get back to the ranch."

Norberta reached into her apron pocket and was about to return the centavos to the boy.

"We could go to the paseo and see who matches the description," a juvenile voice chimed in.

"Herculana Pérez, how many times have I told you to mind your own business?" her mother shook her head and scolded her daughter. "You definitely cannot go."

"Ramón could do it," Guadalupe volunteered. "But it would cost you."

"I gave you all I had," Pedro said forlornly.

"Pedro, why would you waste all your money on someone you don't even know?" Guadalupe said in a maternal tone.

"Because he is in love," Herculana jumped into the conversation. "And people should have the right to love whomever they want."

"Herculana!" her mother pointed her finger. "I'm warning you."

Guadalupe laughed.

"Comadre, your goddaughter takes after you," Norberta looked at Guadalupe and tried to suppress a smile. "Your ahijada is taking on most of your traits. I wish that they were the good ones."

Pedro looked at Herculana and gave her a weak smile as if he appreciated her comments.

"Okay, Pedro, this is how it's going to be," Norberta began. She wanted to earn a little money, but at the same time she felt sorry for the unsophisticated boy. "Ramón is going to try find out who the mystery girl is. There will be a charge for that. When are you coming back this way?"

"My cousin and I come to town every two weeks for supplies," Pedro was quick to respond. "I'll be back a week from today. Sunday."

"You will be charged even if Ramón does not find the girl. However, I will refund the five centavos because I can't write the letter. Agreed?"

"Okay. How much should I bring?"

Guadalupe rolled her eyes. *How naïve is this kid?*

"Herculana, give the young man a cup of chocolate," Norberta instructed her daughter. "And comadre, give him a few churros for his trip back to the ranch."

CHAPTER 4 – NORBERTA'S CASITA

Monday, May 16, 1910
El Pueblito del Valle

The following day, after a meager breakfast in their little casita, Norberta sent her oldest daughter Francisca to the local stream to do the family's weekly laundry.

"And Panchita," the mother warned her. "Don't waste your time gossiping with those other pendejas."

"Yes, mamá," replied Francisca. She was fifteen years old and the firstborn of the three daughters. She was short and had a round, pockmarked face. She had long, black hair that sprouted sideburn strands at the ears. Her dark brown eyes gave no indication that she was the mischievous girl in the family. She constantly picked on her two younger siblings.

Francisca was not happy because she thought she had to do all the chores for the family. She had to roast the cacao beans for making the chocolate; had to cook most of the meals; and had to wash the clothes. She could not go out to dances or just walk around. She felt confined in her little house.

Francisca grabbed the basket of soiled clothes which included some soiled rags from Julia, the second oldest, who had just had her menstrual cycle.

"Vaya con Dios, mijita," her mother called out as Francisca set off.

Norberta took her tree branch broom and started to sweep the dirt floor. Then she examined her burlap sacks hanging from the branch roof above her head.

"Julia," she addressed the middle child. "How are our supplies?"

It was Julia's daily job to inventory the household goods, especially those related to making chocolate that was their livelihood.

"Okay, mamá," the girl said with her dark brown eyes looking up at each sack. "I think we could be running short on bayo beans though."

Julia was also short and heavy for her thirteen years. Her long black hair was tied back with a pink ribbon. She was a quiet child and bore the constant rebukes and commands of her older sister, Francisca. In addition to her daily chores of fetching pails of water from the nearby well and making tortillas, she assisted in making the chocolate with her mother and Francisca.

Both of the older girls had dropped out of school when they reached ten years of age. Without a father around, they needed to help their mother.

Fortunately for her, Herculana was eleven years old and still was allowed to attend the neighborhood school during the week. However, on Wednesdays and Fridays, Herculana would miss classes to go to the market with her mother to sell chocolates.

Norberta put on a pot of pinto beans on the grill atop their outside fire pit. Julia was mixing the masa and salt in a wooden bowl in preparation for making corn tortillas.

"Panchita!" a loud voice emanated from the outside.

"Panchita!"

Norberta untied her apron and went out the wooden front door. Julia did not move. She recognized the voice.

"Oh, good morning, Señora Pérez," the good-looking young man called out as he saw her by the front door. "I thought Panchita was here."

"She's not here," Norberta studied the muscular twenty-five-year-old. Luis Gutierrez had been delivering their milk for the last few years. He usually came on Mondays and Thursdays.

He grabbed a milk jug from the wagon and carried it over to Norberta's front door.

"Do you want me to bring it in, señora?"

"No, thank you, Luis," she replied. She had a strange feeling about this 25-year-old male. He was always trying to talk to Francisca. The girl would get all excited. It was hard to calm her down. Norberta had an even worse opinion about her crazy daughter. All young girls were the same. They fell for every line a boy would make. Norberta should know; she had had it happen to her.

"Please tell Francisca that I said hello," he smiled as he tipped his pointed cowboy hat and drove the wagon off.

"Oye, Julia," the mother called out. "Come over here and help me. We have to bring the milk in."

The morning went by slowly. Francisca came back toting the wet laundry. It was very heavy.

"Hey, chubby," Francisca called out to her sister. "Come out and help me hang up the clothes."

"I'm busy," Julia replied. "I'm making lunch."

"Hurry up, ugly. I had to wash your smelly rags. The food can wait."

Slowly, Julia sauntered outside and took a few items of clothing and draped them on some bushes.

A half-hour later Norberta and her two oldest daughters were eating beans and rice with hot tortillas.

A small human form flashed by the little wooden table and fell into one of the two beds in the one room of the casita.

"Mijita, aren't you hungry?"

"No, mamá," Herculana was lying face down on the bed.

"Come over here, Herculana," the mother ordered.

"I can't," the young girl replied.

"What do you mean you can't?" Norberta's voice rose. She got up from the table and walked over to the bed.

Herculana did not move.

"Look at me, Herculana," the mother commanded.

The young girl squirmed and moved her arms and legs but did not turn around.

"Herculana! Herculana!"

The young girl finally looked around. Her mother noticed a bruise on her daughter's cheek.

"Okay, mijita," Norberta asked in an exasperated tone. "What happened this time?"

"Nothing," Herculana took a deep breath. She was not going to cry.

"Nothing?" her mother exclaimed incredulously.

"Well, there are these three girls at school," the girl began. "They made fun of me. They said my dress has a hole in it. They called me names and said I'm a beggar."

A tear slid down Norberta's cheek. They were poor, but so was everyone else. Herculana had to wear hand-me downs twice over. Her new clothes were made from flour sacks. That was the best Norberta could do.

"Well, mijita," she stroked her daughter's black hair. "We'll get you a new dress as soon as we can. I can certainly patch up any hole in this one." Norberta felt around her daughter's clothing looking for any holes or loose seams.

"But I got them," Francisca said with bravado. "I punched one in the nose. I made it bleed. I pulled another one's hair until she cried. But the third one ran away screaming. I'll get her at school tomorrow."

"Herculana! Herculana!"

"I think that I'm hungry now."

CHAPTER 5 – LA CARTA DE PESAME

Wednesday, May 18, 1910

Teocaltiche

The silver-haired woman in a black veil had been waiting for Norberta as she arrived to set up her booth for the Wednesday market. This was the day of the week when vendors from all over the valley brought their wares and foodstuffs to the plaza to be displayed. Embroidered materials and clothing, carved wooden utensils, and local honey were just a few of the items for sale.

Norberta smiled at her first customer and noticed deep swollen eyes.

"One moment, señora," she was hurrying to ready the booth. "I'm almost ready. Herculana, move the bench over there so the señora can sit down."

"Thank you," the woman said in a soft, almost imperceptible, voice. "I am in no hurry now. It is too late." The lady started to slowly drift off into her own private thoughts.

Norberta recognized the woman as a seven o'clock churchgoer. Norberta did not know people's names, but usually remembered folks by which mass they attended. She seemed to recall that usually a young woman and a tiny girl accompanied this lady.

"Norberta Pérez at your service, señora," Norberta made eye contact while at the same time stirring the chocolate drink in the crock. "How may I assist you?"

"Oh, señora, I don't know how to explain," the woman began.

Norberta offered her a cup of chocolate, which the lady graciously accepted.

Ana Porras de Jesus had a son, Eduardo, who was living near Brownsville, Texas, and was working in the fields as a migrant laborer. He had been there for almost two years when he couldn't find enough work in Teocaltiche. He had left his wife Margarita and his daughter Angelica in the care of his mother. The little girl was a sickly child, and the grandmother Ana was always with her. Somehow Angelica was bitten by mosquitoes and contracted malaria. The local doctor treated her with quinine water, but the little girl's temperature became elevated. Angelica would start shivering or go into convulsions. The girl could not keep food down and was always vomiting. Angelica passed away within hours of having the local priest administer the last rites.

"I am so sorry for your loss, Señora Porras," Norberta always hated dealing with news of death and dying. She thought of her three daughters.

Señora Porras wanted a letter sent to her son detailing what had happened to his daughter. "Do you have an address for your son?" Norberta asked. The lady nodded and handed a wrinkled piece of paper.

Norberta then explained the process. Señora Porras was agreeable. The escribana told her to come back in about an hour. The woman went across the street and entered the church to pray. Norberta began to draft a letter.

"Herculana, go find the bean vendor," her mother ordered. "Go buy a kilogram of beans. The pinto beans."

"Yes, mamá," Herculana stuck out her hand.

"Here, offer him two chocolate tablets," Norberta instructed. "No more than that. Offer him one at first. If he says no, tell him that you will give him two tablets for two kilos. You know how to do this. You've done it before."

Herculana was sometimes a child and at other times a shrewd businessperson, more mature than her elevens years. She ran over with two round chocolate tablets stuffed into her apron pockets.

"Oye, comadre," Guadalupe said having heard the lady pour out her sad story. "Así es la vida. I would be devastated if anything happened to Ramón. I'm going to pray for the little girl."

After Señora Porras left to go into the church, Norberta took out a little copper saucepan. Into it, she put some Indian ink, water, and some chocolate powder laced with chamomile, lavender, and some of her magical spices used to alleviate sorrow. She heated the mixture, constantly stirring it. When it had cooled, she dipped her quill into the mysterious chocolate ink concoction and started to compose the letter.

An hour later, Señora Porras came back. Norberta read her the letter. The lady was pleased. She now seemed calm and at peace. Norberta explained that she would place the letter in an envelope addressed to the lady's son after Ana Porras signed it (or put her X on it).

May 18, 1910

My dearest son, Eduardo,

I have some sorrowful news for you. God has decided to bring your daughter Angelica to heaven with Him. She passed away a few days ago. The doctor said that she was suffering from a case of malaria and her fragile body was too weak to fight it.

I will use some of the money that you sent me to have her buried properly and have a mass said on her behalf.

Margarita is beside herself. She has been crying for three days straight. She doesn't eat or sleep. I cannot comfort her.

We both are praying for Angelica's soul and yours too. We cannot question the Will of God. However, we still feel the pain.

Please do not attempt to come back home. Everything will be back to normal in a short period of time. It is God's Will that you stay in Texas and work in the fields. It is better than starving here. I miss you very much. So does Margarita. May God protect you.

With love,

Your loving mother,
Ana Porras de Jesús

The lady signed it with an "X". As Norberta placed the letter in the envelope and sealed it with her homemade glue, a faint glow and a few sparks seemed to emanate from the drying ink.

Norberta instructed Señora Porras to take the envelope to the town's general store where it would be picked up by the stagecoach that also carried mail.

The woman paid Norberta and gave her a thousand thank you's. She left with a hint of both satisfaction, and sadness for having to be the bearer of bad news. Guadalupe handed her comadre a churro and they gossiped about the townspeople.

Soon Herculana came back lugging a burlap sack.

"How did it go, mija?" Norberta wanted her daughter to learn independence. However, Herculana sometimes had to be reined in. Herculana had a mind of her own and more often than not, expressed her own views.

"Fine," reported Herculana.

"Well? Did he give you a good bargain?"

"Mamá, it was a woman." Herculana narrated that she had found a bean vendor with different types of beans piled on a multicolored blanket. It was a middle-aged woman tending the legumes, Herculana related. Herculana offered the vendor one chocolate tablet for a kilogram of pinto beans. The seller said fine. However, as she was filling Herculana's sack, a man yelled at the woman for being too charitable. The woman ignored the reprimand and smiled at Herculana.

"What a nice woman!" remarked Norberta. "May God bless her."

"And she gave me this," Herculana showed her the pirulí, the multicolor, conic-shaped hard candy that she had in her hand. "May I have it, mamá?"

Norberta was very strict with her daughters when it came to sweets and other treats. They had to ask permission before they could indulge.

"Of course, mijita," Norberta smiled at her daughter. "You did a good job today."

CHAPTER 6 – THE WEEKLY ROUTINE

Thursday, May 19, 1910
El Pueblito del Valle

Norberta and her family had settled into a weekly routine that was designed to ensure their survival. Everyone worked as a team and each had their own responsibilities. This had been their custom for the last two years since Julia had dropped out of school.

On Mondays while Herculana attended the local neighborhood school, Norberta and Julia would do household chores and cooking while Francisca did the washing at the creek. The milkman, Luis Gutierrez, delivered two liters of fresh milk in the morning.

Tuesdays were relegated to making chocolate tablets. On this day the jovial Caxcan-Mexican supplier would steer his mule to Norberta's shack and deliver about ¾ quarters of a kilogram of raw cacao beans to her. Javier Becerra was always polite, and his big smile showed off his large, chipped teeth.

The cacao beans would be used to make the chocolate that would be used to make hot chocolate, and also to sell in bar form at the plaza. Both the older girls assisted their mother in roasting the cacao beans, then grinding and molding them. But for special orders of certain chocolates, Norberta would make the candies by herself while the youngest was at school. Julia was put in charge of packaging the candies in colorful paper wrappers.

On Wednesdays, Norberta dragged Herculana with her to the market. The young girl really didn't mind missing school. She enjoyed spending time with her mother. Norberta also thought that Herculana had to learn to be independent and sociable. The plazita was the place where real learning took place. Also, on this day of the week, Norberta would pick up supplies at Cano's General Store or trade with other vendors that participated in the weekly market. Since money was hard to obtain, she would try to barter her chocolate bars in exchange for goods. She had an open account at the general store where a few chocolate tablets were left on consignment, in order to help pay down the debt.

Thursdays were very much like Tuesdays, but twice as much chocolate had to be produced for the weekend market. Three liters of milk were delivered in the morning. Norberta was becoming increasing aware that Luis Gutierrez seemed to be pursuing Francisca in an amorous way. Francisca, while not directly wanting to confront her mother, seemed to be showing signs of wanting to reciprocate the attention with the milkman. She was fifteen and thought that she knew everything. Francisca knew that she did not want to be a household slave to her family for the rest of her life. She wanted to do something else.

On Fridays Herculana again missed school because she went to the plaza with her mother to begin the business weekend. Most of the chocolate drink sales occurred in the morning and in the evening. Sometimes Norberta would wander about the plaza for about an hour talking to friends. Herculana loved staffing the stall by herself. She loved acting like the boss. At other times Norberta and Herculana would watch over Guadalupe's churros while her comadre took part of the day off.

Saturdays were even more demanding. More people came to the plaza and Norberta and Herculana were constantly busy.

Most of the time Norberta and Herculana would attend the six o'clock mass on Sundays by themselves. Seldom did Julia or Francisca come to town to join them. Their mother did not force them to go to church. She believed that it should be their choice. Fortunately, this day was a day of rest. Or at least a half day of rest. After the twelve o'clock mass crowd, they went home.

Sunday was bath day. In the late afternoon Francisca heated up a few buckets of water on the small wood oven on the outside patio. All four took turns washing their hair with a large bar of soap; they rinsed it out with vinegar if they had some. They bathed modestly behind a blanket in the corner of the patio if the weather was not too cold. They would change into clean clothes and the dirty laundry would be ready for Francisca to wash the next day.

Fortunately for Norberta's family, her godson Ramón had a side job delivering firewood to the barrio. He would deliver firewood to their patio once or twice a week depending on the season. He would also help transport the chocolate and the supplies by cart on the days Norberta went to market.

Her comadre was also a boon to Norberta. When Norberta was not around, Guadalupe would sell the chocolate tablets for her. Unfortunately, Guadalupe could never take a day off because she had to make churros every day. At best, Norberta could spell her for a few hours.

Norberta's work as an escribana was sporadic. Sometimes her work as the town scribe was very slow. She would not have a client for a month. At other times she might have several in one week.

The local government kept trying to tax and regulate the common folk. The workers were barely surviving. At the same time, it seemed that the government was spending lavishly on festivities, political favors, and statues. Municipal contracts and concessions were given to cronies in exchange for bribes and payoffs.

Alberto Nuñez, Norberta's best customer, kept saying that a revolution was on its way.

"The pinche Yanquis are going to invade Mexico and steal our oil," he would rant and rave to his comrades.

"Well, we can have new trains and roads with the revenues," added Mauricio. "It's better than having the oil sit in the ground."

"But the moneys don't go to the peasants," Alberto was getting angry. "The pinche government stuffs its own pockets. Nothing for the poor!"

"Well, I can see both sides," Noe said in a drawn out tone. "It really doesn't matter. It will all end up the same."

Norberta just nodded her head without saying anything. She listened to the men, processed the information, but remained silent.

Herculana always had her back to the obese old man with the big moustache, but she also seemed to be listening.

***

The Mexican Revolution was now gearing up. Díaz relied on support from the upper class and foreign interests. This was at the expense of the poor peasants.

Consequently, socialist and anarchist ideas began to spread throughout Mexico. At the same time, businesspeople and members of the Mexican middle class began to feel that Díaz had allowed foreigners to acquire too much economic power and privilege. Resentment was directed especially against the U.S. and British oil companies, who were becoming owners of what was the country's most valuable resource. In 1910 a revolutionary movement was initiated by Francisco Madero. At the same time, largely because of the support of Pancho Villa, the revolutionaries won several victories in Chihuahua.

And then there was the church. The Mexican Revolution started out as a social movement against the dictator Porfirio Díaz. The liberal progressive faction was anti-Catholic and anti-clerical. The Catholic Church was conservative and to the right politically. However, Díaz played both sides, spouting anti-clerical diatribes while ignoring most restrictions put on the church.

This allowed the church to act with impunity at the local level. The priests would dine with the mayors. The mayors and their families would have special seating at the Sunday masses.

The mayors and major landowners and businesses donated lots of money to the church.

In Teocaltiche, the parish priest, Father Felipe Santiago, would every so often circulate in the plaza among the market booths, trying to extract more donations or actual goods. Norberta always gave money on Sunday mornings. Usually, more than she could afford. The padre, however, was constantly warning the market vendors that they benefitted the most by having the church across the street and they should pay more for this privilege.

Father Santiago would grab at least two churros from Guadalupe's table and then a cup of chocolate from Norberta. While he was pontificating on the need for money, he was gobbling up the baked goods and downing the drink. He would finally wipe his brown beard on his Benedictine habit sleeve.

"And the pinche church always wants more money from us!" Alberto would complain after the priest left. "Look at them. None of them has ever missed a meal. Our people are starving, and they are feeding their faces! They want a new chalice! They want a new Easter garment! They want more flowers on feast days! ¡Qué la chinga!"

Norberta tried to save enough money to buy a new skirt and shoes for Francisca every year. She did not have time to sew clothes for the girls. However, at times she would barter with a seamstress for a sweater or socks. When this happened, Julia got Francisca's hand-me-downs; and likewise, Herculana was the recipient of Julia's old clothes. Makeshift modifications and alternations were made with the benefit of string, ribbons, and pins. More often than not, all three girls went barefoot or wore very primitive leather sandals during the temperate months. They wore long skirts all year around. During the rainy season they used rebozos to protect themselves against the inclement weather.

The daily diet for the family was sparse. They ate rice and beans with tortillas for most of their meals. In the mornings they might have oatmeal. Meat was a rarity unless Norberta bartered for it.

Guadalupe raised chickens and a few times a week Ramón would bring over some eggs. Sometimes at the Wednesday morning market, Norberta would trade chocolate for some vegetables or fruit. Avocados were their favorites. Norberta would split the bounty with her comadre.

Although Norberta and her family were poor, they were not the poorest in the town. She would often say *¡Gracias a Dios!*

CHAPTER 7 – EL CATRÍN

Friday, May 20, 1910

Teocaltiche

Herculana was bouncing along the dirt pathway as she and her mother made their way to the plaza that early morning. The mornings were cold and nippy, and she had a dark brown rebozo wrapped around her. Norberta was chatting with Guadalupe. Ramón had found out the identity of the girl that Pedro was enamored with. It was not going to be good news for the young suitor. Ramón unloaded the cart for his mother and godmother. Herculana helped with the lighter objects.

The morning went slowly, and Alberto showed up on schedule.

"Good morning, ladies," he rubbed his weary eyes as he yawned and stretched his arms out. "Señora Nava, I would like two churros today with my chocolate. I am in a very good mood." He gave them a big smile with his discolored teeth.

Guadalupe walked over to the bench where Alberto was reading the newspaper and handed him two churros that were still reasonably warm.

"Yes, the astronomers have said that Halley's Cometa has left our heavens. We are no longer in danger of being consumed by its toxic gases."

"Who is Halley, Señor Nuñez?" inquired Herculana who normally was quiet around him.

Trying to sound well informed about everything, Alberto answered, "He was some sort of scientist. An astronomer, I believe."

"How high did his kite fly?"

"Mija, why are bothering Señor Nuñez?" admonished Norberta. "Leave him in peace, please."

"It's no bother, señora," he explained that this kind of comet is a type of planet or moon that revolves around the sun. "You are thinking of the other kind of cometa that is a kite."

"Is that the bright light we have been seeing at night?"

"Exactly, Herculana," Alberto winked at Norberta. "She's a smart girl."

"If you only knew the real girl," sighed Norberta. "She is a handful."

It was not uncommon for Guadalupe to take off for a few hours to rest or to do errands. She worked seven days a week and had very little free time. Today was no exception. She and Ramón left in the late morning. Herculana tagged along with her godmother.

Norberta welcomed the solitude. She had so very little of it. She was lost in thought when a figure smoking a cigarette approached.

"Norberta, mi vida," the slick dandy greeted her. "I haven't seen you in a while. How have you been?"

"Fine, thank you," Norberta said curtly. "How can I help you?"

"Well, you can begin by giving me some hot chocolate," he gave her an unctuous grin.

Jorge "El Piojo" Contreras was dressed in a white shirt with a wide embroidered collar and a black leather vest. He smelled of rancid tobacco even though he was doused with Seven Roses aftershave. She hated the cheap cologne almost as much as she detested church incense. It made her nauseous. Jorge was the local womanizer in town and made passes at every woman of any age in town, including Norberta and Guadalupe. He would flatter the mothers and charm the daughters. Every female was leery of him, especially because it was common knowledge that he lived with a woman and had three children.

Norberta really hated when he would talk to Herculana or her other two daughters. She thought that he was a loathsome and conniving man who preyed on women. What made it worse was that he was the cousin of the police captain, Juan

Contreras, who was not well respected either. They were an evil pair.

"I know that you probably get lonely after working all the time," his stained teeth smiled. "We could sit around and relax together. I know how good your chocolate is. Maybe I could sweeten it up for you."

Norberta stared at him. She could not believe his innuendos. "Why would I want to mix my wonderful chocolate with sour milk?"

He gave a loud laugh. "You're something else, Norberta." He swirled the hot chocolate in his cup.

"I could always take one of your daughters off your hands," he offered in a slimy tone.

Norberta's temper was started to boil. She picked up the wooden ladle.

He laughed again. "One of these days you'll be begging me to rescue you."

There was a commotion behind him as an entourage approached.

"Oh, I see we have a cockroach infestation here, comadre," Guadalupe had just returned with the children.

"It is always a pleasure to see you also, Lupe," El Piojo bowed. "I have to go. I hate to leave you beautiful ladies, but así es la vida."

He threw down the cigarette butt and crushed it with his silver-toed boot.

"I can't believe what the cat dragged in," grumbled Guadalupe.

"Thanks for coming to the rescue."

Later, as the Friday twilight approached, young couples started to appear for their diversion in the city plaza. Several mariachi groups would roam from place to place, playing songs for lovers and old timers.

Norberta had not had a serious romantic relationship since her seminarian had left her. Her short "marriage" to the teacher had been out of necessity. There had been no passion, just obligation. Most men did not want to be saddled down with children, especially three young girls. If they did, the machos expected to be the center of the universe and have the offspring relegated to be seen, but not heard. Norberta had made her questionable decisions early in her life and she was willing to live with the consequences. Right now, her immediate concern was survival. The taxes and fees kept increasing. The people were being punished and fined by the government. The church was exploiting the parishioners. A revolution was rumored to be coming. She had to live one week at a time. She had to take care of her family.

By divine providence, Guadalupe had a similar fate. She had migrated down from the Sonoran Desert. When her husband was run over by a stagecoach, she had to assume the breadwinner's responsibilities. Although in this case, the bread came in the shape of churros.

The comadres had met many years before at Cano's general store. Guadalupe was new in town. They were both buying supplies for making their wares. They chatted and eventually became casual friends. Norberta already had her stand at the plaza. Guadalupe sold her churros walking up and down the streets of Teocaltiche. She was not doing so well.

Guadalupe was pregnant with Ramón when she asked Norberta if she would be the godmother. Norberta was honored and said yes. After Ramón was christened, Norberta offered to share her booth at the plaza with her. This was the beginning of a beautiful friendship and a successful symbiotic business venture.

Norberta's older daughters had godparents who had been students at La Virgen de Tepeyac Convent and that she had grown up with. However, when she became pregnant with Herculana, she reciprocated the honor and asked Guadalupe to be the godmother. Lupe was overwhelmed and had literally raised Herculana as her own.

Norberta thought that Guadalupe's traits of being a busybody, complaining about everything, and voicing her opinion on everything, had somehow been transferred to Herculana. Norberta felt that Herculana behaved more like her godmother than her mother.

Pero ¡así es la vida!

CHAPTER 8 – EL POEMA DE AMOR

Sunday, May 22, 1910
Teocaltiche

"Watch out, pendejo!" Ricardo yelled out. "You're going to crash this pinche wagon into a ditch."

Pedro just shrugged. His mind was preoccupied with what he was going to do in town after he and his cousin loaded up the supplies. He knew that he could not simply abandon Ricardo and go straight to the escribana's booth. He already had gotten his cousin in trouble with the mining camp foreman.

"Just wanted to see if you were awake."

"Pinche primo!" The cousin had a sour disposition on his face. "And we are not going to fart around town after we get the supplies. I'll leave your sorry ass there."

"Be calm, Ricardo," Pedro tried to pacify the other. "I know. I know. I won't get you in trouble again."

"¡Sí, chuy!" *Yeah, sure!*

They had departed early that Sunday morning from the mining camp because Pedro wanted to make sure that they arrived in town early and would not be late in the return. Pedro was driving the wagon a little faster than usual and the constant jostling had put Ricardo into a foul mood.

The conversation between the two as they made their way toward their destination was argumentative and contentious.

"I don't see why you are trying to take up with this güera," Ricardo asserted. "You are the wrong color for her. You're too dark and too Indian. She'll dump you like a sack of camotes."

"You're wrong, primo. I know I can win her heart."

"That's not the problem, pendejo!" the other was trying to make his case. "Her parents won't let you get near her. Not to mention her chaperones and brothers. Take my advice and just forget her."

"I can't," Pedro replied. "My heart is full."

"It's not your heart that is full," the cousin was exasperated. "It's your *verga*. We can hit Angela's brothel for a quick one this afternoon."

The bantering remained constant.

The midday church bell was ringing. The eleven o'clock mass had just let out as Pedro and his cousin pulled their supply wagon in front of Cano's General Store.

The owner of the business barely greeted them. There was the smell of liquor on his breath, and he slurred his words. His eyeglasses were almost falling off the end of his bulbous nose. His shirt was half unbuttoned.

Ricardo gave the proprietor the list of supplies and a pouch of coins. Luis Cano crumbled the paper into his pants pocket and started to count the coins. He went behind the counter and opened up a big account book.

"Tell your boss, that you are fifty centavos short," the owner said in a gruff voice. "Plus, what you owe me today. So, what do you need?"

"I gave you the list," said Pedro. Since he could not read, he did not know what was needed. "You put it in your pocket."

Luis Cano clumsily reached into his pocket and pulled the list out.

"Oye, Gustavo," the owner barked to his fifteen-year-old son. "Help me get these supplies for these miners."

The owner rolled up his shirtsleeves and started piling up items on the counter. Some things he weighed on the scale; others he counted.

The pile of provisions started to pile up. A sack of flour. A few slabs of bacon. A couple of tins of coffee . . .

An hour later the supplies had been loaded onto the wagon. The two youngsters made their way to the plaza that was a few blocks away.

By now the cousins were hungry.

"How about this?" suggested Pedro who was trying to be conciliatory with his cousin. "Let's go to the plaza and get something to eat."

Ricardo's head swayed back and forth which indicated his assent.

"We can't leave the provisions unattended though, primo."

"You can stay with the wagon, while I grab us some food. What do want?"

They only had a little money between them, so their options were limited.

Ricardo tied the two horses to a post on the south side of the plaza.

"Let me get the stuff," Ricardo said. "You can relax here."

"No problem."

Ten minutes later they were eating tacos filled with beef tongue.

After he ate, Ricardo's disposition was cheerful. Pedro decided to press this to his advantage.

"Hey, primo, do you want something sweet?"

Ricardo bit. "Sure."

"I'll be back in a few minutes."

Pedro ran through the trees and market booths until he found Norberta's. She was packing up her things.

"Good afternoon, Señora Pérez," he saluted her out of breath. "I'm back."

Norberta looked at the smiling young man. She had dreaded this moment all week.

"Oh, lover boy is back," cackled Guadalupe.

"Hello, Pedro," Norberta said calmly. "How have you been?"

"Fine," he was trying to be polite, but he had an anxious look on his face. "Did you write the love letter?"

"No," the scribe began. "Let me explain why not."

Pedro face dropped. He was almost on the verge of tears.

"First of all, you barely know this girl," she began. "In fact, you don't even know her. This is not the proper way to begin a courtship."

"But you were going to try to find out who she is for me."

"And we did. Ramón discovered who she is. And that is the second problem."

Norberta explained that her godson Ramón had found out that the fair skinned girl was none other than Maria Antonia Sáenz, the daughter of the town's mayor. Don José Sáenz Mejia was a widower and a loyal supporter of Mexican President Porfirio Díaz.

"My boy, their family is gachupin or criollo. They still think they are Spaniards," she continued to explain. "We . .

.you and I, are mestizos. Mixed blood. Their kind don't accept our kind."

"What does all of this have to do with me?" Pedro was frustrated.

"This means that socially you are unacceptable to them," her voice was gentle. "The girl won't even be able to talk to you. You can't always love the one you want." Norberta sighed as she momentarily drifted into an earlier time.

"Why not?" piped up a small voice. "One should be able to love whomever he wants. Who cares?"

"María Herculana!" reprimanded her mother breaking out of her spell. "What are you doing eavesdropping on our conversation?"

"Mamá, that's not fair what you said. Haven't you told me that we should always do what is right?"

"She's got you there, comadre," grinned Lupe who had just joined them. "My advice is don't be a pendejo and find somebody else."

Pedro looked perplexed.

"Writing a letter is not the same as talking," Herculana carried on. "You could still write a letter."

"Oh, Herculana!" her mother sighed.

"What about it, Señora Pérez?"

"Well, I did have an idea in the beginning, especially since I couldn't write a letter because you didn't know the girl's name. You didn't even know the girl!"

Norberta went to the back of the stall and opened up her valise. She found a piece of paper.

"Do you want me to read it you? It's a poem, not a letter."

"Yes, please," Pedro's face was serious. He wasn't quite sure what a pinche poem was, but he trusted Señora Pérez.

Norberta began to recite it slowly:

María Antonia

Your eyes have planted a flower in the garden of my heart.
Your smile has given it sunlight.
The sound of your voice would make it sweet.
The touch of your hand would make it grow.
Please meet with me and make my life complete.

With all my love,

Pedro Campos

As she read the poem to him, small sparkly hearts and flowers seemed to glisten on the page.

"It is the most beautiful thing I have ever heard," exclaimed Pedro. "She will love it!"

Herculana thought that his concept of the world was small and naïve, but at least, he seemed to have a good heart.

They all decided that Ramón would deliver the poem the following day at the Sáenz hacienda that was on a hill on the outskirts of town.

Pedro was elated and he paid Norberta what she had asked.

He started to leave and then said, "Señora, wouldn't it be better if Ramón delivered the love poem tonight. I can't wait for her to get it."

"Go all the way to her hacienda?" interjected Guadalupe. "That's asking a lot."

"No, I mean give it to her at the paseo tonight as she is walking around the kiosk."

Moments later Pedro jumped into the supply wagon.

"Where in the hell have you been?" Ricardo was angry with Pedro again.

"Sorry, I was just trying to settle something."

"And where are the pinche sweets that you promised?"

"Sorry, I forgot."

They started on their journey back to the mining camp.

"Ay, pendejo!" snapped Ricardo at his cousin.

CHAPTER 9 – ARACELI

Monday, May 23, 1910

Don José Sáenz Mejia, the municipal president of Teocaltiche, boarded his carriage and said goodbye to his daughter and her girlfriend. The mayor had a council meeting that morning and he was anxious to get going.

His daughter Maria Antonia waved her white handkerchief until her father had left the hacienda that was situated on a hill about a mile or so from town.

"Oh, Maria Antonia, please tell me!" Araceli pleaded excitedly. "What did he say?"

Maria Antonia walked slowly into the study without replying. She sat down in a casual manner fluffing up her yellow dress as she did so.

"You have to tell me," Araceli begged.

Just then a dark-complexioned woman entered the room. She was short and stocky, and her face was pocked.

"Excuse me, ladies," the domestic servant inquired. "May I bring you anything? Coffee?"

"No, thank you, Jesusita," replied Maria Antonia. Jesusita was the household cook and maid who was entirely loyal to the young girl.

The domestic woman left the room.

"Okay, but this is what you deserve for abandoning me last night at the paseo," Maria Antonia replied in a sassy tone.

"It wasn't my fault," her friend pleaded. "My parents were invited to a dinner with the Aragonez's. I couldn't exactly decline. Besides you were with your cousin Gregorio."

"Don't even talk about him," Maria Antonia shook her head.

"But he was your escort at your quinceañera. I thought your father was pushing you to marry him."

"He is so boring!" Maria Antonia expressed her disapproval. "Besides Renya thinks it is a sin for cousins to get married."

Leyla "Renya" Acle had been the girl's guardian since the death of her mother when Maria Antonia was two years old. Renya was brought up in Veracruz in a traditional Lebanese family. She adhered to the Catholic faith very strongly. She had very seriously taken on the task of raising Maria Antonia in the most proper way for a Christian woman.

"But tell me what happened," Araceli implored again.

"Well, the carriage dropped us off at the plaza. Gregorio and me," Maria Antonia began to narrate. Her hazel eyes looked up to the right. "And Renya also. We started to walk around. Gregorio is such a little boy."

"All of the boys at the paseo seem to be," interjected Araceli.

"We were walking and talking. I don't remember what about, when a teenager ran up to me and handed me a small envelope."

"Was it the same boy from two weeks ago? The one who gave you the palm flower?"

"I don't think so. This one was younger."

"What was in the envelope," Araceli was getting more curious.

"A beautiful love poem."

"From whom?"

"I think it was from that stranger from before."

"I thought you disliked him. In fact, you were going to give him back the palm flower. Did you do that?"

"No. I had it with me last week and I planned to do it," Maria Antonia was on the defensive. "But he never showed up. So, I didn't bring it with me last night."

"Are you trying to hide something from me, Maria Antonia?" her friend asked. "It can't be a coincidence that boys come running up to you. That's not the custom. It's not proper."

"No, I'm not hiding anything. I don't understand this either."

"Did you get rid of the palm flower?"

"No. I have it in my dresser."

"Why?"

"I don't know. I kind of like it."

"That's not what you said two weeks ago."

"I know. I know," Maria Antonia was at a loss for an adequate explanation.

"What are you going to do now?"

Maria Antonia got up from the sofa and started to pace around the room. All of her girlfriends had secret boyfriends, or at least, wanted them. *Well, maybe I deserve someone also! I want to have fun!*

"I don't know," she responded ambiguously. "I can't write back to him. I don't even know who he is. I can try to see if he shows up at a paseo. I know father would not like him. He probably wouldn't even let me talk to him."

"Well, I guess that you are stuck with Gregorio."

"What are my choices, Araceli?" she brooded. "To be stuck for the rest of my life with a dullard of a cousin or risk a scandal by talking to a stranger who is obviously socially inferior. Can you image spending the next thirty years with Gregorio? I think that I'd rather die first. Death by boredom perhaps."

"Well, maybe it would be exciting to meet and talk to the stranger. I'm sure that he is not tiresome," Araceli grinned devilishly. "It might even be fun."

"Maybe."

"Oh, Maria Antonia, you are so fickle."

The girls looked at each other and started to giggle.

A woman dressed in a long, black dress came into the study.

"Good morning, Renya," Maria Antonia bowed slightly to the older black haired, dark eyed woman with a dark complexion.

"Good morning, Señora Acle," echoed Araceli.

"Good morning, young ladies," the guardian replied. "What are you young ladies up to? Maria Antonia, you have studies to do this morning."

"Yes, Renya," replied María Antonia. "Do you think that we could do our lessons this afternoon? I need to discuss the possibility of having a party here at the hacienda this summer with Araceli. Do you think papa would approve?"

Maria Antonia knew how to get around Renya's strict regimen. The seemingly innocent introduction of the notion of a party would start her guardian's mind thinking and planning. It deflected her guardian's plan for morning studies.

"Sure, we can do that," replied Renya. "But as to the party. What date were you thinking of? Maybe we should pick two or three dates and see if they work with your father's schedule. And how many guests are we talking about? We'll have to set a date soon if we are going to invite people from out of town."

Renya went on and on for several minutes brainstorming about a summer party. Maria Antonia's diversion had worked. Unwittingly Renya had permitted her ward to enjoy a leisurely morning. Renya left the room saying that she had to start the planning process for the party.

"How shall we plan for you to meet your prince charming?" Araceli gave an impish grin.

"We could . . ."

CHAPTER 10 – EL GORDITO

Saturday, May 28, 1910

The three older men were smoking and arguing on the benches in front of Norberta's booth. The morning had been chilly, and many people had already finished their shopping.

"That's impossible," exclaimed the old man with the thick glasses. "Only birds can fly."

"Not my chickens," cackled the second elderly man with the knitted green muffler around his neck.

Alberto put down his cup of chocolate and raised the newspaper. He pointed to a photo on the front page. "It says so right here. These gringos flew a machine up in the air . . . and then it crashed!"

But as always, the conversation turned to Mexican politics.

"That pinche Díaz stole the presidential election. What is it? His seventh term?" Alberto was giving a discourse to his two companions. "He was never supposed to have served more than four or six years, as I remember."

"I can't believe he had Madero arrested!" said his companion, Noe. "I never liked Madero, but I hated Díaz. Why doesn't he just turn over Mexico to the yanquis? Their president already stole the Philippines and other territories from Spain. We're next!"

"You can't believe everything you read in those pinche newspapers," Mauricio said "They are tools of propaganda. It really doesn't matter. But yanquis don't want our people, paisano," Mauricio remarked. "They just want to steal our black gold."

The trio went through their routine bickering about the affairs of the world.

Norberta and Lupe had sent Herculana and Ramón on an errand to the market. They were supposed to look for dried corn.

The three gentlemen departed and the comadres were making small talk.

They noticed a very heavyset lady wearing a pea green dress that was bulging out at the seams approaching them. She was waddling side to side in low heels carrying a large floral imprinted handbag. Next to her was a chubby boy who was walking with his head down. The woman looked to the right and then to the left as if she was looking for something or was lost. She walked up to the counter of the booth.

"Excuse me, ladies," she said in a rushed, nervous manner. "I am looking for the mother of Herculana."

"I am her mother, Norberta Pérez, at your service," the wheels in her mind were churning. *What does this woman want with my child?*

Lupe moved closer to her comadre but did not introduce herself. She was interested in what this woman had to say, regarding her goddaughter.

"My name is Silvia Gallegos, señora," the lady began. She smelled of cheap perfume. "This my son is Geraldo." Norberta almost gagged from the cloying scent.

"A pleasure to meet you," responded Norberta. She had a gut feeling that this was not going to be a pleasant encounter. Every once in a while, a customer would complain about the chocolate drink. Too thick. Too watery. Not sweet enough. But being the consummate businessperson, that she was, Norberta learned not to get upset and just try to be pleasant and courteous. She didn't need a bad reputation in the community.

Lupe took a half step closer to her comadre's table.

Señora Gallegos glanced over to Lupe. She was put off a little by Lupe's nosiness, but began to speak, "Señora Pérez, I would like your daughter Herculana to stop harassing my poor son, Geraldo. He came home crying the other day from school. He said that Herculana beat him up for no reason."

"When did this happen?"

"Two days ago. On Thursday."

Geraldo kept a blank face.

Norberta and Lupe looked at each other. The boy was twice Herculana's size and older.

"I'm sorry to hear this, Señora Gallegos," Norberta replied skeptically. "Herculana should be back in a moment."

"Okay," the woman said. "But the girl should apologize to my son and promise never to do it again."

Norberta shook her head but did not say anything more.

A few minutes later Herculana and Ramón came back running with a sack of dried corn.

"Herculana, this is Señora Gallegos," her mother said.

"Pleasure to meet you," Herculana made a slight nod.

"And I believe you know her son Geraldo."

Herculana nodded her head affirmatively.

"What happened at school on Thursday?" her mother asked her very sternly.

"Let's see," Herculana's eyes looked up to the left and drew out her words. "That was the day that I brought a quesadilla to school. I kept it in my handkerchief . . ."

Herculana only attended the little neighborhood school on Mondays, Tuesdays, and Thursdays. On any given day there were between twenty-five to forty students ranging in age from five to fifteen or sixteen in the single room. About two thirds of them were girls.

The school was housed in an old shoe store where the planks were cracked, and the roof had a million holes. It had a dirt floor. It smelled of mold and little critters scurried through the floorboards.

The schoolteacher was a retired librarian from Guadalajara. He was almost sixty years old and stone deaf.

There were only three wooden tables that the students sat around. Some children had to stand or sit on the floor. There was no black board or chalk. The teacher had his lessons on big pieces of paper that he pinned onto one of the decrepit walls. There was an inordinate amount of time when the children took up singing or went outside for a break. Very little "learning" occurred.

The children usually ate a snack at the ten o'clock recess.

"I was starting to eat my quesadilla over by the school building," Herculana continued. "I heard a scream. It was Perla. She was yelling at Gordo to give her food back . . ."

Perla Chou Sota was a slender 11-year-old girl with beautiful almond shaped brown eyes. She was the daughter of Wang Chou, a local merchant, and his wife, Gabriela Soto, from Mexticacan. Perla was bilingual in Spanish and Cantonese.

For the second day in a row, Gordo had snatched Perla's pork filled bun at the mid-morning recess.

Perla had yelled out, "Bei phen ngor ah, lei sei fei chu! Give it back to me, you dead fat pig!"

"Shut your snout!" Gordo screamed back spewing food bits to her. "Chinky monkey!"

Perla replied angrily, "Sei chun! Stupid!" She started to cry.

Herculana had wandered over to where the bully and the victim were. She stared at Gordo.

"What are you looking at, fea?" Gordo's right arm swung around in an attempt to snatch Herculana's quesadilla.

The next thing he remembered was an excruciating pain in his groin area where Herculana had nailed him. She kept punching him. Other children started to gather around and chant.

"Herculana! Herculana! Herculana!"

Gordo had the sudden urge to urinate, but it was painful. Slowly, he struggled to get up in spite of the continuous belting by Herculana. He finally was able to free himself from her and staggered home.

"Hmm," Norberta stroked her chin as if to think. She wanted to support her daughter. She had tried to teach her how to be independent. No girl in her right mind could depend on a man. On the other hand, she did not want Herculana to resolve every problem by physical force or violence. Norberta did not want to make the decision. She did not want to be the "bad guy."

"What do you think, Señora Gallegos?" Norberta dropped the issue on to Silvia's lap.

"I don't know what to think," the woman was searching for a response. "Geraldo, did you take someone else's food?"

The boy blushed. "Well, I was hungry."

Gordo's mother gave him a dirty look.

"Speaking of hunger, Señora Gallegos, excuse my rudeness," Norberta smiled because the woman was trapped. "Would you and your son like some of our hot chocolate and churros?"

Gordo's eyes grew big and he smiled. He started to move forward.

Suddenly, an arm flew out to stop him. His mother nodded her head no.

"Excuse me, Señora Pérez, thank you for the generous offer, but we have to go. We are already late," the woman oozed with insincerity. "It was a pleasure meeting you."

"May it go well with you," Norberta said as the mother and son departed.

In spite of the commotion at the market, Señora Gallegos yelling at her son could be heard everywhere.

Norberta pulled her daughter close to her.

"I am proud of you for sticking up for what is right. That was a courageous thing sticking up for the other girl."

"Well, Gordo is a pig. He was going to steal my food too. That's not going to happen!"

"What did you learn from all of this, mija?

"I don't know. Maybe I should eat my snack with Perla. Gordo wouldn't attack two people. He is too chicken."

"Herculana, try not to get into any more fights," Norberta was proud of her brave daughter, but did not want to encourage her. "But if you do, make sure it is for a good reason."

Herculana nodded her head as if she understood.

"And make sure you win," shouted Lupe.

"¡Ay, comadre!"

CHAPTER 11 – AMIGUITO

Sunday, May 29, 1910

Pedro left early from the mining camp. Half the workers were long term employees; the other half were drifters who earned just enough money to be able to move on. While most of them were Mexican, there were a sprinkling of Yanquis, Chinos, and indigenous natives. Everybody got along. The co-worker next to you deep in the mine was your lifeline.

Pedro had taken a predawn shower and had spruced himself up. El Brujo seemed to like the Sunday rides into town, but the horse was not so happy when he had to make the trek back up the mountain. Pedro compensated him with extra carrots and apples.

There were no clouds visible in the bright blue skies as he descended the mountain. Pedro counted twenty-nine switchbacks before he stopped counting. He knew it was going to be hot, so he took it easy on El Brujo. There was no breeze today.

The sagebrush smells were refreshing, and swallows were darting in and out between the flowering cacti. A gecko skittered across the trail in front of him. Pedro took a cool swig of water from his canteen.

Forty-five minutes later he came to the crossroads and took the way toward town. Nobody was on the camino. El Brujo gave an unusual bray that Pedro had not heard before. A hundred yards later, he found an abandoned two-wheel wooden cart. It was empty and no one was around. Pedro got off his horse and examined the abandoned little dray. It looked like a spoke had broken and the wheel was out of round. That would make this vehicle very difficult to pull.

I don't have any tools with me. Can't be much help here, Pedro thought.

Pedro was within an hour of the pueblo and so he got back in the saddle. A mile later, Pedro detected a small human being, struggling with two burdensome burlap bags. They looked moderately heavy. He came alongside the young boy. The youngster seemed very familiar, but he couldn't remember why.

"Hey, are you going into town?" Pedro asked.

The boy nodded affirmatively. Pedro tried to do some quick calculations in his head. They were probably almost an hour away. He couldn't let this kid carry the sacks in the heat. This was a bad situation for the boy and Pedro felt sorry for him.

"How heavy are your bags?" Pedro asked.

"One is about five pounds. The other is ten," answered the boy.

"Okay, let's tie them to the saddle horn," Pedro reached for one of the sacks. A minute later both sacks were tied on. Pedro handed the boy his canteen. The boy eagerly took some deep gulps.

"Thank you, Señor Pedro."

What the heck! How does this kid know my name! This is strange!

"How do you know my name?"

"I'm Ramón."

Ramón? Ramón? Oh, Ramón that delivered my love poem to my corazón!

"Was that your cart that I spotted back down the road a piece?"

"Yeah. The spoke broke and I don't know how to fix it," sighed Ramón. "I have to get these things delivered to my mom and to my madrina."

"Señora Nava is your mom?"

The kid nodded yes.

"And Señora Pérez is your madrina?"

Another nod.

"Well, you are in luck today, amiguito," Pedro smiled. "I am on my way to see them."

They were walking slowly when Ramón suddenly blurted out, "Señor Pedro, I think I have some news for you."

"Ramón, call me Pedro," Pito thought that this kid had good manners.

"Okay. You remember that I found out the name of the girl that you want to write to," the kid started to narrate. "María Antonia Saenz? The mayor's daughter?"

"Oh, sure."

"Just like you asked me," the boy was sweating in the heat. "I gave her the note. She was at the paseo and I ran up and gave it to her."

"Did she say anything?"

"No.

"Did anyone receive any letters from her?"

"I don't know. You'll have to ask my nina."

The two chatted for the next hour until they reached the town and made their way straight to Lupe's churros.

His mother spotted him from afar.

"Mijo, what happened to you?" Lupe was animated. "You're so late!"

Ramón gave a rendition of the mishap with a tear running down his cheek.

Lupe looked at Pedro. "Thank you for helping my boy. I bet you boys are hungry. Here are a few churros."

A few minutes later Norberta and Herculana came walking over. Ramón had to go through the recital again.

"Herculana, get these boys some hot chocolate," Norberta ordered her daughter. "This was a stroke of good fortune."

The boys indulged and now Ramón was feeling better. Pedro promised to go back with Ramón and help him fix the wheel after he talked with Norberta.

After a crowd of customers, Norberta had a brief respite and was able to talk to Pedro about his love quest.

"Señora Norberta, have you heard anything from María Antonia?" Pedro was apprehensive. "I have been thinking about her all week."

"No, my son. Nada." Norberta said calmly not questioning how he knew the girl's name. *Poor young boy!*

***

Norberta's mind started to wander back to when she was fifteen years old. Even younger than Pedro. She was being brought up at the nunnery. There had been a seminarian assigned to help the elderly priest at the abbey. The other novitiates used to giggle and chatter about how handsome

Reverend Lucero Hinojosa was. He had not yet made his vows to the priesthood and some of the girls wanted to tempt his virtue. A few knew that they would never become nuns. Maybe life could be experienced in a different light before hard decisions had to be made. Nobody said one had to be a virgin, in order to be a nun.

The reverend would tease the girls. It almost looked like flirting. In the beginning he paid very little attention to Norberta. Then one day, he came up to her when she was praying in the chapel.

"Good morning, Norberta," he flashed a big smile as he stood beside her.

"Good morning, reverend," she pulled her black stone rosary into her hand.

"How are you today?"

"Fine," Norberta was puzzled. He had never spoken to her before. *Did I do something wrong?*

"Mother Superior tells me that you are getting excellent marks. She thinks that you are almost ready to go preach the Bible to the people."

Norberta knew that the Mexican government was in a struggle with the Catholic Church. Mexican President Porfirio Díaz was confiscating ecclesiastical properties and banning all religious services and clergy. The Church decided to use lay people in order to proselytize to the peasants. The Cristero War was beginning. This is why she had to excel in her studies.

Reverend Hinojosa began to seek out Norberta. She was more serious than the other silly girls. Norberta thought nothing of it. Then one day the Mother Superior announced to the novitiates that they were going to have a birthday gathering for Reverend Hinojosa. She assigned Norberta to make the cake. A chocolate cake.

CHAPTER 12 – SPOKE

Sunday, May 29, 1910

Pedro was upset that María Antonia had not responded to his love poem. *How can she not be in love with me like I am with her?*

"Señora Norberta, what should we do?" his dark brown eyes pleaded with her. "Maybe she didn't get it."

"Pedro, Ramón said he handed the poem to her," she sighed. "If he said he delivered it, he did so." *What is this "we" stuff?* Norberta was taken back at his words. *It's his affair, not mine. On the other hand, he did help Ramón. I guess I could be charitable.*

"You could wait another week and see what happens," Norberta suggested.

"But I need to talk to her now!" Pedro was frustrated.

"Well, you know that you can't go to her house," Norberta was trying to be direct. "You wouldn't be welcomed."

There was a silence.

"Why don't you send her another letter?" piped up a little voice behind the two. "This way you would know for sure."

¡Ay Dios mio, Herculana! ¡Como friegas! Please don't make more work for me, she silently pleaded. She thought that she was losing money assisting Pedro. The only one who was getting paid was Ramón.

"That's a great idea, Herculana!" Pedro beamed. "Thank you!"

Norberta gave her daughter a dirty look that was ignored by the little one.

"Well, what do you want to say?" Norberta asked.

"I don't know," Pedro's eyes looked askance. "What should I say?"

Norberta didn't reply. She wasn't going to do all the work, especially if she was not going to be paid.

At that moment, Lupe and Ramón walked over. "Oye, comadre, we may have to close up early since we don't have a cart to take our stuff back."

"Well, maybe we could ask Señor Loera if he could take some things with him," Norberta didn't want to go home early. She still had two more masses to sell her goods. "How long until we get the cart fixed?"

Everybody looked at Ramón who shrugged his shoulders. Although he was fifteen-years-old, he was not mechanically gifted. "I don't know," he replied meekly.

"Is there a carretero in town?" Pedro asked.

There were no replies. They never had been a need for a cartwright until now.

"We'll ask around," Pedro grabbed Ramón by the tricep and led him away.

After asking a few people, the boys were directed to a stable with an adjoining shop about a mile away. Ramón rode behind Pedro on El Brujo. The place was easy to find. "Dos Hermanos" read the wooden sign.

The heavy, squat man initially ignored the boys as they approached him. He was named Alfonso.

"Buenos días, señor," Pedro tipped his sombrero. "We're looking for a wheel for a cart. Ours broke down."

"A new wheel, you say," Alfonso echoed. "Follow me."

The trio walked into the stable and pointed to an assortment of wheels of various sizes.

"Which one?" he continued.

Ramón took the lead since he was more familiar with the dimensions of his broken-down cart. He pointed to two. "I think one of these would do."

"That'll be 500 pesos [about $17 U.S.]," Alfonso said.

Ramón looked at Pedro. That was a lot of money and they both knew that they didn't have it.

"Señor, do you have any old ones?" Pedro piped up.

Alfonso knew that these kids didn't have any money. "Let me ask my brother. He's out back."

"My brother says we can give you one this size for 300 pesos [about $10 U.S.]. That's a good deal."

"We don't have that much money," Ramón blurted out.

Pedro and Ramón started to leave when a bigger and fatter man stood in their way. "What's up, young fellas?"

Ramón told him the whole story.

"Hey, aren't you the kid that works with the churro lady?"

"Yeah, she's my mom."

Fifteen minutes later, Pedro was rolling an old wheel down the road and Ramón carrying two wooden spokes with a tin can of some type of pitch glue and another of grease. The deal was the rental of the replacement wheel for 100 pesos for one week plus a dozen churros. This would allow ample time to fix the old wheel and to return the replacement wheel.

Finally, the two boys returned to Lupe and Norberta's stand. Ramón was feeling uneasy. He had spent a hundred pesos with no guarantee that the wheel would be fixed. He knew that his mom didn't have much money.

"You did good, mijo" Lupe said. "And thank you, Pedro, for your help today. You have been a Godsend."

"You're welcome," Pedro started to walk away. He and Ramón would be leaving to find the cart and repair it before Pedro had to return to the mining camp.

"Wait, Pedro, don't you want to see the letter I wrote for you?" Norberta shouted after him.

Pedro was overjoyed. "Yes, please!"

Norberta started reading:

May 29, 1910

My most precious María Antonia,

I keep the memory of your smile in my heart. I can feel it beating. It makes me yearn for you.

I have not heard from you, so I have written you again.

Could we meet? I am only allowed to come to town on Sunday mornings and early afternoons. I could meet you at the plaza when it is convenient for you.

I am anxious to look into your eyes once again.

I miss you very much. May God protect you.

Your servant,
Pedro Campos

"This is great!" Pedro was excited. "Thank you so much!"

"Just remember that since you and Ramón are leaving right now, the letter will not be delivered today."

"Oh?!" replied Pedro deflated.

CHAPTER 13 – COMADRES

Wednesday, June 1, 1910

Norberta rested on a rickety bench in the booth. Lupe joined her. Everybody was still exhausted from having to carry all their goods and materials three days prior without Ramón and the wagon. She now appreciated her godson even more. The sun was hot and the air was dead. No breeze today. There was very little activity at the plazita. Things were quiet. There were very few birds fluttering around.

Lupe looked exceptionally tired.

"I'm glad that Ramón and Pedro got that wheel fixed," Norberta inhaled. "What a pain in the culo!"

Lupe nodded. "They are good boys."

"Well, Pedro was a godsend, comadre. We must be doing something right."

"He's still a pendejo thinking about the güera."

The morning went by slowly. Ramón came back to the booth. He had finished returning the borrowed cartwheel to the Dos Hermanos cartwrights.

"Mom, Alfonso and his brother really liked your churros,"
Ramón reported. "They send their thanks."

Lupe hoped that they would send some business her way.
The hundred pesos had set her back a little.

Alberto Nuñez came by as per his usual custom and
ordered a hot chocolate and a churro. He started to read the
newspaper, muttering ill-tempered commentaries on the
incompetence and corruption of the government.

"The revolution is here!" he said to aloud. "El Presidente
Díaz soon will be paying the price!"

Alberto was soon joined by his two elderly colleagues, Noe
and Mauricio, who also purchased hot chocolate and churros.
They all are argued about this and that. The two companions
warned Alberto that he ought to keep his opinions to himself.
There were too many snitches around who would sell him out
for a song. The mayor didn't tolerate troublemakers. He was
one hundred percent allied with President Porfirio Díaz.

Sometimes Ramón would eavesdrop on the three viejos.
His mother had warned him about this and reprimanded him.

Norberta saw Ramón standing closed to Alberto,
mesmerized by the old men. She knew that Lupe didn't care for
that.

"Ramón!" Norberta shouted at him.

The boy jumped and turned around. He ran over to Norberta.

"Yes, nina," Ramón anticipated that his godmother wanted him to do something for her. Sometimes it meant making a few pesos.

"I need you to take this letter to María Antonia right now," Norberta said in a low voice, not wanting anyone to overhear her. She handed the missive to him.

"The same girl I gave the other letter to?"

"Yes."

"But today is not Sunday," his face frowned.

"I know, but it needs to be done today," replied Norberta.

"But where do I take it?"

"To her house."

"Where is that?" Ramón wasn't liking the sound of this.

"I think it is about a ten or fifteen-minute walk from here," his godmother said. "I think it is north of here. In the foothills. Ask around. Somebody should know how to get there."

Ramón shrugged and started to leave.

"And Ramón this is sort of a secret," she said softly. "Don't go to the front entrance. Try to find the kitchen door. And be careful."

Ramón sighed. *This is going to be a long walk. But I know this is for Pedro. I owe him for helping me out with the cartwheel. And besides, I know my nina will give me a peso for the delivery.*

After Ramón had left and there was a break between the customers, Norberta walked over next to Lupe as was her usual custom.

"Old man Alberto is crazy!" Lupe remarked. "He is going to get himself shot if he doesn't watch his mouth."

"Hopefully, he will be okay, comadre," Norberta countered. "By the way, have you heard that the government is sending troops into our town. I think the mayor has requested them. This can't be good."

"And Yoli told me this morning that they want to increase the taxes on our booths. I think they want to raise money for the military."

"It's bad enough that we can barely eke out a living for our children, comadre," Norberta stated sadly.

A woman with her baby came by and ordered a hot chocolate and a few churros. They chatted for a few minutes and then the pair left.

"Oye, comadre, I'm glad the boys fixed the wheel," Norberta was repeating a prior conversation. "It must have been expensive."

Lupe nodded without saying a word.

Norberta knew what this meant. Lupe didn't complain. Well, not too much, anyway. She would never ask for help. She was too proud.

"Anyway, if you need any help, just let me know," Norberta said trying to tactfully offer her comadre money. They had a history of helping each other out since they pooled their resources many years earlier and opened up their chocolate and churro businesses. Norberta had the advantage of being the village scribe, and that allowed her to earn extra income.

"Thanks, Norberta," Lupe gave a weak smile. "I'm good."

"We need to expand our business, comadre," Norberta said. "Especially if they are going to raise out rates."

Lupe paused for a few moments. "What can we sell? Tamales? Rosalinda makes good ones and everyone buys from her. That wouldn't be fair. Maybe something that we can make at home and bring to the plaza."

"So, you are thinking of food?"

"I can't sew. What else could we do?"

They brainstormed and discussed this and that. Somethings would take too much time and effort to make. Others were sold by other vendors. And certain things had expensive up-front expenses.

"Comadre, maybe we should be thinking about providing some type of service. Like washing clothes or something?"

"Well, that's what the criadas do," Lupe answered. "And I am certainly not signing up to be a wet nurse or puta!"

They both started to laugh. Their exhaustion was overwhelming them.

Ramón came back about an hour and a half later. He had been successful. He had delivered the letter to the maid at the back door of María Antonia's house. He didn't wait for a response.

At the end of the day, Norberta and Lupe and their children started walking back home. Norberta sidled over to Lupe and slipped fifty pesos into the latter's apron pocket.

Francisca and Julia greeted the entourage upon their homecoming. The homemade tortillas whetted everyone's appetite.

CHAPTER 14 – THE HUMMINGBIRDS

Friday, June 3, 1910

Crunch! Crunch! Crunch! Herculana was trudging on the gravel alongside her mother that early morning on the way to the plaza. There was a cool high desert dew on the succulents that bordered them. A few birds flew around the saguaro cacti. There was the smell of wood being burned in the casitas throughout the valley.

"Mom, why do hummingbirds fight?" Herculana looked up and asked her mother interrupting the latter's thoughts.

"How do you know they fight, mija?" Norberta was curious about her daughter's observations.

"I see them. One sits a branch. He is green. And is red around the throat. And white around his belly."

"Sounds like a real Mexican hummingbird to me," laughed Norberta.

"No, really, mom. He sits on a little branch next to the red flowers behind the casita and when other hummingbirds come around, he chases them away. He goes really fast. And they go really high in the air."

Too early to tell her about the birds and the bees?! These kids grow up so quickly, Norberta pondered.

"It almost like they are sword fighting."

How would she know anything about that?!

"Well, mija, we are all put on earth to work and have children," Norberta began. "In order to do that, we need to have food and water. For the hummingbirds, it is the same thing. The macho has to protect the food supply so his family can eat and survive and make babies. He is just guarding his territory."

"But what about the other birds. Are they going to starve?"

"Well, unfortunately, in this world, only the strong survive. And that is why men control the world."

"But, mom, no men protect us. You and my nina look after us just fine. We don't need anybody else."

Norberta stared at Herculana. *She's a handful.*

"Mom, when I grow up, I'm going to get me a canary. A whole bunch of them. They can sing for me."

They arrived at the plazita and began to set up before the six o'clock mass. A few parishioners braved the cool air and bought hot chocolate from Norberta and fresh churros from Lupe.

The morning went slowly as usual. The regulars like Alberto came and went.

Around noon a dark-skinned woman in her mid-thirties approached Lupe. Her face was pockmarked, and she was short and stocky. While her clothes were plain, they seemed to be of good quality. She stopped in front of Lupe.

"Señora, are you the escribana? The one who wrote the letter to María Antonia?" she seemed uneasy talking.

"No, paisana," Lupe felt sorry for the woman. "She's right over there talking to one of her customers."

A minute later, the woman was introducing herself to Norberta.

"Señora, I am Soledad Lopez. I am here at the request of my mistress, María Antonia Saenz," she gave a polite bow.

"I am Norberta Pérez. A sus ordenes. What can I help you with?"

"María Antonia wants to know more about the boy who has been writing to her. The delivery boy says that the letters come from you. She can't talk to the young man without her chaperone. She is very proper"

Norberta's forehead furrowed. The visitation did not make sense. *Why is Soledad here on the sly?*

"Maybe she should meet with him with her chaperone," Norberta countered. This put the other woman on the defensive.

"Señora, María Antonia does not want to do that. She doesn't want to embarrass her father. He's the mayor of the town. He can't have gossip circulating."

"Soledad, if I may call you Soledad, what do you think about your mistress writing Pedro a letter explaining all that? She can even suggest a two-minute conversation. Then she could get a quick impression of him and make a decision."

Soledad didn't know how to respond. "Yes, maybe she could do that."

"It couldn't hurt."

"Is Pedro around right now?"

"No, Soledad, he works at the Atepoca mine," Norberta wanted her to report all of this to her mistress. "He only comes to town on Sunday mornings."

"Does he go to mass?"

Norberta shrugged. She didn't want to say one way or another on this subject. "He'll probably be around here this Sunday."

Soledad nodded and thanked her.

Norberta handed her some wrapped chocolates. "And maybe this will help."

It was getting close to two o'clock and Norberta and Lupe were starting to clean up. Ramón and Herculana were doing their share.

"I'll take two of those," a gruff voice demanded as a hand reached out and grabbed two churros.

The voice was attached to a slovenly-dressed police sergeant. He was obese and had a big moustache and long sideburns. He toted a large pistol at his side. He was loud and ill-mannered.

Lupe and Norberta looked up. Geraldo Montez was a nightmare. It was rumored that he was part of an enterprise that abducted young girls from the poorer areas of Mexico with false promises of work only to be sold to brothels. He was a friend of Jorge "El Piojo" Contreras and was involved in numerous dirty deeds.

Oh, no! This pig is here again. What does he want now? Norberta was concerned.

"Señoras, have you seen any revolutionaries around here?" Geraldo inquired in a nonchalant manner.

Norberta and Lupe automatically nodded their heads no. Ignorance was always the better alternative to answering an infinite number of questions.

"Well, that is good news!" he gave them a large unctuous smile. "That means that the police are protecting the fine people of this city."

Norberta and Lupe continued to clean up.

"But do you know what that means, ladies?" he took a step closer to them. His foul breath could wilt flowers. "We'll need more funds to continue this level of public service for you. Everybody wants to have a safe city. And everybody should be willing to pay for it. It could be very dangerous otherwise."

The two women could feel another mordida coming.

"The mayor thinks that an increase of ten percent for the privilege of doing business in this town seems fair. The vendors are making money and have the most to lose. We don't want revolutionaries here stealing our goods. This levy went into effect two days ago. We will start collecting at the end of the month. Thank you for your support."

¡Ay demonios! Norberta was shaking her head as the pig left. *We are barely eking out a living now! We can't raise prices.* What are we going to do? Where is that macho hummingbird to protect us?

CHAPTER 15 – FATHER KNOWS BEST

Saturday, June 4, 1910

Araceli walked into the salon of the Sáenz home. María Antonia was just finishing her French lesson. Mayor Sáenz was a strong supporter of President Porfirio Díaz and the Porfiristas. Like Días, he wanted a whiter, more European looking Mexico. He wanted modernization and foreign investment. Everyone loved the monuments and buildings in Mexico City, he thought proudly. Why shouldn't they? He believed in patriarch and that men should rule the world! They did not have to live like animals, like the mestizos and indios. Díaz and his government knew best.

"De quelle couleur est ton chat?" the governess Cybele Dumas recited.

"Elle est orange avec des rayures noires," replied María Antonia with perfect pronunciation and rhythm.

"Très bien!" replied the tutor. "C'est tout pour aujourd'hui. Continue le travail. Jusqu'a le semaine prochaine."

The student and teacher exchanged kisses on the cheek. Mademoiselle excused herself and left the salon. Leyla "Renya" Acle escorted Araceli into the study so the two friends could entertain themselves.

"María Antonia," directed Señora Acle, "you should change your dress if you have any inclination of going outside. It's warm out there. Take a parasol." Finally, María Antonia's guardian then exited the room.

Araceli rushed over to María Antonia. "You're going to have to tell me everything. I can't wait to hear it."

The pair ran up the stairs and flew into María Antonia's room where they both jumped on the bed giggling.

A half hour later they were walking to the far ends of the immense garden filled with red and white bougainvilleas, far from earshot. They stopped and huddled under a tall sycamore tree.

"Come on, María Antonia," Araceli pleaded. "Tell me! Tell me!"

Her friend loved the attention and hesitated a moment before speaking.

"I had to be careful after receiving that poem. I didn't want to get caught," María Antonia began. "I sent Soledad to the plaza to buy some chocolate tablets to make hot chocolate . . ."

"Why? I don't understand," Araceli frowned.

"The poem came from the escribana in the plaza."

"I still don't understand."

"The lady is a scribe, and she sells chocolate," María Antonia was starting to exhibit signs of frustration trying to explain things to her best friend.

"Okay."

"Soledad met this lady. I think that her name was Señora Pérez. She admitted to Soledad that she was the writer of the poem. Soledad said she wanted to talk with Pedro, but the lady said he was not around. He works in a mine or something like that. He only comes around on Sunday mornings."

"That doesn't sound good, María Antonia."

"I really want to give him back that shabby flower that he gave me. Can you imagine me accepting it?"

Araceli nodded her head no.

"What are you going to do now, María Antonia?"

"Soledad said that the boy, his name is Pedro, wanted me to write him a letter. He said that his heart stops when he thinks of me."

"How would you get a letter to him? Renya and your father are watching you all the time. It's impossible!"

In the early afternoon the two friends wandered back into the mansion. There they were met by Soledad.

"Señorita María Antonia, would you like your lunch now?" the cook asked.

"No, thank you, Soledad," the girl paused. "Let's do tea in the salon. A little bread and cheese too. Better yet, serve some of those chocolates you got yesterday."

A while later Renya walked in on the two girls who were wildly chattering away. She scanned the afternoon fare and called out.

"Soledad, where is the tea?" Renya yelled out.

Señor Sáenz was pretentious about serving tea in his home, rather than coffee. Tea was European. Coffee was for the indigenous people.

Soledad came in and obsequiously bowed. "Yes, señora," and returned to the kitchen.

"María Antonia, what are you eating?" Renya was bent over examining the chocolates that were situated on a China plate.

"Chocolates," the girl smirked.

"Those were used as part of the pagan Aztec human sacrifices," Renya barked angrily. "Their use is sinful!"

"But Renya, everybody eats it or drinks it," countered María Antonia, cautious not to appear confrontational. Her father always deferred to Renya in all matters, especially since she was raising his daughter.

"The apple that Eve gave to Adam was sweet," scolded the guardian. "And look how we have suffered for it."

"But didn't the Aztecs drink it every day as a beverage?"

"I don't know," Renya retreated a little. "We can ask Padre Bocanegra tomorrow when we go to mass."

María Antonia nodded. "I just wanted Araceli to have something special for her visit with us today." It was a white lie, but it caused Renya to become silent.

At nine o'clock that night, María Antonia was dining with her father and Renya. The mayor was sipping a red French Bordeaux; he eschewed Mexican and Spanish wines.

"How was your day, my dear?" the father asked.

"Fine. I did my French lesson. Señora Dumas said that I am making excellent progress." Another white lie.

"And I heard Araceli came visiting."

"Yes, we had a nice time," María Antonia took up a forkful of green beans and casually added. "Father, is eating chocolate sinful?"

Her father almost choked with laughter. "Who told you that tontería? It was a staple of the Aztec civilization. All of Europe is raving about chocolate. We should travel to Europe next year and visit some of its chocolate houses. I should have thought about this a long time ago."

"Father, I have a few pieces of chocolate," María Antonia did not look at Renya. "I can have Soledad bring them to you for dessert."

"Perfect, my dear. It would go well with my red wine."

At that moment María Antonia had devised a plan for the next day.

CHAPTER 16 – MISFORTUNE

Sunday, June 5, 1910

There was a light early morning drizzle as Pedro and Rico entered Teocaltiche and made their way to the supply store. The church bell tolled ten times.

"Pito, I want to get the stuff and get back on the road," the cousin said. "I don't want to waste all day looking for your little girl friend."

Pito nodded his head. He was in his passive resistance stance. Rico had incessantly berated Pito over the latter's infatuation with the mayor's daughter during the two-and-a-half-hour journey.

"Oye, pendejo, she is too smart for a feo like you," Rico kept haranguing. "You stink like something between a skunk and an old goat. You're going to make her throw up when she sees you. Or shall I say, smells you. You can't even afford to buy her a gift. Even if you could, she would throw it back in your face!"

Pito ignored his cousin. He just whistled his little tunes. Fate had brought María Antonia to him the first time. Fate would bring them together again.

The supply wagon pulled up next to the warehouse door at the back of La Compañia Los Olivos. They went into their biweekly ritual, loading the regular food staples, and supplies needed for repairs and the like. Rico was the one in charge and he signed his "x" on the invoice. Neither could read, so they trusted old man Olivo or his store manager. No money ever exchanged hands. Payments were made by a bank draft from the mining company.

Contrary to Ricardo's original statements about wanting to get back to the Atepoca mining camp early, the two were fatigued after loading the forty kilo sacks onto the wagon.

"Pito, let's go over to the plaza and lay on the grass. We can keep an eye on the goods while we rest."

Pito nodded in agreement. He knew that this cousin wanted a siesta. He thought a minute. He could run over to Norberta's and see if María Antonia had answered his letter. He would grab something to eat for both of them in order to avoid suspicion.

"Oye, Rico, I'm going to look for something to eat."

"Bring me a taco."

Pito zigged and zagged between the stands until he came upon Norberta's booth. The eleven o'clock mass had just let out and there were a dozen customers procuring hot chocolate and chocolates. He waited patiently. Finally, the line died down.

"Buenos días, señora," Pedro greeted the escribana.

She stared at him, and a sad look enveloped her face.

"You're too late, mijo," Norberta replied in a soft, dejected tone. "¡Qué mala suerte!"

***

After the ten o'clock mass, Mayor Sáenz exchanged greetings with the high society of Teocaltiche. The municipal president was deep in conversation with Señor Moreno, the local minister of public works. Renya had been very quiet since the night before.

"Father, I'm going to find Araceli and we are going shopping in the plaza," María Antonia had deliberately bypassed Renya in seeking permission. He inattentively nodded approval and she left in a hurry before anyone could say anything.

The night before Araceli and Maria Antonia had arranged to meet at the chocolate stand after the ten o'clock mass. Araceli was waiting for her when she arrived. After a few customers had finished, María Antonia casually walked up to Norberta. Araceli stayed behind.

"Good morning, señora," the girl smiled furtively. "I love your chocolates. My whole family does." She was trying to appear inconspicuous.

"Thank you, señorita," Norberta knew exactly who she was. *Why is Pedro enamored with her? Her skin is too white. She seems very spoiled. Not a match!* "How can I help you?"

"I need a tablet of Mexican chocolate. Make that two," the girl was looking up to the right, trying to remember something. "And six pieces of chocolate."

Norberta complied and María Antonia paid her.

"And I need you to give this to him," she handed la escribana a crème-colored envelope. "It's an answer to his request." She knew that Pedro probably couldn't read, and that Norberta was the go-between. It didn't matter if Norberta knew. She would be reading the note anyway.

Norberta slipped the note into her apron pocket. *I don't know what to do. But the customer must always be obeyed. This is going to break Pedro's heart.* She gave a deep sigh.

María Antonia turned around securing her purchases and grabbed Araceli's. They rushed away.

***

"You're too late, mijo," Norberta informed him. "She's already gone. She was here an hour ago."

Pedro rushed up to her. "Did she say anything?" His worried eyes searching her face for any clues.

"She left you a note," Norberta reached into her pocket and pulled it out. She handed the envelope to him.

He handed it back. "Please read it to me." He looked like he was about to cry. His forlorn look hurt Norberta's soul.

"Okay," she said as she tore open the envelope and started to read it.

Dear Pedro,

Thank you for your intentions. I know that they are honorable. I know we can't be together. We're just too far apart. You understand that, and I am sure that you see that. I wish you luck in finding someone that is more compatible with you.

Therefore, I can't see you, not now, not ever.

May God be with you.

Sincerely,
María Antonia Sáenz

To Norberta's surprise, Pedro was remaining calm. The boy is finally going to come to his senses and leave this nonsense alone, she thought.

"Why don't you write her another letter?" a squeaky voice said behind them. "You have nothing to lose."

¡*Ay, Herculana! You are going to be the death of me! God give me strength!* But Norberta started taking out her stationery.

CHAPTER 17 – BUREAUCRACY

Wednesday, June 8, 1910

Wednesdays were slow days at the plazita for Norberta and Lupe. There were only two masses and only a handful of parishioners attended them. That meant that there were fewer religious customers for them. On the other hand, most of the households in town bought their supplies for the weekends on these days. The two women made up the income by volume sales. The family cooks and delivery boys tended to be more friendly and often chatted with Norberta and Lupe. It was better for them than being back in their respective patrons' kitchens doing the cooking.

Today Norberta and Lupe were talking about how abusive Carmelita's husband was to her. The wife had been seen with a black eye.

"She should leave that hijo de puta," opined Lupe.

"But first, she needs to talk to the padre. Maybe he can help."

"All he will say is go back to your husband. What the man

says goes," Lupe was a strong feminist who would not tolerate spousal abuse.

"You're probably right, comadre," Norberta yielded.

"Of course, I'm right!"

Alfredo came around more or less on schedule. He ordered his hot chocolate and two churros from the ladies. He was in a huff. "That pinche presidente is trying to stop priests from saying mass!" he shouted to his two friends who were sitting on the low wall with him.

"But you don't go to church anyway!" countered his colleague, Noe.

"That's not the point! The government steals our money to build bigger statues. Now they want to rob the church! That's not right!"

"Do you even pay taxes, Alfredo?" asked Mauricio.

They argued and argued.

Finally, Alfredo stated, "I am going to write a letter to the presidente and ask him to desist from this outrageous abuse of power!"

His friends knew that he would never do it.

Suddenly, the fragrance in the air changed from cigarette smoke to Seven Roses after shave lotion. The slick Jorge "El Piojo" Contreras sauntered up to the trio of men. "Talk like that might get you shot, viejo. Or maybe thrown in jail. This sounds

like treason. I hope that you are not one of those
revolutionaries who are causing trouble here in Mexico." He
put his thumbs in the little pockets of his black leather vest.

The three old men didn't say a word. They knew that Jorge
was the cousin of the police captain Juan Contreras and a
minion for the mayor. He was not a man to be crossed. After a
few minutes they got up and walked away.

Jorge laughed and spit out a toothpick he had been chewing
on. He walked over to the booths of Norberta and Lupe. "Give
me a chocolate. And a churro. Those guys should be smart like
you ladies and learn to keep their snouts shut." He laughed
again.

Normally, El Piojo liked to get Norberta and Lupe alone.
Then he would alternate between teasing and intimidating. But
today he was being arrogant.

"I hear that the government needs money to fight the crazy
revolutionaries. They are going to raise the prices of you doing
business here," he laid out the scenario.

The two women didn't say anything.

"I could help you out so you wouldn't have to pay so
much," he boasted. "I would only take a fraction of what it
would cost you. And for you, Norberta, I could try to get some
work for one of your daughters."

"Go fuck yourself, desgraciado," Lupe blurted out angrily

before Norberta could respond. "Please leave us. Your stink is too much."

Jorge laughed and slowly walked away. "You'll need me sooner or later," he shouted as he left.

"That cabron makes me so angry! I wish someone would shoot him!"

Norberta thought the same thing, but knew she had to keep her cool. She would protect her daughters no matter what.

The comadres then started talking about the new fees that they would have to be paying. They couldn't afford them. However, they would support each other in any event.

The second mass was over, and the last customers had left. Norberta and Lupe were starting to put things away. Ramón had just started to load the cart with their provisions when a skinny man in a baggy uniform carrying a large leather bag suddenly appeared and handed Norberta and Lupe some forms. He looked like some local official. He was Felix Arias, and everybody thought of him as the village idiot.

"Fill these out and return them to the municipal palace," he officiously shouted as he delivered them. "Don't be late!"

The comadres gave each other a puzzled look. *What were these papers? Why did they have to fill them out?*

Norberta read the forms and frowned. "They want us all to get licenses to run our businesses. They will issue us some license plates, but we have to pay for them!"

"And do we still have to pay the monthly rent, comadre?" Lupe anxiously asked. "We have to pay twice?"

"I think just once for the license. But they want to know what we sell, what hours we work, and how much we make."

"They are going to rob us legally!" Lupe was irate. "What are we going to do? I don't keep good records."

"We'll just do what the government does. We'll overestimate our costs and report less money and hours."

"That's good business, comadre!" Lupe finally let out a grin.

"Let's start filling out the forms now, Lupe." One thing less to worry about at home. "Children, relax. We're not leaving for a while." She was talking to Ramón and Herculana.

Norberta started to do Lupe's form first.

"Besides churros, what else do you serve, comadre?" Norberta began the tedious process with Lupe.

"Nothing," Lupe answered. "Do Ramón's errands count?"

"Let's forget about what he does. We'll just put down what the main business is." Norberta was thinking at the same time, that she would not mention that she did writings for people as a scribe.

They went through a list of questions. It took about twenty minutes to complete the form. Then Norberta started to do hers.

Unexpectedly, Herculana approached her mother from behind. One of the other plaza vendors, Josué, the leather goods maker, accompanied the young girl.

"Señora Pérez, buenas tardes," he stepped forward and said meekly. "Do you know how to fill out these forms? Could you please do mine?"

Norberta put down her own form and began to do his. She looked at her daughter. She asked Josué a series of questions and filled out his form. She only charged him ten pesos.

Norberta was about to finish her own form, when Leticia, the flower vendor, came forth and requested assistance with her licensing form.

"Children, it's going to be a while. We have more customers," she shouted to Herculana and Ramón. She gave Lupe a shrug. *What is going on?*

By last Saturday afternoon, Norberta had completed the licensing forms for most of the vendors of the plaza. As part of the deal, she was able to barter a new dress for Herculana at a good price. *Life was good!*

CHAPTER 18 – THE SECRET

Thursday, June 23, 1910
El Pueblito del Valle

Herculana had gone to school, and the other two daughters were washing clothes down at the stream. Today Norberta had to make chocolate. For the last few days, she was concerned about the surprise visit from Soledad, María Antonia's cook. The servant had informed Norberta that her mistress was going to meet Pedro near her booth but did not want to be seen. Norberta had an ominous feeling about such a meeting.

Norberta remembered distinctly the letter that she had sent to María Antonia. If any writing could move the girl's heart, it would be this one. She thought that Pedro was still making a grave mistake pursuing the mayor's daughter. Everything was wrong about it, except that Pedro had the passion.

The morning sun was climbing higher in the sky, and it was getting hot. Norberta had placed the roasted cacao beans on two wooden boards supported on adobe bricks. She draped a few cloth towels over them to let them cool off and keep the flies away.

The fragrance of the chocolate essence stimulated repressed memories of her time in the nunnery.

***

Norberta was fifteen when she made a chocolate birthday cake for Reverend Hinojosa. Originally, she was a ward at La Virgen de Tepeyac Orphanage at the abbey where her aunt was a nun. Norberta's parents had died of food poisoning when they attended a family wedding reception, along with the cook and several guests. The suspected culprit were some wild skullcap mushrooms that had been part of the meat sauce. Norberta had been only four years old. Her aunt sold Norberta's parents' house and used the proceeds to pay for the child's room and board. It seemed to be a win-win situation for all concerned. Two years later the aunt passed away from breast cancer.

Norberta was a bright child and throughout the years demonstrated skills for being a lay preacher for the Church. Since President Díaz was persecuting clergy, the Catholic Church fought back by having lay persons evangelize the village peoples.

When Norberta was about fourteen years old, Reverend Lucero Hinojosa had joined Padre Rogelio Salas at the abbey. The girls were ecstatic about the young and handsome seminarian who was now in attendance. The other priest was old and smelled like rotten onions. He never bathed and had a constant snow drift of dandruff on his vestments. The girls would make fun of him when he walked by. He was nearly deaf and couldn't hear their laughter. For confession, he would assign ten Our Fathers and ten Hail Marys, no matter what their sins were.

By contrast, the other girls would fall all over themselves trying to attract Hinojosa's attention. A furtive wink here. A bosomed sigh there. A casual bump into him on the narrow staircase. They were young and hormonal. Most would not become nuns anyway. Why should they pray when they could fantasize about the seminarian? The exception to these puerile antics was Norberta. She was very serious about her studies and her future calling. The Mother Superior was well aware of this. It was no surprise to Norberta when she was asked to make a chocolate birthday cake for the reverend. She was the best cake maker in the nunnery and could do magic with chocolate.

The birthday party was a huge success. The girls complained when they could not have second servings of the delicious cake. Reverend Hinojosa even sought Norberta out and thanked her.

The seminarian had been assigned to conduct the evening prayers with the girls before they retired. One night after the litanies, the reverend casually asked Norberta to remain behind after all the others had retired.

"Señorita Norberta, it has come to my attention that you are the star pupil here. Soon you will go out into the world to preach the Gospel," Hinajosa gave her a disarming smile.

She blushed.

"I think we should give you some advanced lessons." He stepped a little closer to her. "Some theological teachings and some practical approaches to the problems that we face in the community. Would you be willing to participate in these special sessions?"

"Yes, father."

And so, it began. The next evening after prayers, they walked into his little office.

"And what do you know of St. Paul?" he quizzed her. She recited what little she knew.

"Why do you think his works are important?"

She didn't know. She was not being taught to think. She was being taught to memorize religious doctrines and then regurgitate them.

"Norberta, I want to know what you think," he probed. "Not necessarily what you have been taught. Do you understand the difference?"

She did and she didn't. Why would anyone care what she thought or if she could think for herself?

The next night he invited her to walk outside. "This will allow you to think freely." She obeyed without question. They walked to the church cemetery about a hundred meters from the nunnery. They sat on the headstones and conversed.

A few days later, the Mother Superior approached Norberta. She was in an agitated mood.

"Norberta, where have you been at night?" There was an edge to her voice. "What are you doing?"

"I am with Reverend Hinojosa. He is teaching me things," she said without shame.

The eyes of the nun, shifted from side to side. "He didn't notify me." She wanted to say more but was afraid to.

"Sister, you can ask him if you wish," Norberta offered.

The nun shook her head and walked away. Over the next weeks, Norberta was not bothered by anyone.

Then one night, the air was breezy and cool.

"My child, are you cold?" Hinojosa looked at her. It was a deep stare. He put his hand on her shoulder. Then he drew closer. He looked into her eyes. Her eyes met his. He could feel her body shaking. He put his arms around her. She did not resist. He slowly bent over. His lips met hers. They held steady for several seconds.

Over the next month, the trysts became more passionate and intimate. Norberta was happy. *This was God's way!* she thought. She was so happy!

Then one morning she woke up nauseous. She threw up all over herself. Norberta was given hot tea and toast. For the next three days, the same thing happened. She was spending most of the day in bed, not able to do her tasks. Then the Mother Superior appeared before her.

"Norberta, I think it is time you went to confession," and walked away.

Two days later Norberta struggled to go to confess her sins. She went into the confessional booth.

"Bless me, father, for I have sinned," Norberta began. She was relieved when she recognized the voice of Padre Salas on the other side of the screen.

How could she admit having carnal knowledge with the seminarian? Besides it was God's will. Wasn't that what he told her.

When she admitted the affair, the normally deaf priest yelled out, "What! That is not possible!"

"I think I am having his child," she said meekly.

"What kind of enchantress are you!" he shrieked. "Get out of my church, you . . . you, harlot! Don't come back."

Norberta struggled to get back to her room. Tears dripped
down her cheeks.

The next day there was a loud argument going on
downstairs. It sounded like it was between a man and a woman.
All the girls were gathering outside the Mother Superior's
room.

"She must leave!" shouted the man vociferously. "She must
go now!" It sounded like Padre Salas.

"Padre, she is with child," the Mother Superior asserted.
"We can't abandon her under the circumstances."

"But she has disgraced the nunnery and our church! What
will our parishioners think about us sheltering a shameless
harlot?"

Norberta felt faint listening to the dispute.

"It is our Christian duty to protect all sinners. And this
case, an unborn child."

Norberta struggled back to her room.

In the afternoon, the Mother Superior came into her room.
"Norberta, what you did was wrong. You can no longer be
considered for being our missionary to the people."

Norberta nodded in affirmation. More tears flowed down
her face. Her stomach ached. She felt like throwing up.

"We will find a suitable place for you to live and deliver
your child. Do not worry. God looks out for everyone."

"Thank you, Sister," Norberta kept her head bowed.

Three months later Norberta and her bundle were transported to the city of Encarnación, and was married to a very devout José Anaya, a schoolteacher who had recently lost his wife and baby in childbirth.

CHAPTER 19 – HOT CHOCOLATE

Thursday, June 23, 1910

After moving in with José, Norberta delivered her baby safely on April 14, 1895. Her husband José treated her with respect and loved the newborn, "Francisca." They evolved into a married couple, and they had two more children, Julia and Herculana.

Since José was a teacher and Norberta was literate, the children were taught to read at a very early age. Unfortunately, the husband died trying to break up a fight at school when Herculana was four. He was stabbed to death.

Norberta was forced to leave her home in Encarnación after selling off what she could. She moved to Teocaltiche where she knew a girl from the nunnery.

***

The day was getting hotter, and Norberta started scooping up cooled cacao beans from the comal and putting some in a big wooden cuenco. Slowly, she ground the roasted beans with the rounded tejolote. The fragrance of the chocolate awakened her senses. She inhaled deeply. Her fingers rubbed and squeezed the concoction. There were crackles as the mixture scraped the sides of the molcajete. She felt the beans coming to life. She gently massaged the mixture. She added some cinnamon. It was coming together. Harder and harder she beat the chocolate substance. Her shoulders heaved up and down, in a slow rhythm.

She had been so innocent when she was a young girl. She did her marital duty when she was married to José. He was a gentle lover. He respected her. He loved her and the children. They would both pray together before going to bed or making love. She believed that she was fulfilling the will of God and propagating the faith. If she couldn't do it by preaching to the villagers, she could do it by producing children.

The first batch of chocolate was done, and she rolled the mixture into balls and filled the round and low wooden molds. She evened them out with a big spoon. And then she put the first set of molds on a long wooden board. She placed a cloth over them to protect the chocolate. She licked her fingers to clean them. The taste was sweet. Her mouth watered. Her whole body tingled.

Reverend Lucero Hinojosa had taken her without her permission. But she did not resist. He was not a tender lover, but he was passionate. He wanted her in every way, and she wanted him. He did not give any explanations for his bestial behavior. He did not say it was the will of God. He did not say it was not a sin. She didn't care. She craved the attention. The physicality of their love making made all of her joints ache with pain and pleasure. She wanted him.

Norbert began crushing the second batch of roasted cacao beans. She was consumed with the process. Gripping and squeezing the molinillo. The chocolate paste oozing between her fingers. Sweat beading on her forehead. With her left hand, she wiped her brow and resumed the gripping and grasping. Another deep sigh. Her shoulders and back gyrating up and down. She let out a moan. The second batch was done, and she made these into chocolate spheres like the prior ones. She stuffed them individually into another mold.

He touched her shoulders. He kissed her eyelids. He bit her ear lobes. Lucero let his tongue trace her body from top to bottom. She cried out with pleasure. If this was sin, she wanted more. If this was hell, she was ready to go. God had created these desires. It was natural. This could not be wrong. It had to be blessed things.

The reverend never said much after they consummated the act. He would put his palm on her forehead. It felt warm and comforting. Since Norberta had been a virgin, she did not know what to expect. None of the girls at the nunnery had experiences like she did or at least, they did not confess to them.

Norberta did not take note when she missed her menstrual cycle. She did feel some slight changes in her body and her breasts seemed to be getting slightly swollen. But she was still growing. This was all natural.

Norberta labored to make four more batches of the hot chocolate disks. Each batch became more sensuous. Each one exhausting her more. Moisture from her body was wetting the concoctions. Her fingers were cramping. After she stuffed each mold, she sucked on her fingers. Her eyes started to glaze over. She wanted to take a rest. Maybe even a little siesta, but she decided to keep going.

He had said "yes" when she had asked Lucero if he was still part of the priesthood. She didn't understand how he could be after he had violated his vow of celibacy, but she didn't care. She was in love with him. He was older and wiser. She would trust his decisions.

She had gone to him for Confession, and he gave her five Hail Marys. He did not reprimand her or tell her to refrain from doing it again. She never wondered if he was confessing all of this to Padre Salas. She wondered if the Mother Superior suspected something, since Norberta was returning to her room later and later each night. Surely, she would have said something by now if she had concerns.

Now Norberta needed to make the chocolate sweets. She crushed the remainder of the roasted cacao beans and put them into a smaller wooden cuenco. She took the wooden spoon and separated out a third of the mixture. Norberta set it aside in a small bowl. Then took the molinillo and mixed the remaining paste in the cuenco and added brown sugar, cocoa butter, and a touch of vanilla. She dipped her little finger in the mixture from time to time to test the sweetness. Norberta added a pinch of salt.

Thrust, she felt pain. Thrust, she felt pleasure. Thrust, she felt moisture. Her body responded with tingles and tickles. Her senses were increased tenfold. Her lips tasted everything. Her fingers felt the feathers of a hummingbird. Her pezónes hardened. She closed her eyes and fell into a bottomless ecstasy. Stop! She felt pain! More! She felt pleasure! Her thighs crossed. She felt moisture.

Norberta shaped the chocolate mixture into balls and sprinkled powdered cinnamon on top of each one. Finally, she put the dozen chocolates on a small plate and placed them on the wooden boards with the chocolate tablets. She was almost done.

Her mind wandered to Pedro and Maria Antonia. She was halfway between being angry and sympathetic to their dilemna. She didn't want to interfere with Pedro's destiny. It was a bad idea to go after something outside of one's station.

On the other hand, she had been subjugated most of her life because of her indigenous appearance and the fact that she was a woman. She had decided long ago not to tolerate the Spanish "whiteness" doctrine, nor the Mexican version. Norberta wanted to give Pedro an even chance. What would happen would happen.

Against her better judgment, she took the rest of the chocolate paste and some secret ingredients that served as a love potion. She mixed it with determination.

"Lucero, you are not going to leave me, are you?"

"I have to."

"But I love you!"

"You can't!"

He had broken her heart. But she knew it was her own fault. Never again would she trust a man.

José had changed her mind, but she was still jaded. After José's death, she swore off men. Why buy the pig, when one can get the sausage free? she thought in her later years.

She formed the last batch of the chocolate into six small balls and wrapped them into pretty cloth sack and tied a ribbon to it. Now she was ready for a siesta. As she climbed into the hammock, she felt wet from her exertions.

CHAPTER 20 – THE TRYST

Sunday, June 26, 1910

Pedro woke up and started his whistling. He washed up in the cold water. He lathered his hair twice and rinsed it out both times. He grabbed a clean shirt (only one of the two that he owned). He wanted to look nice and smell good when he was supposed to meet up with María Antonia at ten o'clock.

He grabbed some warm tortillas and hot coffee from the mining camp mess hall. His cousin, Ricardo, was eating by himself.

"Do you still think she is going to meet with you, pendejo" His cousin inquired. "After today, maybe you will realize she's not interested."

Ricardo had continued tormenting Pedro relentlessly for the last few weeks. Pedro had been hovering around camp in a daze, whistling all the time. He seemed to be walking on a cloud.

"Ay, pendejo, what's wrong with you?" Ricardo finally inquired on their Sunday supply run into town.

"I think I'm in love!"

"Ay, pendejo, you can't be in love," his cousin shook his head. "Even if you were, you can't even talk to her."

It was then that Pedro told his cousin about the scribe, Señora Pérez, and the love letters. Ricardo's mouth dropped.

"But she hasn't even contacted you back!"

"After loading up the supplies, we can stop by Señora Pérez's stand."

Later that Sunday afternoon the two cousins were sipping hot chocolate and eating churros with Norberta and Lupe. Herculana was hanging around them. Pedro talked privately with Norberta. Then Pedro and Rico had to leave.

"I think I am supposed to see her next Sunday, according to Señora Pérez," Pedro confided to his cousin.

"I don't believe it! You're throwing your life away, primo!"

"At least, I'm trying to do something with my life," Pedro countered coolly.

"Like what?"

"Trying to find love," sighed Pedro. "Trying to find happiness."

"Oye, pendejo, love and happiness don't exist for people like us," Ricardo said despondently. "We are poor indigenous people. The wrong color. Uneducated. Nothing to offer."

"I have plenty to offer!"

"Pito, we are destined to work hard, earn a little money, fill our panzas, get bien pedo," lectured Ricardo, "and every once in a while, get some nalga."

"I want more than that. I don't want to just work at the mine, get drunk on Saturday nights, or look for putas." Pito looked at his cousin. "One day, sooner or later, I will leave the mine when I have a little money and find a good woman. I will settle down and raise a family. That is what I am going to do."

***

The following Sunday arrived, and Pedro made his way over to Norberta's booth. He gave her some money for the services that she had rendered on his behalf, including some for Ramón.

The church bells rang ten times.

"She is supposed to be coming here after the nine o'clock mass," Norberta informed him.

Pedro started to whistle nervously.

"Pedro, what did you bring her?" Norberta inquired.

He looked puzzled. "Like what?"

"Flowers?!" Norberta rolled her eyes. *This kid can't even wipe his own butt.*

"Oh, I forgot."

"Okay, give her these then," Norberta handed him a cloth sack with a little red ribbon tied around it.

Pedro took the small package into his hand.

A minute later a young girl came up to Norberta. "María Antonia is still talking to her father and the padre. She is running late. She says that she can't meet here. She doesn't want to be recognized by anyone."

Norberta said to the girl, "You can wait here. Pedro, go over to the palm tree orchard over there. It should be secluded. Herculana, please show him."

Pedro obeyed and left. Norberta handed Araceli a cup of hot chocolate.

Herculana's return coincided with the arrival of María Antonia.

"Araceli, thank you," María Antonia kissed her best friend on the cheeks. "I will meet you in front of the plazita before eleven o'clock. This shouldn't take too long.'

Araceli waved and left. Herculana boldly grabbed María Antonia hand and started to lead her to the secluded palm tree orchard. Suddenly, María Antonia turned around and ran back toward Norberta.

"Señora, could I trouble you for some hot chocolate?" she seemed nervous, and her mouth was dry.

"Surely, señorita," she handed the girl a cup.

María Antonia started to pull out her leather coin person, but Norberta waved her off. It was gratis.

The girl and Herculana trudged through the grass-covered path. Pedro was standing next to a fallen palm tree.

María Antonia and Pedro faced each other, several feet apart. Neither one said anything. Herculana was standing to the side.

The girl noticed the child still there. Quickly, she reached into her leather pouch and pulled out a hundred peso note. "I forgot to give this to your mother." Herculana took it and ran back to the plaza.

There was still a moment of silence. Then Pedro took a deep breath.

"Good morning, señorita. I am Pedro Campos," he looked into her hazel eyes. They were big and brown and beautiful. "Thank you for coming to see me."

María Antonia took a sip of her hot chocolate. She flicked at her reddish-brown hair and then she gave a slight bow. "You already know my name and you know that my father is the mayor of this town. While I appreciate being the object of your affections, I cannot accept them."

Pedro did not flinch with the sharp words. Instead, he handed her the bag of chocolates that Norberta had given him to give to the girl. "These are for you."

Good manners dictated that she had to accept the token. She opened the bag and saw what they were. Her eyes sparkled. She was hungry. She had not eaten that morning because she was anxious about her meeting with Pedro.

She would taste one just to be polite. María Antonia put one up to her mouth and the chocolate essence overwhelmed her. She took a nibble and then remembered to offer Pedro one. He took a bite.

Suddenly, there was a hiss from her piece of chocolate. Her hand started to shake. She licked her lips. Her eyes started to sparkle.

Pedro stepped closer to her, and his hands began to feel warm.

She took another bite. A bigger one. Her heart started to effervesce. She couldn't move. She couldn't breathe. María Antonia wanted to cry out.

Pedro reached over and put his hands on her shoulders. He stared directly into her eyes. Her eyelids fluttered. He stretched his arms around her. She trembled.

She looked up and turned her head toward him. She lifted herself on to her tiptoes. Slowly, she forced her lips to meet his. Her body became alive. All of her senses were overactive. Her soul melted into his.

When she later saw the pair, Norberta smiled. She had transformed her chocolates into a special love potion with the addition of cinnamon, nutmeg, chiles, ginger, and saffron along with her magical spices.

CHAPTER 21 – FOLLOWING THE HEART

June 1910

Atepoca Mine

The warbler was perched on the red oleander singing. Pedro whistled along. After his meeting with María Antonia, Pedro thanked Norberta profusely for her intervention. He knew that it was her and the mysterious chocolates that had helped get María Antonia to express her affection for him just before the summer solstice.

Norberta was of a mixed mind. *What have I done? This obsession of Pedro's can't last. He is going to get hurt. I shouldn't interfere!* She sighed. *On the other hand, youth cures a broken heart.*

Now he was inflamed to write another letter to María Antonia. Pedro didn't know what he wanted to say, but he was in a feverish mood. Norberta captured his temperament and magnified it.

June 26, 1910

My most precious María Antonia,

Since I left you, I have been constantly overjoyed. My happiness is to be near you. Incessantly I live with your caresses, your kisses, and your words carved in my memory. Your charms kindle a continually burning and glowing flame in my heart. My greatest desire is to be able to spend all my life with you, having only to love you, and to think only of your happiness. I want to devote my life to proving my honorable intentions to you.

May God protect you.

Your faithful servant,

Pedro

Norberta read it to him, and Pedro could barely understand it. But the sound of her voice was mellifluous, and he surrendered any reservations. He knew that Norberta understood love.

The next weeks found him in an ecstatic frame of mind. He did his chores at the mining camp with a smile on his face. He was whistling more than ever now. His cousin Ricardo had stopped harassing him.

Pedro wanted to see María Antonia secretly two weeks later at the same place. Ramón had delivered the love letter to the Sáenz residence. Specifically, he had delivered it to Soledad, the cook, whom María Antonia trusted. Again, Araceli was involved in the ruse.

Pedro confided in Norberta every step of the way what he was doing. She would roll her eyes and pray to the Virgin of Guadalupe to protect him. *What have I done? May God forgive me for tempting fate.*

Then, of course, Norberta would share the intimate details of Pedro's infatuation for María Antonia with her comadre, Lupe. Norberta made Lupe promise not to share the secret, but she knew that Lupe did what Lupe wanted to do.

Norberta concocted more magical chocolates for Pedro to share with his love interest. After the second rendezvous, Pedro was whistling and whistling. His head was in the clouds.

"I know she loves me, Señora," he confided. He continued paying her for the love letters and the chocolates. Norberta knew that it was probably all the money that he had, but she was just providing a service. *I'm not his guardian.*

This routine continued for the following month. But it was interrupted when the mayor took his family to Guadalajara and then to Matzamila for cultural exposure and to relax in the Sierra del Tigre foothills. María Antonia had sent Pedro a note saying that she would miss him. He took some comfort in that but was glum back at the Atepoca mining camp.

"What's wrong, primo?" Ricardo asked after noting the sudden change in Pedro's behavior.

Then Pedro spilled his guts and told Ricardo everything.

"I can't believe it, puto!" the cousin shook his head. "I'm surprised that the mayor hasn't put a noose around your neck!"

"But she loves me, Rico."

"How can she love you, pendejo? She's in a different class. It will never work, You're too poor for her."

"But one day, I will have a lot of money!" Pedro countered.

"How, pendejo?" Rico scoffed at him. "Besides we're mestizos."

Pedro wouldn't give up. In late July while he was making his weekly visit to Norberta, he received a message from María Antonia. She had returned from her trip and wanted to resume their meetings. They would meet at the same place at the same time, the following Sunday.

"Señora Norberta, I hate to ask you again," he gave her a sad-eyed look. "Could you make some more of those special chocolates? They work magic."

"Well, of course, mijo," she replied. *What am I doing encouraging this? I am enabling this ill-fated assignation.*

After Pedro had left, Herculana approached her mother.

"Mamá," her little eyes looked up in a quizzical manner. "Why are boys so dumb when they get around girls?

Norberta wanted to laugh, but she didn't. "When they grow up, their bodies and minds change, and they think they can conquer the world. They act from the heart, and not from the mind."

"I'm sure glad that I'm not a boy."

"It happens to girls too, mija."

"Not me. It's not going to happen to me," Herculana frowned with determination. "I'm not going to act like a stupid boy."

¡Ay, Herculana!

***

Norberta knew that she knew was young and innocent when she was at La Virgen de Tepeyac Convent sixteen years prior. She didn't even know what a boy was, much less a man. What she had done with the seminarian was wrong. Or was it? Her body had tasted him. Had tasted his flesh. That was natural.

How could this be wrong? But someone said it was forbidden. It was a sin. Reverend Lucero Hinojosa did not act like it was wrong. He yearned for the carnal knowledge. He was a holy man. He couldn't do anything sacrilegious.

Norberta could still taste the chocolate that was on his lips when they "celebrated" his birthday. Was this the forbidden fruit of Eve? How could Adam have rejected her offering? God made them in his own image. They had to be perfect. They were incapable of sinning.

Am I leading Pedro astray? Am I helping or hurting him? What should I be telling him? I know this is wrong, but it is not sinful. I think that Love is predestined. I will help him win over this girl, even if it costs me my soul.

CHAPTER 22 – TROUBLE BREWING

July 1910

El Pueblito del Valle

Herculana happily marched on the dirt trail alongside her mom and Lupe at dawn. The days were long, and the sun rose so much earlier. The smells of the barrio were a mixture of mesquite trees and dust. The mother and daughter were on their way to the plazita to sell their products. Ever since Norberta had bought her a new dress, Herculana liked going to school and didn't care what the other kids were thinking about her clothes.

Herculana was an obedient child, although a bit too precocious at times. She rarely complained. But lately, Norberta noticed that Francisca and she were getting into arguments and Herculana didn't back down. *Was her baby being a brat or growing up?*

Norberta sensed that something was in the air. Francisca was fifteen and at times was highly emotional. Then Norberta started noticing that Francisca was being lax in performing her tasks. There was not enough water in the kitchen. The house was not swept. The meals were not ready when she and Herculana returned home from the market.

One day Norberta found unwashed menstrual clothes on a back bench.

"Francisca, what is the meaning of this?" the mother barked.

"Oh, I've been busy," Francisca replied nonchalantly.

"Doing what?" Norberta was angry. "This place is a pig sty! Hurry up and clean up this mess right now!"

Francisca sighed and slowly went through the motions.

What is wrong with that girl? Norberta wondered.

Back at the plaza, Norberta had been filling out many more municipal licensing forms for the other vendors. Her supplies were running low. She sent Herculana to the Machado Stationery Store to purchase some ink and some quill pens. Unfortunately, Señora Machado wouldn't barter chocolate for writing materials. Plus, the elderly woman didn't give discounts. She was a shrewd businessperson. However, the owner did give Herculana a brand-new red pencil. The young girl had never had anything more than pencil stubs that were barely useable.

Herculana returned to her mother's booth and found that her mother was busy talking with Señora Bustamontez. Herculana was drafting a letter of congratulations to the lady's daughter for the arrival of a healthy grandson. Norberta was reciting the letter to the woman who kept nodding her head.

July 8, 1910

My dearest daughter Esperanza,

Congratulations on the birth of your new son, Samuel. Your father is very proud that you named the baby after him. We are so happy to have this little angel in our family. We are all blessed with this gift from God.

Please rest and take care of yourself. Remember not to lift anything heavy.

We are sorry we can't be there now, but papá has to work. We would so much love to take care of you and the baby.

Don't eat foods that give you gas. It is bad for the baby. Also, remember to

have a blanket over the baby at all
times. Keep the baby warm and protect
him against the mosquitoes.

God willing, we will try to see you
when the baby is going to be christened.
Have you chosen the compadres yet?
Your sister would be hurt if you didn't
ask her to be the madrina.

And don't forget to get a lock of
hair when he is older. It is for good
luck.

May everyone be in good health.
¡Gracias a Dios!

Con cariño,
Mamá

Señora Bustamontez was quite pleased.

"I thank you," she said as she paid Norberta. "And may
God bless you." She turned around and left.

Business for Norberta was good. If there was a lag during
one of the market days, Norberta would sometimes teach

Herculana how to fill out the forms. Herculana was a good reader and a quick study. She even tried to write a letter for one of her school mates but got caught. She had to promise not to do it again. However, Norberta told her if one of the school kids came to their booth at the plaza, Herculana could compose a letter and keep any money she earned.

A few days later, Norberta and Lupe were chatting between masses. Norberta's mind was in a different universe. Lupe knew her comadre well.

"Oye, why the sad face?" Lupe was never shy about asking. "You seem preoccupied. Is anything wrong?"

Norberta's forehead furrowed. "I don't know, comadre," she answered in a disconcerted tone. "The other day, we came home, and Julia had a big red mark on her face. It didn't look like an accident."

"What did she say when you asked her?"

"That's the problem. She wouldn't say," Norberta revealed.

"What did Francisca say?"

"I don't know," Norberta looked sadly into Lupe's eyes. "She wasn't around."

On Monday Lupe walked over from her casita to Norberta's and shouted for her comadre. Herculana and Norberta came out and greeted her.

"Comadre, let's take a walk."

Norberta was apprehensive but trusted her comadre. After they had walked for about five minutes into the brush, Lupe said, "Norberta, I don't want you to get mad." Lupe put her hands on Norberta's shoulders, "but the other day, Francisca yelled at Ramón."

"Why?"

"Ramón said he was trying to protect her, and she told him to mind his own business. She didn't need his help. And then she called him a mama's boy."

"I'm sorry," Norberta's eyes started to tear. "She has been acting strangely lately. I don't know why."

"Maybe it's because of the boy she is seeing," interjected Herculana.

"What boy?" the comadres shouted out in unison as they turned around. They hadn't realized that Herculana was following them.

"You know. The milkman, Luis."

CHAPTER 23 – THE TEMPEST

August 1910

Atepoca Mine

Ricardo had noticed that Pedro was happy and whistling all day, no matter what sort of arduous tasks he was doing. The crew manager Nacho and several other miners noticed the change in Pedro and started making comments, mostly directed to Ricardo. Everybody knew that they were cousins.

"¡Qué la chinga! What is that idiot chamaco smiling at?"

"He's so cheery, what's going on here? Even when he is sweeping up horse shit and working like a slave. I don't get it!"

"He must not be working hard enough if he is so content. Send him down the mineshaft and let's see what happens!"

Rico was loyal to Pito and kept his thoughts to himself. However, one night the two were walking around camp looking upward at the millions of stars in the sky. They could see the Evening Star. Pito was whistling a happy melody.

"What's up, primo?" Rico asked nonchalantly.

At first Pito was silent, but he was bursting to share his secret. Who better than his cousin and best friend Rico to confide in?

"I'm in love!"

"Still?" his cousin shook his head. "With whom now, pendejo?"

"The girl you said would never even look at me."

"The Spanish blood?" Rico remembered her. But that was months ago, he thought.

"She's the one with the long reddish-brown hair," Pito's mind was drifting upward. "Her hazel eyes are so beautiful!"

"Not the mayor's daughter, pendejo?!" Rico recalled. "Not the güera! You are crazy!"

"But she loves me," Pito sighed. "And I love her!"

"Do her parents know?"

Pito spent the next quarter hour explaining how the town scribe Norberta and María Antonia's best friend, Araceli, were helping the lovers meet secretly.

"But you're going to get caught, pendejo!"

"And what can they do to me?" Pedro spoke with an air of bravado.

"What do you plan to do?" Ricardo was deeply concerned. "You can't get married. Nobody will marry a white girl and a mestizo."

"We'll run away together."

"And go where? Her father will hunt you down like a pinche deer."

"Probably Texas." Pito inhaled and thought. "Or maybe Arizona."

"And how will you live?" Ricardo was shaking his head. "You have no money. You've been wasting your money on stupid letters. You can't even read."

"Well, you can't either," Pedro was starting to get defensive.

"But I'm not going any place," Ricardo said. "I don't need to read. I can just ask one of the miners. A few of them can read."

"What will you do for money?"

"I have a little saved up. Not much. I don't know if María Antonia has any. We haven't talked about this."

"You're a pendejo."

"I could sell my saddle," Pedro countered. "The one I got from Guillermo when he died. It should be worth a lot."

"Who would buy it? The miners around here don't need horses or saddles."

"Somebody might."

"When are you going to see her again?"

"Next Sunday."

Pedro was counting the days until his next date with María Antonia. He had bartered for a blue cotton shirt and a pair of brown leather boots. They fitted him big, but they were presentable. He was trying to bathe more often these days.

The weather was getting hotter and more humid. It started to rain during the nights. The mornings were then cool and smelled of fresh flowers. Pito wanted to give María Antonia a present. He really didn't have any money to buy anything. Maybe he could make something out of a pinecone or give her flowers. The more he thought about it, the less confident he was. *She wouldn't want some cheap trinket, especially if it looks indigenous. She is used to European finery. But I can't afford that. I wouldn't even know where to look. I could ask Señora Norberta for her advice.*

Sunday morning arrived. Pedro hadn't slept well. It had rained hard all night and the winds had shaken the communal dormitory. He got up early and grabbed a tin cup of turpentine-tasting coffee and a few tortillas.

Pedro saddled up the horse. He had no rain gear. Ricardo tried to discourage him from going.

"Ay, pendejo, it is too dangerous going down the mountain with all the mud. Watch out for the holes. If the horse breaks a leg, Nacho is going to be very angry," Rico cautioned him. "Just be careful."

Pedro's mind was elsewhere. As usual, he was to meet María Antonia after the nine o'clock mass at the orchard near Norberta's stand. Pedro had hoped to arrive early and chat with Norberta. He knew that she would give him good advice.

The showers started to pick up again as he started down the mountain. The wind swirled the rains up and down and all-around Pedro. He and the horse were getting soaked. The sarape Pedro was wearing felt like it weighed ten pounds. A few sparrows dared to challenge the storm and flew from tree to tree.

The visibility was poor, and Pedro had to be vigilant for potholes. He was walking the horse slowly. The path started to get steeper and the footing for the horse was difficult. The squall was becoming fiercer and fiercer. Pedro knew better than to rush. The side of the road looked like it was going to collapse. Pedro hoped to remember to tell Nacho of this danger. The wagons that delivered tin came down to the loading depot in town at least once a day. Besides the miners, no one else used this narrow road.

After about an hour, Pedro spotted some dark objects in the middle of the road in front of him. As he approached, he saw hundreds of jagged rocks in the middle of the path. Part of the cliff wall had collapsed and was blocking his way. Pedro stopped and looked. He assessed the damage and realized that he had less than an even chance to negotiate his way through the rubble.

I have to see María Antonia! She is waiting for me. I can get through this.

Pedro dismounted and left the horse. He scrutinized the fallen rocks. There were one or two places a man could get through. But with a horse, who knew?

I promised her I would come. I love her. We can't be apart!

Pedro started forward slowly with the reins of the horse in hand. He stepped on a flat rock and then another. The horse was hesitant. Then Pedro slipped and almost fell down.

She will be angry with me if I don't come! But she loves me! She would forgive me. What should I do?

Pedro reluctantly turned around and led his horse slowly back up the mountain.

CHAPTER 24 – EL LECHERO

August 1910

El Pueblito del Valle

Norberta was speechless when she learned that her daughter, Francisca, might be sneaking around with the milkman. *I can't believe it! I don't believe!*

For the next few days Norberta's mind swung back and forth. With the tempestuous storms and worry, she couldn't sleep. She watched every move that Francisca made, looking for anything suspicious. She couldn't ask Julia or Herculana to spy on their sister. What could she do?

Lupe had been silent on the subject. She was Norberta's comadre. She could offer some sage advice. That was her obligation.

Norberta related what little she knew to Lupe. "What am I not seeing, comadre?"

"I think you're not seeing a fifteen-year-girl who wants to be a woman."

"But she is just a child, Lupe!"

"How old were you, comadre, when you were with child?"

But that was different, Norberta thought. I was educated. I was chosen by God to spread the faith.

"Have you even looked at your daughter?" Lupe blew out a breath. She hated talking to Norberta like this. *What do I know?*

Norberta thought, *of course, I see my daughter. Every day! From the early morning to late night. She is my apprentice. I'm her mother. I have to protect her!*

"Girls her age want to experience life," the comadre continued. "And that means boys. They want attention from boys. Not mothers. Not family. Boys."

"But she is so young!"

"Look at where we were at her age," Lupe said. "We were impetuous and didn't listen to anybody. But the choice was ours."

Later that afternoon when the entourage returned from the plaza, Norberta went looking for Francisca, but couldn't find her. It was her oldest daughter's responsibility to cook dinner. Norberta couldn't smell anything and when she looked at the comal, nothing was prepared.

"Where's your sister?" Norberta asked Julia.

The second oldest daughter hesitated in answering.

"I asked, where is your sister?" Norberta barked at Julia.

Julia stepped back. She had frightened look on her face. She turned slightly to the right and pointed to the woodlands nearby.

"Did she go alone?"

Julia nodded her head no.

"Whom is she with?"

Julia's shoulders started to fold over and she cowered. She was reluctant to say.

"I asked you with whom?" Norberta was fuming with impatience.

"Luis," Julia answered in a whisper.

Norberta furrowed her forehead. Her mind was frozen with anger. Luis Gutierrez was the lechero who delivered dairy products to her. He had a horse drawn cart that supplied goods to her twice a week, on Mondays and Thursday. But the provisions were delivered in the mornings. Now here it was late afternoon and Francisca was nowhere to be found.

Norberta knew Luis casually. He was of medium height with a muscular built. His dark skin was offset by his curly black hair and dark brown eyes. However, she knew that Luis had to be at least twenty-five. He could prey on Francisca like a wolf chasing a lamb. Her daughter had no chance against him.

An hour later, Francisca nonchalantly waltzed into the house.

"Dinner is not ready!" Norberta said coldly to her oldest daughter.

"Oh, I'll get it started."

"I'm already preparing it."

Francisca did not react and was about to walk away.

"Where have you been?"

"Out," replied Francisca coolly.

There was a thud as Francisca fell backward. She was holding the side of her head, sniffling in pain. Then she quickly sprang up and ran out the door.

"I hate you! I hate you!" Francisca shouted. "I'm not going to rot in this pig sty!" She disappeared into the woods.

Norberta was shaken. She had not meant to strike her daughter with the stirring spoon, but she was not going to tolerate any disrespect from her children. Herculana came close to her mother and wrapped herself around her. Norberta stroked the little one's hair. *Am I cursed by having three daughters?*

That night Norberta waited for Francisca to come home. *Did she want her to return? Or would she banish her and let her fend for herself?* She fell asleep and tossed fitfully. The roosters were crowing when she woke up. She looked in the corner of the room where normally her three daughters slept atop a mat. Francisca was wedged between her two sisters with her shawl over her head in a dead sleep.

Norberta decided not to wake Francisca but did wake the youngest. They had to get ready to go to the plaza. *What she had to say to Francisca could wait until she returned that evening. She was calmer now and she would ask Lupe for advice.*

At their booths the comadres discussed Francisca. It wasn't a contentious dialogue, but every angle was looked at.

"You could just pretend that nothing has happened," Lupe was talking. "But I know you. You want to take control of the situation."

"I just don't want her to make the same mistakes that I did when I was her age. At that age, we believe everything a man says. "

"Comadre, I can tell you one thing not to do," Lupe looked at Norberta sharply. "You can't tell her not to see this guy. It's not about right or wrong. At their age, they will just defy authority."

Norberta knew that Lupe was right.

***

The seminarian, sixteen years prior, had convinced Norberta that their carnal relations were necessary in order for him to carry out his sacred mission. And that she was the chosen one. Her mind told her that he was not telling the truth, but her heart told her otherwise. When his hand touched her breast, a warmth spread throughout her body. Is this the fire of Hell? How could it be? Hell is for punishment and suffering. These sexual liaisons were pleasurable. Doesn't he cry out the Lord's name when we are making love?!

"Norberta, we have a religious duty to spread the Faith. And that includes Hope and Love. Together we will find Salvation for ourselves and others," Reverend Lucero Hinojosa said. Then he kissed her shoulder.

This sent shivers throughout her body. She tried to cross her legs. They kissed and there was moisture there.

"They taught me this is a sin," the young Norberta looked up at him.

"Judge for yourself."

She thought that she knew better. She thought everybody else was wrong. But she really didn't care. She was in love.

***

A beleaguered Norberta and her daughter Herculana rambled back home late that afternoon. They found Julia by herself. Francisca and all of her meager belongings were gone.

CHAPTER 25 – THE APOLOGY

Monday, August 8, 1910
Atepoca Mine

On Monday morning, the day after the aborted trip down the mountain, Pedro was called over to see Nacho, the foreman.

"You're in trouble," warned his cousin. "He never talks to anyone unless they have screwed up."

Pedro was nervous. His hands were shaking. Maybe he shouldn't have tried to travel down the mountain. His horse could have injured himself and then Pedro would have been in deep trouble. On the other hand, he had promised María Antonia that he would meet with her and he didn't do it. She would never forgive him.

"Come in, Pedro," Nacho sat behind a pine table. "Take a seat."

Pedro sat on a short wooden stool. Nacho was smoking a hand- rolled cigarette.

"I want to talk to you about yesterday."

¡Demonios! Here it comes! Pedro thought. His body twitched and an odor of fear oozed from his pores. He broke out into a sweat.

"They told me that you went down the mountain in that terrible rain. You were crazy," Nacho spoke in a serious tone. "And you found a rockslide." He paused.

Pedro mumbled a weak yes.

"Do you realize what you did?"

The boy nodded his head no.

"You saved the company one, if not two, days, of delays in our tin deliveries. It would have been a nightmare," Nacho leaned forward in a friendly manner. "Because of you, we have almost repaired the road and our wagons are ready to continue down the mountain with very little delay."

Immediately, Pedro felt relieved.

"As a thank you, I'm going to give you a five peso per week increase in your wages. Keep up the good work, kid."

Pedro was whistling all the rest of the day, talking to the horses about love and how he was going to try to soon see María Antonia.

Two weeks later the cousins were making their routine Sunday supply run into town.

"This is where the rockslide was," Pito pointed out to his cousin Rico. "There were hundreds and hundreds of gigantic stones."

A few hours later the two entered the town of Teocatliche and parked the wagon in front of the La Compañia Los Olivos supply store. A young boy who worked there, helped the cousins load up the wagon. He lifted the heavy bags of beans and rice like they were feathers. The owner went over the charges with Ricardo, even though the latter couldn't read. Rico would simply nod his head affirmatively and agree with Señor Olivos. The truth of the matter was the clerk at the mining camp would peruse the invoices to determine accuracy and then come to town once a month to pay the supply company (and spend an afternoon getting drunk and seeing a lady). It was all part of doing business.

"Rico, let's ride over to the plazita," Pito said. Normally, he would have his cousin wait for him in the wagon. Rico didn't mind because he could take a nap. But today was different. Pito wanted to share. He whistled as they pulled up as close as they could to Norberta's stand.

"Remember that delicious hot chocolate I got you a while back?" Pedro asked. "This is where it comes from."

Ricardo was not impressed. *So?*

"This is where Señora Norberta is the scribe and writes my letters." A minute later Pedro was introducing his cousin to Norberta and Lupe.

"Pleasant to meet you, señoras," Ricardo tipped his straw hat. "Pito has told me how much you have helped him."

Then, out of nowhere, a small figure appeared. "Hi, I am Herculana. I help around here. Would you like some hot chocolate?"

Pleasantries were exchanged among them and Lupe added a few churros for the boys. Pedro very discretely handed over some pesos to Norberta who quietly shook her head in appreciation. *He is such a nice boy.*

"Señora Norberta, I need another favor," Pito hemmed and hawed. "I need another letter for María Antonia." He assumed that she knew that he had not shown up the week before for his secret meeting with the girl of his dreams.

"Wait a moment!" Norberta went into her leather pouch where she kept her stationery supplies. She pulled out a small envelope, looked at it, turned it over, and then handed it to Pedro.

"Soledad, the cook delivered this earlier this week," Norberta stated. "It is for you. Do you want me to read it to you?'

"Yes, please."

Norberta unsealed the letter and showed it to Pedro. She then started to read it in front of all present:

August 8, 1910

My darling Pedro,

I miss you! I am so sorry that I was unable to meet with you yesterday. It was raining jugs and jugs. After we went to mass, Renya and my father made me come home. They did not want me to catch my death of cold.

I hope that you are not upset and will forgive me!

I will do my best to see you in less than two weeks. I can hardly wait. I miss you so much.

I dream about you all the time.

Con cariño,
María Antonia

Pedro blushed as the letter was being read. Now everybody knew his business. He felt the weight of everyone's eyes on him.

"Señora Norberta, I think we should write her back. What do you think?"

"It's probably a good idea," she reluctantly replied.

"Señora, unfortunately I can't wait here while you to write it. We have to be getting back so we don't get in trouble. Can you just write it and have it delivered?"

"Sure," Norberta thought this would be better so she wouldn't have to be rushed. "But why don't you put your mark here on this piece of paper." She handed him a blank sheet.

"Perfect!" Pito's face had a full smile. "Thank you."

Five minutes later the cousins were on their way back to the Atepoca Mine. Pedro started his whistling as the wagon bounced along the rough road.

"So, is this what you have been hiding from me?" Ricardo reproached his cousin.

"What?" Pedro was startled.

"You know, the chocolate and churros."

CHAPTER 26 – LA MORDIDA

Friday, August 19, 1910
Teocaltiche

On that warm morning, the smell of hot chocolate wafted through the air as Alberto was finishing up his drink. He swirled down the dregs and used his forefinger to wipe the inside of the terra cotta cup, salvaging the chocolate mud.

"There are more and more uprising every day! Everywhere!" he yelled at Noe and Mauricio. "Thank God that coward Díaz is in exile. He will be the lapdog to the yanquis or the alemanes!"

"He was too old anyway," Mauricio commented. "Let's see what Madero can do, if anything."

"At least Porfiriato has ended," Noe added. They thought the Porfirio Diaz days were numbered.

Suddenly, there were nearby sounds of hammering, followed by shouting. The elderly Señora Ibarra was in tears as she struggled to walk by them.

"What is happening, Matilda?"

"They are throwing us out," the old woman said.

"Why?"

"Because we can't pay the fee."

All the vendors in the plaza had been hit hard by the monthly municipal assessment to fund the defense of the city against the revolutionaries. But everyone knew that the mayor was really lining his own pockets. Several booths had closed down and the merchants had moved out of Teocaltiche.

"Mamá, he is nailing papers onto some of the booths. Pink ones," Herculana excitedly blurted out to her mother and Lupe.

"Why, mija?"

"The paper says for not paying."

Lupe turned ashen but did not say anything.

"Who is doing it, mija?"

"That man who wanted all the forms signed."

Norberta recalled Felix Arias, the crony of the mayor. He was an officious underling who took pleasure in harassing the market vendors.

Norberta was barely able to survive. She was making the payments, but she was a little behind with the grocer.

In the middle of the day, a dozen or so men milled around the municipal palace, screaming for the mayor to come out. A handful of local police and some soldiers on horseback blocked their access.

"We want to talk to the mayor!"

"Down with Díaz and Sáenz!"

"The end to tyranny!"

Norberta had never seen the revolutionaries but she imagined that this was very close to the real thing. She did not recognize any of the men protesting and knew they were very angry. She knew that the mayor would react in less than a conciliatory manner and that there could be potential violence.

"Mija, I think we are going to leave early today," she tried to sound calm. "Try to find Ramón and tell him to get packing. Is that all right with you, comadre?"

Lupe nodded her head. She could read Norberta's mind.

Ten minutes later, the foursome was traveling back to their El Pueblito del Valle casitas with Ramón pulling the cart.

"Mamá, who were those men who were yelling?" Herculana asked innocently.

"I don't know, mija," her mother answered.

"I heard that they were miners from around here," Ramón chimed in. "Someone told me that they are on strike, whatever that means."

A million thoughts crossed Norberta's mind. *Is the revolution here in Teocatliche? Will the revolutionaries overrun the city? Will the federales come here? How safe will*

*the city be? How can we survive? How can I protect my
family?*

They were almost home when Lupe started coughing and
almost stumbled. She was bent over on her right side and
looked like she was going to faint.

"Are you all right, comadre?" Norberta said in an alarmed
tone trying to prevent Lupe from falling. "Let's stop over here
for a moment."

Ramón pulled the cart over to the side of road. Lupe was
helped down by Norberta and sat on the grassy knoll. Norberta
thought that Lupe seemed skinny and frail. Lupe had beads of
sweat covering her brow and she felt feverish. Norberta hadn't
noticed her comadre's physical condition before. Lupe coughed
again.

"Mija, give her some water," Norberta directed Herculana.

Lupe took a sip. She seemed to regain her composure. Her
color came back, flushed with embarrassment.

"I'm fine, comadre," Lupe tried to give a smile of
assurance. Her son and Norberta helped Lupe to her feet.

They walked home slowly. Everybody was carefully
watching Lupe. It was still early afternoon when they arrived at
Lupe's casita. They settled Lupe onto a little mat on the floor
where she normally slept. They draped a sarape over her. Lupe

closed her eyes and was trying to sleep. Norberta noticed the sparsity of the little hut.

Norberta escorted Herculana and Ramón toward her own house.

"Mijo, has this happened before? What is going on?"

"I don't know," Ramón said with a sheepish look.

"Has she been sick?" Norberta drew nearer to him and gently grabbed his shoulders. "Has she been in pain?"

"No, but I think she has been worrying about not having enough money. She doesn't eat very much. I think she gives me her food."

Before entering her house, Norberta pulled out some pesos from her apron and gave a few to Ramón.

"Go to the Chinese story and buy some bones. Chicken ones," The Chinese enclave was about a ten-minute walk across the main road. "Get some wing bones and thigh bones too."

Norberta took some dark roasted cacao beans from a canister she had tucked away in the corner of her sleeping space. She ground them up into a fine powder and put it into a cup of hot water. She mixed in some ginger root pieces, willow bark shavings, and elderberry leaves. She also put in some of her magical chocolate shavings. Norberta wanted to reduce

Lupe's fever. She let it cool for about fifteen minutes and told Herculana to take it to Lupe.

Norberta sighed. Francisca had taken off. She hadn't paid much attention to Lupe. She had strived to restructure her household. Julia had assumed her older sister's duties. She had to carry the water, clean the house, and cook the meals. She was slowly learning the basics in the kitchen and she made great corn tortillas.

And then there was Herculana. She had been forced to drop out of school and now did the tasks that her sister Julia had been responsible for. She had to help make and package the chocolate. Herculana had risen to the challenge and was acting seemingly more mature. However, Norberta felt bad about Herculana having to drop out of school. She had wanted to give her daughter a chance at survival in the world without having to rely on men. Norberta promised herself that she would continue teaching Herculana how to write letters, with her daughter hopefully becoming an escribana also.

Norberta came back into the kitchen. Julia was about to help Norberta start dinner.

"Mija, get the big pot and start getting it to a boil. Throw in some cilantro, cumino, salt, a chile, and a carrot. Do we have an onion?"

Julia obeyed. She began making the soup.

"Mija, go back to Lupe's casita and see how she is doing," Norberta directed Herculana. "If she is not better, we should have Señora Pacheco see her. Stay with your madrina."

Señora Pacheco was the local doctor, curandera, and midwife for the little community of El Pueblito del Valle.

"Maybe we should have Señora Pacheco see her anyway," Norberta heaved a sigh.

CHAPTER 27 – LA CURANDERA

Friday, August 19, 1910
El Pueblito del Valle

It was near dusk when the small Purepecha woman found her way to Lupe's casita. Norberta escorted Señora Pacheco, whose leather parched face had a thousand wrinkles. The medicine woman wore a blue turquoise and black onyx necklace and a wide leather bracelet with tiny bells. The curandera had on a white blouse with purple flowers embroidered on it and a deerskin skirt.

Señora Alicia Pacheco had settled in El Pueblito del Valle forty years prior. People could not discern if she was sixty-years old or two hundred. She was full-blooded Purepecha. Her family had been systematically killed off by the Apaches and Mexicans. She has taken refuge under the protection of her tribal shaman. He taught her about medicines, magic, and the walking spirits. When the shaman passed away, she inherited his position and became known as the curandera of the

Teocaltiche Valle. Now she was a poor person's doctor, the agnostic's spiritual advisor, and the pueblito's midwife.

It was under the latter circumstances that Señora Pacheco and Norberta had become acquainted. Norberta had trouble with the delivery of her second pregnancy. The curandera treated Norberta with a magical tea and gentle massaging that relaxed her and led to the successful birth of Julia.

Since Norberta didn't have any money, she had paid the curandera in chocolate and it was readily accepted.

"This is the blood of the gods," the curandera shouted. "I will show you how to make magic with it."

Back when Norberta was at La Virgen de Tepeyac Convent, she had learned to make chocolate in various forms. But Señora Pacheco had instructed Norberta how to concoct teas, balms, and foods with chocolate and cacao beans that would create powerful and magical medicines. One potion could change a person into a goat; another could grow back a missing toe. Over time, Norberta had slowly disassociated herself from the curandera. However, they remained on friendly terms and occasionally would socialize. Norberta had children to raise and that was her priority.

"Buenas tardes, señora," Norberta greeted Señora Pacheco and walked her over to Lupe who was lying on a mat with her eyes closed. Ramón grabbed a little wooden stool for the curandera.

Lupe seemed to be asleep, or at least resting. She did not seem to be awake.

The old woman turned to Norberta and asked what had happened. Norberta did the best that she could reciting the afternoon events. The entourage of Ramón, Julia, and Herculana were close by and nodded in agreement.

"Is there any bleeding?" the old woman asked. She had an indigenous accent that made her sound like she was stuttering but with a rhythmic flow.

"I don't think so," Norberta answered.

She was interrupted by Ramón. "Madrina, sometimes there is blood when she coughs. She wipes her mouth with her sleeve. It looks like red spit."

The old woman nodded and put her right hand on Lupe's chest and applied a gentle pressure. "Is she in any pain?"

Lupe stirred and weakly opened her eyes. The curandera touched Lupe's forehead. The fever was gone.

"Lupe, do you have pain? Does that hurt?" probed the old woman.

Lupe slowly nodded yes.

"Are you coughing and sneezing?"

Again, Lupe moved her head signifying yes.

The old woman put her wizened hand back on Lupe's head and then on her neck for several seconds.

"I am going to examine her, Norberta," Señora Pacheco said. "Please have the children leave. And can you bring me some clean towels or rags. And some water. Not cold."

The youngsters left and went back to Norberta's casita.

"Norberta, has she eaten anything today?"

"I don't know, señora," Norberta replied. "We gave her some chicken soup last night. She ate a little. And she drank some of my special cacao bean tea. According to her son, I don't think she has been eating much lately."

She's probably not making much money. And that pinche mayor keeps raising the fees. He is going to starve us all out, thought Norberta.

Señora Pacheco did a thorough physical examination of Lupe. Norberta had gone to the other end of the room to give them more privacy.

Afterwards, the medicine woman walked over to Norberta.

"She is weak. She needs to build her strength back up," the medicine woman's black eyes emitted a spiritual warmness.

"That means that she shouldn't work for a while," said Norberta.

The old woman nodded in agreement. "I need to do a few things. Is there a candle or oil lamp around here?"

They found a candle. The medicine woman balanced a bundle of herbs next to the candle making sure that it would not fall. Then she lit the smudge. The wonderful scents of eucalyptus and sage permeated the air. "This will purify the room."

Norberta had repressed her hunger but now her stomach was growling. "Con permiso, señora," and Norberta left to go to her own casita.

Five minutes later, she returned with Herculana carrying two cups of chicken soup.

When the old woman was done, she took the soup and slowly slurped it. Norberta did the same.

Finally, the medicine woman was getting ready to leave. Norberta thanked her profusely and gave her some pesos and chocolate bits which brought a big smile to the old woman's face.

"A few more things, Norberta. Plenty of liquids. But nothing cold. Your cacao tea is good," she was picking up her things. "And wash everything she touches. A little lime juice would help. Don't use her dishes without washing them first."

"Thank you, señora," Norberta waved. For the first time that day she felt hopeful.

The next day Norberta and her daughters got up extra early. They had worried about Lupe all night. They had even brought over an extra blanket for her.

Julia prepared some soft-boiled eggs, beans, and tortillas for Lupe and Ramón. Ramón was really happy. He hadn't eaten like this for weeks. Norberta was now trying to decide who would take care of Lupe during the day.

Ramón would have a hard time taking care of his mom. Lupe is modest and probably wouldn't want him to. I don't think he can cook. I need him to help me wheel the goods to the plaza.

"Ramón, please load the cart. We're going to the plaza today. Bring along any churros that you have left."

Who is going to take care of Lupe while we are away? Julia needs to wash clothes and cook. She probably will not have much time to do much cleaning. But maybe she can straighten a few things out at Lupe's, and for sure, cook her some food.

Norberta gave some instructions to Julia who assented by nodding her head. She was an obedient girl and began gaining self-confidence after Francisca had left.

Herculana was no longer attending school. She would be excellent for looking after her madrina, Norberta thought.

"But mamá, I want to go with you," the youngest started to whine.

"Mija, somebody has to look after your madrina. That has to be you. Make sure you carefully wash her dishes. And her clothes." *Herculana needs to grow up,* Norberta realized.

Herculana didn't look happy.

"I'll tell you what. I have an idea that might be fun. Go get your sister. Meet me at Lupe's when you find Julia."

Norberta went over to her comadre's casita with more freshly brewed tea of cacao that she had recently concocted with her dried cacao leaves, chiles, and herbs. Then she had added three roasted cacao moscas and some of her magical spices to Lupe's brew for good measure.

"How are you feeling, comadre?" Norberta saw that the patient was awake and sitting up on the mat.

"Better. ¡Gracias a Dios!" the color was starting to come back to her face.

"Your favorite ahijada is going to keep you company today," Norberta put on a game face. "And Julia is going to feed you. You have to drink your tea. All of it. If you need anything else, just ask the girls. This is your revenge for having to change their stinky diapers when they were babies."

Lupe struggled to make a slight grin.

"Now drink the tea. It's good for you," Norberta was now in charge. "I want you to eat whatever they bring you."

Herculana came into the casita with her sister Julia.

"Ramón and I are leaving for the plazita in a moment," Norberta looked at her two girls. "Comadre, I want you to give them the recipe and instructions on how to make your churros for tomorrow's market. Señora Pacheco says that you are not allowed to cook. Do you understand this, comadre?"

Lupe nodded her head slowly.

Herculana beamed. "This is going to be so much fun!"

CHAPTER 28 – CHURROS

Saturday, August 20, 1910

Norberta and Ramón had departed from the casitas a little later than usual, so they were walking at a little quicker clip. Norberta asked her godson about his mother's health during the prior month. He wasn't sure but thought that she had been having respiratory problems. She had sporadic sneezing and coughing attacks. Lupe had shrugged it off as a common cold.

I think that I need to have a serious talk with my comadre. She is probably not going to like what I have to say. But she is my comadre and Ramón is my ahijado. I have to take responsibility for both of them.

"Mijo, how has she been sleeping?"

"Good," Ramón knew not to hide anything from his godmother. "But last night, she was moaning really loud. I think she was having a nightmare. I tried to shake her but she did not wake up. She kept shouting things."

Norberta was worried. She had given Lupe cacao tea that was said to have special properties. Many thought it had magical curative powers.

"What was she screaming about?"

"I don't know," Ramón was flustered. "She just kept yelling, 'Run! They're coming! Hide! They're going to kill you!'"

"Who are they?"

"I don't know," Ramón put out his hands. "She never told me."

I will have to ask Lupe about this tonight. Was it a portentous dream or was it a hallucination?

When they arrived at the plaza, there were fewer vendors around. Old man Jiménez was lugging a big sack over his shoulder. His dark face was creased with sadness. He greeted the pair. "They're kicking me out! Cabrones!" he was trying to sound brave. "They want more money. I can't even feed my family!"

Norberta exhaled a gush of air. Ramón helped her set up and put the old churros on one side of the booth.

Alberto and his two friends were the first to arrive. They purchased hot chocolate and the old churros. Alberto made a face as he bit into it. Norberta knew that it was cold and stale but what could she do about it? Lupe needed to earn a little money.

"Where is Señora Lupe?"

"We think she has a cold," Norberta told a whitish lie. "She should be back here in a few days."

The morning went by slowly.

"Mijo, go over to Señor Cano's grocery store and buy some limes. Make sure they are soft and ripe. Maybe about six. Thanks, mijo." She sent him on this way.

Norberta was rinsing some earthenware cups when she smelled the cloying smell of Seven Roses after shave. She did not even have to turn around to know that's Jorge "El Piojo" was behind her. She took a deep breath. She pulled the chocolate and churros closer to her person.

"Good morning, dearest Norberta," the dandy gave an unctuous smile. He had his black hair slicked back and a three-day old stubble. His black shirt was covered by a black leather vest. He wore silver-toed black leather boots. "How are we today?"

"Good morning," she really did not want to engage in conversation with the village womanizer.

"I see that some of the merchants have left the plaza. What a shame! Maybe if they can't pay the fees, they don't know how to run a business."

Norberta gave him a stare that could have excised his villainous heart. But she kept herself under control. She knew better than to argue with a snake. Especially a serpent who was in collusion with the mayor and Sergeant Montez. She didn't respond.

"I don't see your wonderful companion Lupe around," he gazed at the empty booth next door.

Ramón arrived in the nick of time. "I got them, madrina!"

Jorge gave a sly smile as he started to leave. "Let me know if you need any help. I can get jobs for your daughters. You can make lots of money and still sell your chocolate. All you have to do is ask." He slowly walked away.

Norberta was livid. *¡Ese cabrón!*

For the remainder of the day, Norberta was in a foul mood. She did manage to sell a few churros, but she observed that the customers were only eating half of them. There were still about a half dozen left in the basket.

"Mijo, take these over to the family that is camped out on the front steps of church." There was a young girl with three kids dressed in indigenous garb that begged there every day no matter what the weather was. "And don't forget to bring back the basket!"

The way back home was uneventful. Norberta began to calm down and needed to talk to her godson.

"Mijo, what do you think about your mom staying with us a few days?" It really wasn't a question. "It would be easier for us to take care of her."

He nodded.

"You're a young man now and can stay in your casita by yourself. You can come over for breakfast and dinner."

They reached their place in the mid-afternoon only to find Herculana and Julia laughing around the area where Lupe usually made her churros. Norberta walked into the casita and saw that Lupe was sitting up and doing some embroidery.

"How are you, comadre?" Norberta asked.

"Good. The rest and the tea really worked. Thank you," she smiled. "And the girls kept me company. They are so silly. They will drive their future husbands crazy."

The two chatted for a while. Then Norberta broached the subject.

"Comadre, tell me about your dream from the other night."

"I don't really remember. I just felt like a white light was shining on me. Making me well. Giving me back my energy. I really don't recall anything. But I've been feeling good all day so far."

"We'll make sure your rest some more. Did you finish your tea?"

"Yes, it gave me energy. I have so much to do."

"In due time, comadre," Norberta gently rubbed her comadre's arm. Then she turned around and yelled for Julia to come in. The middle child ran inside.

"Julia, go to our house and fetch some tea of cacao that's in the pot. Heat it up before you bring it over here." The daughter obediently left.

Herculana was in the doorway. She was acting bubbly.

"What did you do today, mija?"

"We tried to make churros. My nina gave us the recipe."

"How did they turn out?"

"Not so good. We forgot to put in the baking soda."

"So, what happened?"

"We had to throw the first batch away. My nina said they looked like dog turds."

¡Ay Herculana!

CHAPTER 29 – CHOCOLATE KISSES

Sunday, August 21, 1910

The morning blue skies were being overcome by puffy dark grey clouds from the southeast. Norberta and Ramón felt their clothes becoming a little damper and clingy with the increased humidity. There was a slight breeze behind them.

Norberta was quite happy that Lupe had awoken happy and energetic. Her comadre wanted to get up and do things but she followed Norberta's cautious advice. Lupe had slept next to Norberta while Ramón remained alone in his own casita. What bothered Norberta was that Lupe had been moaning and talking in her sleep. Lupe warned of people coming to harm others. Norberta was afraid that this was an omen induced by her cacao tea. In her experience it had happened to others. The dreams always seemed to come true. Some of the ingredients that Norberta had concocted to make the cacao tea had magical properties, and usually she was very reluctant to use her enchanted chocolate products, but this was an exceptional circumstance.

Little drops of rain started to pitter-patter in front of Norberta and her godson. By the time they arrived at the plaza they were entirely soaked but pleasantly cooled off. The morning went by as usual but Norberta did not go to mass. She did not want to leave Ramón alone.

The regular customers came by. Alberto bought some churros and shared them with his friends. Today they were arguing about who the greatest president of Mexico had been.

"Benito Juarez! He really gave it to the Frenchies!"

"No! No! No! Agustín de Iturbide! He beat back those arrogant Spaniards! That's why there is a Mexico today!"

Alberto was about to give his position when he started choking. His colleague Iván started pounding him on the back. Alberto started to spit up the churro that he had been munching on. After a minute of spasmodic coughing, Alberto shook his head.

"¡A la madre!" he cursed.

Norberta rushed over and gave him a tin cup of cool water.

"Señora," he tried to be calm. "I think the churros are malcocinados." He pointed to the doughy inside of his churro. It was raw and doughy.

"I am so sorry, Señor Alberto. Señora Lupe will be back soon. I'll make sure she gives you a some gratis when she comes back."

The loyal customer nodded his head and resumed the political discussion with his cohorts. "Madero is being attacked by the old guard. Mark my words. That pinche Díaz and nephew will have him killed."

Norberta was embarrassed. Her daughters had cooked the churros the day before in too high a heat. The outside was nice and brown, but the interior was undercooked. *¡Ay Dios Mío! I can't wait until Lupe is back!*

Norberta hesitated for a moment. *What should she do with the churros? Throw them away? Give them away?*

"Ramón, did you give away the churros to that poor family on the church steps yesterday?" she asked.

"Yes, madrina."

"Okay, take the rest of these to them today," She let out a deep sigh. She hoped that they wouldn't get sick from the undercooked dough. "And don't forget to bring back the basket, mijo!"

Five minutes later a horse pulled up with a young man in the saddle.

"Good morning, Señora Norberta!" Pito had the biggest smile on his face. Very soon he was going to see his love.

"Good morning, mijo. Did you remember to bring her a present?"

He nodded no.

"I want to buy her some of your magical chocolate. It's the best," he was trying to charm the older woman. "And I need to pay you what I owe you for the letters." He gave her some pesos and she handed him a packet of her special chocolates.

She wanted to warn him about being too naïve, but she kept herself in check.

"Señora, I'm going to 'the place.' Thank you. See you later. He rode his horse down to the grove where he and María Antonia had their assignations.

The church bells rang ten times. The nine o'clock mass was over, and customers would be coming from the church. María Antonia remained at the back of the group. She caught Norberta's eye and tilted her head to where Pedro had just gone. In a flash she disappeared, and Norberta could see the back of the young girl as she hurried toward the palm grove to meet with her lover, Pedro.

She rushed into his arms, ecstatically pushing him against a tree. Their lips met.

"I've missed you so much, mi vida," he struggled to say, panting.

"Me, too!"

"I thought that I would die if I didn't see you again."

"Me, too! The hours away from you seemed like years," her eyes longed for his attention and affection. They talked and embraced for the next half hour.

"Would you like to go for a ride?" Pedro asked her with his devouring look.

"Sure!" María Antonia knew better but she was in love. "But we have to be at Araceli's no later than two o'clock. She is going to give me a ride back to my house. I said that I would be with her this afternoon."

Pedro unhitched the horse from the tree and helped María Antonia onto the saddle. She was used to riding horses. He flung himself behind her.

"Where would you like to go?" he asked her.

She thought for a moment. "There is an old chapel over that hill. Nobody ever goes there anymore."

For the next half hour, they moseyed up the incline with Pedro's arms wrapped tightly around María Antonia's waist. Her body permeated heat. The grass was gently trampled by El Brujo traipsing up the overgrown path. Purple sage bordered the way with a sweet, after rain smell. The greenery turned into barren ground and there were tall cypress trees above them. They stopped at an old adobe chantry with peeled white paint and a missing bell.

"Here we are!" Pedro got off El Brujo and helped her down. He tied the horse to a bush next to a good place for it to graze.

The building was old and dusty. The lumber was rotten, and the inside was stacked with old benches and picture frames. The two found a spot behind an old stone holy water fountain.

They giggled.

"Are you hungry, my love?" Pedro looked deeply into her hazel eyes. He gently stroked her shoulder.

"For you," she said with an impish grin.

"I brought us some chocolate."

"I love that chocolate."

Pedro undid the ties on her blouse. He took a piece of Norberta's chocolate out of a little paper and put it on her lips. It started to melt. She, in turn, duplicated his maneuver. They both laughed and started to lick the chocolate on the other's face. A piece of chocolate fell on to her shoulder. His mouth lapped it up slowly. She sighed.

María Antonia unbuttoned Pedro's shirt. Then she took another chocolate and put it on his nipple. She savored it.

More and more chocolate melted as the passion heated up. Two molten bodies liquefied.

"You taste delicious!"

"So, do you!"

CHAPTER 30 – DANGER

Sunday, August 21, 1910

Renya was feeling a little beside herself as she and Don José Sáenz Mejia rode back home after going to mass. She was upset that the mayor's daughter, María Antonia, had been trying to exercise her independence lately and circumvent her as a guardian. Renya wanted her ward to be more serious and studious. Within a few years she would marry a gentleman, hopefully her cousin Gregorio, to carry out the family traditions. She didn't understand why María Antonia wanted to spend the day with Araceli. They were not in the same social class, although she thought Araceli was a likeable young lady.

After Renya had changed out of her Sunday church clothes, she decided that she needed to do a few things before the afternoon lunch. She really didn't like the idea of María Antonia starting to eat more chocolate lately. Her father should have put an end to this indulgence or least limit it. She decided to go into María Antonia's room and get rid of the chocolates. She looked about the room that had been tidied by the maid.

She found nothing. She walked over to the double set of clothes drawers and pushed the clothes around. Still nothing,

She started to leave the room but decided to check the vanity table. Renya saw herself in the mirror. She had aged. But being a caretaker for the mayor's daughter had been her calling and he was good to her. The jewelry box on top had earrings and necklaces. The two left drawers had hairbrushes and sweet-smelling soaps. The middle drawer had some stationary and quill pens. The top right drawer emitted the stimulating smell of chocolate as she opened it. There were at least a half dozen pieces. Renya scooped them up and put them into the front pocket of her apron. She would dispose of them later on. For the sake of curiosity, she opened the last drawer, the lower right. She was surprised to see a small of stack of letters held together by a pink ribbon. *Who would be writing to María Antonia? Certainly not her cousin Gregorio.* She unwrapped the bow and unfolded the letter on top. She was shocked. María Antonia was corresponding with someone without her knowledge. How could she have done this without Renya's knowledge? Renya felt betrayed by her ward. She opened the second and could not believe the letters that oozed of love and passion. She was taking panicky shallow breaths as she went through all of them.

Five minutes later she was knocking forcefully on the mayor's study.

"Come in, Renya. What is it? What's all the fuss?"

Renya rushed in and spewed out what she had learned about María Antonia's recent amorous antics. The mayor lost control when he found out that a meeting between his daughter and her seducer was occurring as they were speaking.

"How could this have happened?" the mayor was apoplectic. "Why didn't you know about this? This is going to be the scandal of the century! We will be the laughingstock of Teocatliche!"

"I'm so sorry, Señor Sáenz," Renya's head was bowed in supplication. "But she has been scheming with someone. Probably with the help of Araceli. That is where she is supposed to be right now."

"Go over to Araceli's house and fetch her!" Mayor Sáenz ordered. "We'll get to the bottom of this. Heads are going to roll!"

"Yes, señor," Renya replied meekly.

"But before you go, tell Rodrigo to go to town and talk to Sergeant Montez. Have him find this Pedro creature and take care of him," the mayor screamed.

"Yes, señor." *How did María Antonia receive these letters? Who had helped her?* She put her rebozo back on and twenty minutes later the two-horse carriage had drawn up before Araceli's yellowish two-story house.

"Jaime, knock on the door," Renya remained in the carriage as her driver jumped off the rig. "Fetch María Antonia."

"As you wish, señora," the middle-aged man wearing his black and gold household livery replied.

Renya was growing impatient when the girl did not appear. *Is she really here? Could she be with that boy?*

Finally, María Antonia rushed out of the door. Her face was flushed, and her clothing looked bedraggled. It looked like she had thrown herself on a forest floor. Her hair was wet and tangled. Renya gave her a disapproving look.

Goodbyes and thankyous were said to Araceli. Then Jaime cracked the whip, and the horses started their prancing back home.

After they arrived back home, Renya went directly to María Antonia' room.

María Antonia seemed to be panting. She was looking away from Renya. *I barely made it back in time! It was difficult leaving him. Oh, that chocolate!*

"How was your day?" Renya asked neutrally,

"Fine," María Antonia wanted to keep her responses short. She had hoped that Renya would not interrogate her like she normally did. The young woman was not a criminal. She was just in love.

"What did you do?"

"Oh, just talked," María Antonia was thinking about her rapturous time with Pedro. "We took a stroll through the fields. We saw beautiful flowers and heard birds sing. We had a good time."

"Besides Araceli, did you talk with anyone else?"

"Like whom? Just Araceli's mother," the young woman started to get nervous.

"I don't know," Renya smiled craftily. The fly was getting lured in by the spider. "Maybe a boy perhaps?"

María Antonia's heart stopped. *What does Renya know?*

"We found the letters. Your father is furious," Renya was taking great pleasure in this. "You'd better tell me everything."

***

During this time, one of the mayor's security guards, Rodrigo, rode into town and stopped at the tiny adobe police station. He walked in and asked for Sergeant Montez. Montez was always doing favors for the mayor, legally (and illegally). Rodrigo was pointed to the back of the building where he found the big and fat policeman taking a siesta in a chair.

"Geraldo! Wake up!" Rodrigo shook the snorer. "The mayor has a job for you. He needs it done yesterday!"

Montez rubbed his long black right sideburn that melted into a droopy moustache.

"Okay! Okay! Just let me clear my head!"

Rodrigo began to explain that a person named Pedro had to be found and be "taken care of."

"What's he look like?"

"We don't know. But here's a letter that he wrote."

The sergeant looked at him. He couldn't read very well, and besides, what good was the note to him? However, he couldn't disappoint the mayor. He needed help. He and El Piojo had collaborated on many things. He would talk with his friend.

The sergeant reluctantly told Rodrigo not to worry. He would do whatever it took to find Pedro.

Montez left the police station and first went to La Vispera Cantina. Jorge "El Piojo" was not there. The bartender told him to try the tobacco shop. The sergeant went there. No luck. Finally, he went to the barbershop where Jorge had just finished getting his hair cut and greased down.

Montez related the problem to him.

"How are we going to find this Pedro without a description? ¡A la madre!"

"I think he is the boyfriend of the mayor's daughter."

"¡Ay Dios Mío! I pity the poor kid," El Piojo shook his
head. "Well, that's a clue. He should be young."

"Oh! I have a letter that he wrote," he handed one of
Pedro's letters to El Piojo.

El Piojo read the letter and then laughed. "I recognize this
letter. Norberta the scribe writes them. I think I have seen a
young guy hanging around her booth. I think his name is Pedro
and he works at the Atepoca mine."

***

Pedro had dropped off María Antonia about a hundred
yards from Araceli's house. He never wanted to leave her. He
still felt the ecstasy of their tryst flowing from his veins.
Afterwards, he went to the plazita in town. He wanted to write
her another love letter. Maybe even a love poem.
Unfortunately, Norberta had left and was unable to do it. He
went to a panaderia and grabbed a torta for his lunch.

As El Brujo slowly trotted back to the mining camp, Pito
was whistling in between goofy smiles. The air and grass
dampened by the rain smelled sweet and fresh. He could smell
the chocolate on María Antonia's skin. He closed his eyes and
let the horse guide him back to the camp.

Bamm! Suddenly Pedro felt himself flying through the air
as El Brujo reared up on his hind legs and kicked out his front
legs. Pedro was thrown to the ground. The air gushed out of

him, and he doubled over. He tried to look up, but a flashing object smashed his left eye. He fell backwards stunned.

"Did you think you were going to get away with messing with the mayor's daughter?" a glib voice sounded above him.

Then there was a flurry of kicks to the ribs and body. In the front. In the back.

"This will teach you never to come back here again!" panted another voice.

Pedro was left lying on the ground, not moving a muscle.

CHAPTER 31 – RESCUED

Sunday, August 21, 1910

The rain had stopped but the skies were still cloudy. The air was moist with a fine mist. Norberta was struggling to finish up the quinceañera invitations she was doing on behalf of Señora Gloria Guzmán and her daughter Sibila. The girl was turning fifteen years of age the following month. Her mother was a social climber who bragged about how smart and beautiful her daughter was and how lucky a young man would be if she married him. Of course, the Guzmán family was not rich, and put on airs. The husband, Señor Abdel Guzmán owned a tapestry business in Teocaltiche. The family lived in Colonia Las Flores that was situated between Teocaltiche and El Pueblito del Valle.

Two weeks earlier Señor Guzmán was enjoying hot chocolate and rosquetes with her daughter after mass. She overheard a customer ask Norberta to draft a letter of condolences. She made an inquiry and found out that Norberta was a scribe. She engaged the services of Norberta to

handwrite fifty invitations to Gloria's quinceañera. She
stipulated that the stationery had to be of the highest quality
and was to be done by August 21.

Norberta agreed. She drafted several examples and finally
Señora Guzmán settled on one:

Señor and Señora Abdel Guzmán

Request the Honor of your Presence

In Celebration of the Quinceañera

Of their Daughter

Sibila María Guzmán

Saturday, the Tenth of September

At the Home of the Guzmán Family

Colonia Las Flores

Norberta did not realize that it would be difficult to procure
the formal stationary paper. Finally, the local bookstore

ordered some from Mexico City and it took ten days to arrive. Norberta had been scurrying madly to finish the invitations. She ran out of ink once and had to buy a more expensive kind in order to complete the work.

Today Norberta had brought the invitations for Mrs. Guzmán but could not find her. Norberta panicked. She did not know where the lady lived or how she could deliver them on time. She asked around and someone told her that the Guzmáns lived in Colonia Las Flores about thirty minutes from town and thirty minutes from El Pueblito del Valle. After talking to Lupe, it was agreed that Ramón would make the delivery in the afternoon.

After escorting his mother and godmother back home from the plaza, Ramón devoured some caldo with corn tortillas. He had wanted to take a nap but his mother insisted that he deliver the invitations to the Guzmáns. He had to walk there, but he thought he knew a shortcut.

"Make sure you keep them dry, mijo," Lupe worried. "Don't dawdle. I think Señora Guzmán has warts on her nose. Don't stare at her."

Ramón walked at a quick pace on the established paths. He did not want to get lost or delayed. When he got close to the next village, he asked a couple of people for directions. Everybody, of course, knew where Gloria Guzmán lived.

He knocked on the door of a large house covered with ivy. It was old and stylish but still elicited a bit of charm. Ramón was shown into the drawing room by the maid and offered a cup of hot tea. There were Oriental carpets and tapestries from floor to ceiling.

Mrs. Guzmán entered the room and greetings were exchanged. Ramón handed over the invitations. He had successfully kept them dry and in good order. *Oh my God! She does have warts on her nose!*

Ramón was offered little tea cakes. He grabbed a few and made a feeble excuse that he had to get home.

He made haste trying to get back home. He saw a deer trail that veered to the right. He tried to recall if it was a shortcut. He set off in that direction. It was a pleasant jaunt with a gentle mist falling on him. Several warblers were singing and every so often he would see a squirrel scurrying up a tree. Ramón stopped at another fork in the road. He didn't know which way to turn but he decided that the left path looked more worn and therefore more promising.

This trail was quieter with bigger trees and bushes. *Maybe a future source for more firewood?* The path turned to mud, and the wind started to pick up. Ramón looked up and saw dark grey clouds above him. He felt a few drops. *¡Ay demonios! I'm*

*going to get caught in the rain. I don't have a coat! Blessed
Virgin take pity on me!*

Five minutes later the rain had ceased, and patches of blue
could be seen in the skies. He whispered a thank you for the
divine intervention. He was shivering from his wet clothes
when he looked up to evaluate the weather. He noticed a wake
of grey-headed zopilotes circling above a clearing, two
hundred paces ahead. This piqued Ramón's curiosity. As he
approached, he saw an object partially hidden under a tree. He
stared in that direction and finally discerned it was a horse. It
had a saddle. It wasn't tied to anything. There was no rider.

Ramón looked around. *Should I call out? I don't know.
Probably the guy is taking a pee in the bushes.* As he got closer
to the horse, he thought he recognized it. He couldn't
remember from when. At least the horse was smart enough to
get out of the rain, Ramón smiled to himself. Then he noticed
the ground. Its grassy growth looked like it had been thrashed.
The rain wasn't that forceful. *I should just leave. The horse
isn't mine. Someone will come back for it.* Then he noticed
reddish-brown splats on the leaves. He bent over and saw a
disarray of muddy footprints.

Then he saw a boot. It was attached to speckled jeans.
There was a form. It was a body. He reached over slowly and
carefully turned the figure over. The face was rust colored. The

form was breathing shallowly. Ramón looked hard. He knew that face. It was the guy that his madrina wrote the love letters for. He then remembered that the horse belonged to this guy.

Ramón tried to awaken the guy but had no luck. He took off his wet shirt and tried to wipe the guy's face and cover the bloodied eye. He was shivering but the adrenaline kept the cold away.

What am I supposed to do? Well, I can't leave him here. My mom and my madrina will know what to do. I need to do whatever it takes to help this poor guy!

Ramón tried to pick up the body. Although Pedro was not large, the wet and bloody clothes made it a challenge to lift him. Ramón pitched him over his shoulder. The body emitted a groan. The horse made no effort to retreat as Ramón approached. Ramón threw the body across the wet saddle. The horse gave a little whinny after being spooked. A few reassuring pets and Ramón were leading the horse and body forward.

By good fortune they found the main thoroughfare between Teocaltiche and El Pueblito del Valle a hundred paces away. They passed a doe and her three fawns grazing on the grass on the side of the road.

Ramón was exhausted and feeling faint. *I gotta get home! This guy needs help!*

CHAPTER 32 – FIREWOOD

Monday, August 22, 1910
El Pueblito del Valle

It had rained cats and dogs all night. Every nook and
cranny of Norberta's casita was soaking wet. Pots and bowls
were strewn over the floor. Ramón helped Norberta make the
morning fire. Today was her day to make chocolate. But before
she could start, she had to make breakfast for everyone. Julia
helped her by stirring the rice porridge.

"Mijo, how did Pedro sleep?" Norberta asked her godson.

"I think okay," Ramón replied. "But he was wailing all
night."

"This morning I want you to rub that balm on him again. I
hope it will help. Also, I will make him some cacao tea with
cinnamon." She knew that would help relieve some of the pain.

"Yes, madrina," he politely answered. "How's my mom?"

"¡Ay Dios Mío! She must have eaten a dozen chiles. She is
so full of much energy. She wants to do everything. But la

Señora Pacheco says no. She has to rest." Ramón nodded his head in agreement.

"Mijo, I am a little worried. We're going to be out of money soon. Then they will kick us out of the plaza. That Arias makes sure everybody pays every month. He is uncharitable," Her dark eyes looked at Ramón for some kind of counsel. "What are we going to do? We need to take care of each other, verdad?"

"Madrina, is it okay if I do my firewood job today for Señor Caraballo?" On the one hand he did not want to abandon them, but it would be better if he could earn a few pesos. "Or I can stay here and help."

"Go, mijo," Norberta said. She too knew that they needed the money. Ramón was acting like a man. That had to be respected. "Have your breakfast first! I think the tea is ready for Pedro. Don't forget to rub him down. And please be careful in this rain."

Ramón acknowledged what his godmother had said. He felt that his madrina still treated him like a child. He wanted to be the man of the merged families. He sat down at the small table. Julia came by and scooped up an earthenware cup of the rice porridge. These two didn't talk much with each other. He inhaled his hot cereal. But before he finished, Julia took the cup from him and refilled it with more porridge dripping over the edge.

He gave her a nod of appreciation. When he was finished eating, Ramón grabbed another cup of porridge and a cup of Norberta's special cacao tea. These were for Pedro. He went over to his mom's casita. He saw that the bare-chested Pedro was staggering back into the dwelling. Pedro had had to relieve himself in the bushes outside.

Inside, Lupe was in the corner talking with Herculana. Lupe pulled Ramón close and whispered something in his ear. He nodded.

Ramón went over to where Pedro was sitting upright on a straw mat. "How are you feeling?" Ramón asked as he handed Pedro the oatmeal and some tea.

Pedro answered with a primal grunt. "Where am I?" he asked in a dazed tone.

"You're with us. You had a terrible accident and we brought you here," Ramón looked over to his mother for reassurance.

"Where's El Brujo?"

"Who?" Ramón thought that Pedro was hallucinating. *Who was El Brujo? Did some sorcerer do this to Pedro?*

"My horse."

"Oh. I don't know. I didn't see him this morning."

Pedro started to shake his head in frustration, but it was painful to do so. He lifted up the steaming hot tea and took a sip. And then another. Then he took a spoonful of porridge and slowly savored it. The second spoonful he gulped quickly. He continued until he finished half of the porridge.

"Pedro, what happened?"

Pedro took another sip of tea. "I don't know. All I remember is that El Brujo and I were riding back to camp. Then suddenly I felt a tremendous pain in my left eye. I got very dizzy." Pedro was straining to talk. Ramón could feel his agony. "I fell off my horse and hit the ground. Hard! It knocked the wind out of me. And then I felt kicking. Somebody was kicking me. I felt the sharp points of boots."

Ramón was having a difficult time understanding. "Did someone do this to you? Do you know who?"

"I don't know. I can't remember. One guy. Maybe two. One smelled very sweet, I think. Cologne or something."

Ramón padded Pedro on the shoulder. "Compañero, gotta rub you down before I go to work. We need money since my mom hasn't been working. Tú sabes."

Gingerly, Ramón put dabs of Norberta's special cacao-based balm into the palms of his hands and rubbed them together. Ramón could feel the heat being generated. Pedro then laid down, face down. Ramón massaged Pedro's body.

His skin turned red emitting little sparkles. Pedro moaned. Beads of sweat secreted all over this body. By the time Ramón finished, Pedro was asleep.

***

It was midmorning and Norberta was already exhausted. Sweat was running down her brow. In addition to making her chocolate discs and chocolate pieces, she concocted more mesquite-cacao balm. It was one of her special magical salves. Julia was attentively assisting her after she finished her morning chores.

A cart led by a roan-colored horse drove up to Norberta's casita. A short, dark-skinned man with a white handlebar moustache got down. Abelardo Gutierrez was the owner of a small dairy in El Pueblito del Valle. Until several weeks earlier, his son Luis had delivered milk and dairy products throughout the neighborhood. But all that changed when Luis and Norberta's daughter ran away together. Now old man Abelardo had to make the deliveries himself. He couldn't afford to hire anyone else.

"Good morning, Señora Pérez," Abelardo greeted her in a very polite manner. "I think the rain is over now. But we really need it."

"Good morning, Abelardo," Norberta said in an impersonal manner. Normally, Abelardo dropped off two liters of milk on Mondays.

Neither of them dared to talk about his son, Luis, taking off with Francisca. *What could they do? Así es la vida.* Abelardo felt guilty about it. The payment for the milk was based on a barter agreement between the two. Today Norberta took advantage of his discomfort and asked for a half kilo of queso casero. She, in turn, gave him extra chocolate.

"Qué le vaya bien!" he called out as he left. Norberta resumed her duties. "Oye, Herculana, you're in charge of washing everyone's clothes."

The youngest daughter resented this. She wanted to escape and be with her godmother Lupe. She had Lupe, Ramón, and now Pedro to look after.

In the afternoon, Herculana brought some quesadillas and more cacao tea to Pedro.

"Does it hurt?" she asked him.

Pedro tried to give her a brave smile, but instead nodded yes.

She began talking to him, firing dozens of questions at him. She was a pest, he thought, but at least she was keeping him company.

"Do you know how to read?" she prompted. "I do."

He shook his head no.

"Would you like me to teach you?"

Pedro nodded yes.

That evening Ramón came home with a chicken. He also brought some extra firewood that he had scavenged with his machete as he had made his rounds. They would enjoy a tasty dinner that night.

CHAPTER 33 – FIVE COINS

Tuesday, August 23, 1910

The next day's routine was a repeat of Monday. After breakfast, Herculana returned to Lupe's casita to pick up Pedro's dishes and do other chores.

She approached Pedro who was sitting upright on a mat. "Take off your pants!" Herculana commanded. "And cover yourself with this." She handed him a brown and tan sarape. She then left the room. Pedro noticed that his trousers were filthy and smelly. He went through the pockets and emptied them. He recovered several loose pesos and placed them on the mat next to him. He counted out five coins.

Herculana returned and took his pants.

"You better give me your shirt too," she directed him. "And everything else. I'll turn around now."

A few minutes later she had all of his dirty clothes. He was naked under the cover. "They sure do stink," she commented.

Pedro was embarrassed. "Here," he tried to shove the five coins toward her.

Herculana's head rocked back. *What is this?* "Mamá won't let me take money or gifts from strangers."

Pedro didn't consider himself a stranger, but he respected what she had to say.

"And Pedro, don't forget we're going to teach you to read and write," she looked at him sternly, way beyond her years. "And you have to whistle for me."

He hadn't whistled since his accident. He gave her a weak smile as she left.

Meanwhile, back at the other casita, there was an animated conversation going on between Lupe and Norberta.

"Oye, comadre, I have to go to the plaza with you tomorrow," Lupe insisted. "We need the money."

"Señora Pacheco wants you to wait until Saturday."

"By that time, people will have forgotten my churros," Lupe complained. "You told me how bad the last two batches were."

"A couple more days won't hurt," Norberta tried to pacify her.

"But comadre, now you are supporting not only your own family, but mine too!" Lupe was adamant, "And God forbid,

now that pendejo Lover Boy. May La Virgen save us from all
of this mess!"

"Ramón brings in some money. He's a good son."

"But we are behind with our accounts," Lupe persisted.

"We see our friends leaving the market. It's only a matter of
time for us."

"I have an idea, comadre. Let's combine our businesses.
We'll only need the one booth and only have to pay one fee.
That would teach that scoundrel Arias for trying to gouge us
with all these fees."

"But you do the scribe work. You make more money."

"Well, I need to ensure that my godson Ramón is protected.
Besides, four eyes see better than two. Especially two viejas."

They both laughed.

"Okay, I'll think about it," Lupe took on a surrendering
look.

"One other thing," Norberta added. "Why don't you make
the churros for tomorrow. Maybe we could go to plaza together
on Friday. This is with the understanding that if you get a
relapse, I'll send for Señora Pacheco. And you know that she
will sentence you for more bed rest. She means business."

"Yes, mi general," Lupe gave a mock salute. They both
laughed again.

For the remainder of that Tuesday, everybody was busy. Herculana had picked up Pedro's dishes and then grabbed the laundry, drying on some nearly bushes.

As Herculana started to wash his cup, she saw that it contained several coins inside.

"Mamá, Pedro put some coins in the cup," she showed them to her mother.

Norberta looked at them and frowned.

"You said that I'm not supposed to take money from strangers or men. Isn't that right? Is Pedro a man?"

Norberta put down one of her cooking trays. She knew that they desperately needed the money. They had to pay the cacao bean supplier, Javier, the next day. Lately, Señor Becerra preferred pesos rather than bartering for chocolate. On the other hand, she had a healthy respect for Pedro. She felt safe. She trusted Pedro, but she had to err on the side of caution.

"Mija, thank you for telling me. I will talk to him."

In the late afternoon, Norberta marched over to Lupe's casita. She placed herself in front of Pedro.

"Hijo, how are you feeling?"

"Better."

"Are you still in pain?"

"Not too much," he did not want to whine about the constant throbbing around his left eye. It still bothered him.

"Have you been eating, and drinking your tea?"

"Sí, señora. Thank you."

"That's good. One more thing," she returned the five coins back on top of his blanket. He was still naked underneath the cover. "Mijo, we can't take your money."

"Señora, please. I respect your charity and dignity, but I want to contribute somehow. I need to pay my fair share. Otherwise, I have to leave."

Norberta, for her part, could understand where he was coming from. Pedro was respectful and was trying to do the right thing.

"How about this? When you get better, you can help with the chores around here. I think Ramón likes you being here."

"Señora, please take the money. I can see that you need it" he stated very seriously, but with an air of gratitude.

"Still no, mijo."

He smiled. She was stubborner than the mules he took care of back at the mine.

"Besides, Herculana is going to teach me how to read and write. This could count toward the payment for my lessons."

¡Ay Dios Mío! This poor boy! He doesn't know what he is getting into. Herculana will make him a victim!!

Norberta would have to have a frank conversation with her daughter and give her ground rules. *What book would they start*

with? He would need paper and a pencil. Norberta filled her
head with a thousand questions.

"One more thing, señora," Pedro looked a little
uncomfortable as he squirmed under the cover on the mat.
"When can I get my clothes back?"

¡Ay Herculana!

CHAPTER 34 – SOLEDAD

Wednesday, August 24, 1910

Teocaltiche

There was a refreshing sprinkle that fell upon Norberta and Ramón as they traveled toward the plazita.

"Ramón, I'm trying to talk your mother into combining our little businesses," Norberta had her right hand on her godson's shoulder. "Our expenses are too high. We need to save money. But your mother is not too sure about this. And you know how stubborn she can get if she doesn't want to do something."

Everybody in our families is stubborn, Ramón rolled his eyes. Ramón had thought about getting a fulltime job, working six days a week, but how would his mother and godmother get their goods to the plaza? *Not such a good idea.*

"Madrina, is there anything else we could sell and make more money? How about hot coffee?"

"Mijo, if the people buy coffee, they don't buy our hot chocolate. And coffee beans are more expensive."

Ramón felt stupid. His mom and madrina were savvy businesspersons. He knew that he still had a lot to learn.

"We can't do cookies. Gloria, who had a booth on the other side of the plaza, sells them. She's a good friend."

"How about tamales?" Ramón knew that everybody liked them.

"Too much work, mijo."

"Burritos?"

"Get too cold too fast. The tortillas start to crack after a while."

"I give up, madrina."

"You have a good head on your shoulders, mijo. You'll think of something. Nobody is born knowing what to do. Paso a pasito. We just have to learn slowly."

An hour later, Alberto, the regular customer, seemed very happy. A missing tooth highlighted his broad smile. Norberta had given him a free churro to compensate him for the last churros he had bought that were unsatisfactory.

Ramón, a little while later, was standing close to Norberta when a middle-aged short and stocky woman with short black hair approached them. She was carrying a worn-out pink cardboard suitcase.

She rushed up and wagged her crooked finger in Ramón's face. "You, naughty boy!" Spittle was spouting from her mouth as she ranted. "I was fired because of you!"

Norberta, the lioness, swung her body between the woman and Ramón. Her arms folded back to protect him.

"Mijo, what is she talking about?" Norberta had her back to her godson. She was sure that she had seen this woman before but couldn't recall where.

"She's the cook for the mayor," Ramón answered. "I used to deliver Pedro's letters to the girl he liked."

Norberta recalled the woman now. *I think her name is Soledad. She once delivered a letter from María Antonia here at my booth.*

"Soledad, we are sorry for this terrible tragedy. We were only sending letters to two young people in love."

The woman stopped moving. She started to calm down.

Norberta handed her some hot chocolate.

"Ramón, hand me a churro." He quickly obeyed.

Soledad took a bite and then a sip. "Thank you. As always, they are delicious, Señora Pérez. But is it true?" Soledad asked incredulously. "Is he dead?"

"Who?" Norberta frowned.

"The boy who was writing the letters to María Antonia."

"Pedro?" Norberta replied quickly. "No, but he was beaten up. He might lose an eye."

"Please forgive my bad manners, señora," there were tears in Soledad's eyes. "I should never have given those letters to María Antonia. That crazy girl! Señor Sáenz found out about the secret rendezvous. He became furious. He was going to send some men to teach that mestizo a lesson."

"Do you know who he sent?"

"That pig, Sergeant Montez. And I think, his friend, El Piojo. María Antonia knows nothing of any of this."

Norberta squeezed herself just above the bridge of her nose. Now it made sense. She knew who the players were.

"Soledad, where will you go now?"

"Guadalajara. My sister Hortensia has her family there. I can stay with them for a while until I find a job."

"Soledad, I am deeply sorry for the pain that you have had to suffer."

"Me, too," chimed in Ramón unexpectedly.

"I was supposed to have written another letter from Pedro to María Antonia. I can still do it if you think I should."

"It's too late," responded the former cook. "María Antonia was sent to Spain two days ago. She is supposed to marry a cousin in Madrid."

The faces of Norberta and Ramón dropped.

"Vayan con Dios." Soledad said, then took her leave from Norberta and Ramón.

"Pedro is not going to be very happy," Ramón tendered.

"Mijo, go to the grocery store," Norberta told Ramón what she needed.

He left with the cart and stopped at the grocer's. Norberta and Lupe had a running account there. Ramón started stacking bags of flour, beans, rice, and sugar on the wooden counter.

The skinny, middle-aged man with wire-rimmed glasses, Luis Cano, who was the owner started to count up the purchases and gave Ramón the total.

"Please put this on the Norberta Pérez account," Ramón tried to complete the purchase.

"Can't do that, son"

"Why not?" Ramón was bigger than Cano.

"The mayor says that you people need to be taught a lesson. He will not be made a fool of," the owner replied meekly. "And besides, I have a wife and two kids."

"I don't understand," Ramón was bewildered.

"Just go away. I can't sell you these things," Cano muttered with his head down. "Tell Señora Pérez that she doesn't owe me anything. Sorry!"

"How about Lupe Nava?"

"Don't know. Please just go."

Ramón slowly wandered back toward Norberta's booth. He was shaking his head. He didn't want to give his godmother the bad news. Finally, he manned up and went back to tell his godmother the evil tidings. He disclosed his conversation with Señor Cano. If he expected Norberta to get angry or cry, he was disappointed. Norberta took it stoically. *Así es la vida.* She was the matriarch. She needed to find another solution.

CHAPTER 35 – THE RESCUE

Thursday-Sunday, August 25-28, 1910
El Pueblito del Valle

The raindrops lightly pelted El Pueblito del Valle. There was a cool wet smell of lavender in the air. Lupe was feeling better and making jokes. They had sold all the churros the day before without any complaints. Life was good. Several customers asked Norberta when Lupe was returning.

"I'm ready, comadre!" Lupe yelled. "I'm tired of doing nothing."

"You seem fine," Norberta stroked Lupe's hair and smiled. "Why don't we bring you to the plaza on Friday?"

"That would be great!" Lupe's eyes were the size of two moons. "Thank you!"

"But if I see you getting sick, I'll send you home. Agreed?"

"Of course!" Lupita thought. *Just let them try to stop me!*

The two women talked more about combining their businesses. Lupe still did not want to make a commitment.

"How's Pedro?" Lupe tried to change the subject, even though Ramón was always giving her periodic updates.

"Fine. His bruised ribs are healing fine. Most of his pain is gone. I think that he'll be able to fully recover in another month. We'll see. May the Virgen protect him! But his left eye is still swollen. I don't know how to treat that."

"Comadre, how about this? I can make him a patch. You know, to protect the eye," Lupe offered. "We can call him El Pirata."

"Ay, comadre!" They both chuckled.

A little piece of cloth and a string should do the trick, Lupe thought. And it would be simple.

"Oye, comadre, I appreciate you taking care of me in your casita, but I should be moving back. Ramón needs me there."

"If you ask me, Ramón is doing just fine being alone. He's starting to act more independent. He's a nice young man. And he and Pedro have become good friends."

Lupe nodded her head. "And I think Pedro should stay with us. There's more room there." Lupe knew that Pedro could not move into Norberta's because she had two young daughters. That was a no-no.

Norberta hadn't thought that far ahead. She was worried about how to eat tomorrow and pay her bills.

That evening after dinner, Ramón rubbed Pedro's body with the special cacao bean balm from Norberta. Its magical properties were working. At times sparks emanated from Pedro's skin. The skin tended to turn red and heat up. The purple and black bruises had been transformed into yellow patches.

"How did you make out today in the rain?" Pedro asked Ramón about working with the firewood deliveries.

"It was harder than usual. The cartwheels kept getting stuck in the mud," Ramón tried to explain. "But I made more money because people wanted more firewood. When I make more money, Señor Caraballo gives me an extra bundle of firewood."

"Maybe I can help you when I get better," Pedro offered.

Ramón had never thought about how long Pedro would be staying.

"I need to contribute for my keep and repay you for caring for me," Pedro handed him the five coins. Unlike Herculana, Ramón took the coins. He would give them to his mother. She wouldn't say no.

The remainder of the week was uneventful. Lupe went to the market on Friday. She was so elated. She gabbed with all of her customers in a bubbly fashion. She was the center of attention, telling stories and making everyone laugh.

By mid-morning Lupe was tired out, but always put on a happy face when Norberta was around.

Sunday finally arrived. Business was good. Lupe had almost depleted her inventory. At one level she really wanted to leave to go home. Her eyes showed her weariness.

The ten o'clock mass was finished and most of the parishioners had left.

A young dark-skinned boy of about eighteen years of age slowly approached Norberta and Lupe.

"Good morning, señoras," he said politely. "I am Ricardo Campos. I met you a few weeks ago. I'm Pedro's cousin."

Norberta remembered him and nodded her head. He was there when Pedro received his letters. She shook her head in disbelief as she thought about all that had happened since then.

"Yes, I remember you."

"I'm searching for my cousin, Pedro. He's missing. His horse came back last week without him. Something must have happened."

Nobody had come looking for Pedro until now. Norberta sighed and pulled him to the side of her booth. She told him about the attack on Pedro and his current recuperation.

"Do you know who did this to him?" Rico was agitated. "Do you know who attacked my cousin?"

Norberta didn't say anything, avoiding answering the question. "You could follow us home." She had changed the subject.

"Señora, with your permission, I will do so," then he hesitated. "But I must return to camp before the late afternoon. I have to unpack the supplies. Since Pedro has been missing, I've had to assume his duties."

"Comadre, would you like to guide Ricardo to your casita so he can see how Pedro is doing? It'll be a short visit."

"Why, of course. No problem," Lupe was exhausted and this was a good excuse for her to leave. Also, it would be nice not to have to walk.

"Don't worry, comadre," Norberta continued. "Ramón and I will pack your things and come home as soon as we can."

Ricardo escorted Lupe to his supply wagon. He assisted her up. It wasn't easy.

"Which way, señora?"

She pointed to the opposite end of town. They made a few turns here and there and finally found themselves in front of Cano's grocery store.

"Ricardo, I need a small favor. I need you to buy a few items for me," she recited out a litany of goods and handed him all of her coins, including the ones that Pedro had given Ramón.

Ricardo did not understand what was happening, but he was in no position to say deny her.

His task went without a hitch and fifteen minutes later they were slowly riding back to Norberta's casita.

What a treat not to walk! I thank La Virgen! Lupe sighed.

It took almost an hour to get back to El Pueblito del Valle. Lupe had Ricardo unload some of the supplies at Norberta's casita. Sugar, flour, etc. Then she led Ricardo to her house where he delivered the remainder of the merchandise.

"Pito, is that you?" Rico flew over to the corner where his cousin was sitting up on a mat.

"Ow!" Pito's ribs hurt from Rico's powerful embrace.

Ricardo stared at Pedro for an instant. "How are you feeling? What happened to your eye? Are you in pain?" Rico barraged his cousin with dozens of questions.

They conversed for a bit with frequent gasps and nods.

"The jefe thought at first that you had stolen the horse. But El Brujo came home late that night. Then the jefe got worried. He thought that you had been robbed. I thought that you were dead, pendejo!"

Then Pedro got serious. "Primo, I don't know if I'm going back to the camp. With my bad eye, I can't do my job with the horses. Next time you come back, bring my things. I've been wearing poor Ramón's clothes."

"No problem. El jefe will understand."

They continued talking a little more and then Rico said that he had to leave. But Lupe intercepted him before he reached his supply wagon.

"Ricardo, I need a favor," Lupe explained that she wanted him to purchase the same supplies from the Cano grocery store the next time he rode into town. He thought that this was a very strange request, but he didn't ask why.

"Don't worry! I will pay you back for the purchases," she reassured him.

Rico thought that he would have to front the money. But that was all right. They were taking care of his cousin. This was the least he could do.

CHAPTER 36 – WORK

Monday, August 29, 1910

Once or twice a month, Ramón burned the accumulated trash from his and Norberta's households. He tried to do it early in the morning. He separated out any tin cans or glass bottles. The latter would be picked up by the town scavenger. Ramón had to be sure that there were not any winds when he lit the fire. He didn't want to burn down the village.

When he finished the task this morning, he went back to the casita. Pedro was wheezing and tears were running down from his good eye.

"What is all this pinche smoke?" Pedro coughed out.

"Trash. Burning trash," Ramón noticed that Pedro was having difficulty breathing. He handed Pedro a wet cloth.

"Pedro, do you think you could walk with me. We need to get away from this smoke and I have to do my firewood deliveries."

Pedro was elated. *I get to escape from my prison after all of that confinement. I need some fresh air! I need to stretch my legs!*

Ramón proceeded very slowly. He certainly didn't want to have to carry Pedro back to the casita.

The two casually talked about this and that. Ramón informed Pedro that a few days prior, María Antonia had left for Spain in order to get married. Pedro did not respond. He thought *¡Así es la vida! Maybe Rico had been right.*

Ramón described his work routine to Pedro. He had divided his deliveries into eight sectors. He did at least one section on those days he was not at the market (Mondays, Tuesdays, and Thursdays). He loaded up about two dozen bundles from Señor Caraballo's storage area, about five minutes away from his mother's casita.

Most deliveries consisted of one bundle of firewood per week. A few people could only afford a bundle once every two weeks. Others, like his mother and madrina, needed two bundles of week. While Señor Caraballo was generous in letting Ramón have two free bundles per week, Ramón had to scavenge to make up the difference that was needed for his mother and Norberta. He would pick up loose branches or chop off available dry boughs with his machete as he sauntered along his route. Unfortunately, lopping off green branches produced terrible firewood and stirred up a lot of smoke.

The deliveries that morning went well. Some people were home and gave Ramón warm greetings. Ramón would introduce Pedro to all of them.

"This is my good friend Pedro!" he would shout.

"Mucho gusto," they replied.

The loads were not heavy and Ramón was accustomed to lifting them by himself. Pedro tried to assist but was more of a hindrance. After the second attempt, Pedro stopped trying to help his friend.

Otherwise, Ramón and Pedro were chatting nonstop and the time went by quickly. Ramón sensed that Pedro was waning and decided to head back home.

They were greeted by Lupe who had hot bean burritos ready for them. She normally had a pot of beans cooking. After lunch, Ramón went back out by himself to finish his deliveries.

"Señora, thank you for taking care of me," Pedro said sincerely to Lupe as they were now alone. "I know that I'm extra burden for you and Señora Norberta."

Lupe felt guilty about having badmouthed him earlier for being infatuated with the mayor's daughter. She had been in love once, or at least she thought she had been. Love, or passion, plays funny tricks on the young.

"You can thank La Virgen," Lupe replied tactfully. "She protects all of us. La Virgen has protected you."

"Señora, I don't know when I will be well enough to return to Atepoca."

"Don't worry about it. Ramón needs a friend like you," Lupe stopped. She realized what she had said. It was true. Ramón had no friends. *Had she kept her son isolated? He didn't even have a girlfriend. Oh, what a selfish mother I am! Was this an opportunity to make amends?* "And thank you for the money. It helped a lot," Lupe added. *Am I getting sentimental?* She left the casita and went outside to do her chores.

Pedro was exhausted and decided to take a nap.

Then the storm hit. "Pedrocito! Wake up!" Herculana came strutting into Lupe's casita. "It's time for our reading lesson."

He moaned.

Herculana had started to teach him the alphabet. He had to practice on Norberta's scratch paper. They were not allowed to even touch Norberta's private stash of stationery that she used for her business as an escribana.

"The letter '*f*' [efe] is written like this," she demonstrated on her own blank piece of paper with a sharpened pencil.

Pedro stared at the character.

"Now you try to write it," she instructed. "Lots of them."

He wrote a line of them.

"It makes a 'fff' sound as in 'frijoles.' Now another line."

They practiced for about a half hour. Pedro's bad eye started to water. He was getting tired. They decided to end the lesson. Herculana started to leave.

"Pedro, do me a favor."

"Sure. What?"

"Whistle a song for me."

He was elated and his mouth formed a big smile. He started whistling an old corrido that he had learned back in the mining camp.

After he was done, Herculana clapped enthusiastically.

"That was beautiful, Pedro," Lupe shouted from outside the casita.

Twenty minutes later Pedro was taking a nap with a big grin on his face. This was the best day he had had since the accident.

Norberta came to visit him in the later afternoon in order to check up on him.

"How are you feeling, mijo" she inquired.

"Better."

She pulled up his shirt and examined his chest. Most of the bruising was gone. There was very little discoloration.

"Breath in, mijo."

He inhaled.

"Breath out."

He exhaled.

"Any pain?"

"Just a little." He was trying to be brave.

"Any more blood?"

"No."

"You seem to have made a quick recovery." Norberta frowned. "But I'm still worried about your left eye. Can you see out of it?"

"Not really. Everything is blurry."

Norberta placed her hand on his shoulder and gave him a serious look. "Just remember this. In the land of the blind, el tuerto [one-eyed person] is king." They both laughed.

CHAPTER 37 – CHINESE TOY

September 1910

The weather was morphing into the autumnal season. The breezes seemed to be getting cooler. Trees were hinting at changing their colors. The birds and squirrels seemed to be constantly foraging. Norberta and Lupe wore their dark rebozos in the plaza. People who were attending mass had on sweaters or light coats and scarves.

The cold was good for business since customers consumed more hot chocolate and churros after the church masses to stay warm. The downside was that Norberta had not been getting many clients for her scribe services. Nobody was getting married, having babies, or dying.

The exception to this came in the form of a visit from Wang "Juan" Chou and his daughter Maya. Wang owned the El Cielo grocery story in the Barrio Chino. He was married to a Mexican woman named Gabriela Soto. His Spanish was passable. The daughter Maya was fully bilingual, Spanish and Cantonese. Norberta had assisted them previously when

Wang's friend Ping "Grant" Leong had been injured in a mining accident.

"Good morning, Señora Pérez," Wang said in long drawn-out syllables.

"Good morning, Juan," Norberta gave a big smile. "Oh, hello, Maya, you're getting to be such a young lady. How can I help you?"

Maya blushed. Then Herculana came over and gave her a big hug. "Haven't seen you in such a long time," Herculana said. "I had to drop out of school to help my mom."

"Me, too," Maya turned around as her mother approached the gathering from behind. "I have to work at the grocery store."

"Mamá," Herculana cajoled her mother. "May we have some chocolate?"

"Let me talk to Señora Chou first," Norberta saw through her daughter's ploy immediately. *¡Ay, Herculana!* she thought.

"Tell me, Juan, how can I assist you?"

There was an old friend of the Chous that Maya called "Auntie." Auntie was eighty plus years old and occasionally took care of Maya. Auntie had a middle-aged nephew Fang Ho who had a poor work ethnic and had never been married. Yielding to peer pressure, Fang decided to take the plunge into matrimony. However, the choices in the Barrio Chino were very limited and everyone knew of Fang's character.

Fang was finally able to contact a couple named Toy that specialized in matchmaking. They promised Fang a young virgin girl from Guangzhou in the Canton Province in China. Fang gave the Toys five hundred pesos. The delivery would happen in two months.

However, there were delays and the Toys made a dozen excuses. The transport ship had sprung a leak. Pirates had attacked the boat. There was an epidemic aboard. Finally, the delivery was made. At the depot Fang found himself staring at an obese, thirtyish woman with very unpleasant physical attributes. Fang was flabbergasted. He ran over to the Toy residence and complained. He wanted his money back. Señor Toy replied that he had delivered the merchandise as agreed upon. Unfortunately, this was the woman that was already purchased, and she couldn't be returned. Fang argued profusely. He wanted his money back. Mr. Toy replied that they had no money; it had already been spent. There was nothing he could do.

Norberta's forehead crinkled. She was racking her brains on the course of action that should be pursued. This was like the purchase of a horse that turned out to be a burro. It would be very difficult for Fang to get his money back.

"If you want, we can write the Toys a letter on the behalf of Fang. We can threaten to have them thrown in jail for fraud."

"That's a good idea," Juan perked up. "I will talk to Fang today. He works for me at the grocery store."

"Now, mamá," Herculana tugged on her mother's rebozo. "Can we have some hot chocolate, please?"

"Yes, mija." *¡Cómo friegas!*

Norberta gave the girls some hot chocolate. And then Lupe gave them a churro. They took turns taking bites.

Norberta then began composing the demand letter:

Dear Señor Toy,

This is to inform you that you must refund me the five hundred pesos I paid you. You have made terrible misrepresentations in the sale of a suitable wife.

You have ten days to comply. Otherwise, I will turn this matter over to the police. They will make you pay what you owe me plus a heavy fine. They can even put you in jail.

Very disappointed,

Fang Ho

Norberta knew that the letter was really a bluff. When she read it to Juan, he nodded his approval. She made a duplicate copy.

"Take these to Fang," she instructed Juan and Maya who had taken up the place next to her father. "Read it to him. If he agrees, have him sign both letters. He needs to deliver one of them to the Toys. He should bring a witness when he does so. When he does this, come back here with the other signed letter."

"What will happen then?" Juan asked.

"I don't know," Norberta confessed. "Let's find out!" Everybody said their goodbyes with Herculana and Maya exchanging hugs and promising that they would get together soon. "¡Y saludos a Gabriela!" Norberta yelled as the Chous were leaving.

***

Saturday came and Lupe was in the booth. She called Herculana over to her.

"Mija, I need some baking soda," her godmother requested. Her churros were selling out quickly and she needed to increase her inventory. "Here is some money. Go to Cano's. Take Ramón with you."

Ramón was nervous about returning to this grocery store after the disagreeable reception he had received from Señor Cano on that last visit. He hoped that Herculana would have better luck. He had to protect her in any case.

At the Cano's grocery store, Herculana waltzed in nonchalantly. She looked at the shelves until she found the tins of baking soda. She took one and brought it over to Señor Cano who was standing behind the counter. He had just finished with another customer.

"How much is this?" Herculana asked.

"Three pesos."

She turned around and walked back to the shelf where she had originally found the baking soda tin. She grabbed a second tin and returned to the counter. Señor Cano's head bent down and he looked at her quizzically.

"How much for these two?" Herculana asked.

"Six pesos."

"Five!" Herculana countered abruptly.

"But each costs three!" Cano responded in disbelief.

"And I want a discount for buying two."

"I'll lose money."

"You'll lose money anyway. These are old products. You should throw them away. I guess you're going to lose some money."

Two minutes later Herculana walked out of the grocery with the two tins.

Ramón was in complete shock. His eyes stared at her. He had overheard the entire exchange. The pair returned to the booth.

"Here you go, madrina," Herculana plopped the tins in front of Lupe.

"Any problems"

"None."

Ramón shook his head from side to side. *¡Ay, Herculana!*

***

Finally, Sunday arrived. Juan and Fang were standing in front of Norberta's booth. Juan handed over to Norberta a signed copy of the letter and she verified Fang's signature.

"Did you give a copy to Señor Toy?" Norberta looked at Fang who in turn looked at Juan.

"Yes," Juan said. "I was his witness. Toy get mad. He says he won't pay. Bad luck! No money!"

The grownups talked and talked. Norberta was about to advise Juan and Fang to take the demand letter to the police. But she knew that in reality they wouldn't do anything. Why would they want to help the Chinese?

Then a head popped up next to Norberta. Herculana let her eyes wander over the three adults.

"Why don't you auction off the girl?" Herculana suggested.

"¡Ay, Herculana!" Norberta let out a gasp of embarrassment.

CHAPTER 38 – GOING ONCE

September 1910

Norberta cringed when Herculana made the suggestion.
¡Ay, Herculana!

But Norberta was business savvy. She had to be if she
wanted to survive as a woman and as a businessperson. There
were so many factors that had to be considered and weighed.
Fang needed to recoup his five hundred pesos and rid himself
of his prospective mail order bride. Juan had to be
acknowledged as trying to resolve a problem among his
Chinese community. The Toys had to be held accountable. And
Norberta needed to make a little money for her troubles.

The permutations in Norberta's mind were going a mile a
minute She thought and struggled and then thought some more.

Norberta, Juan, and Fang discussed the auction proposal,
with Maya translating when necessary. Finally, a decision was
made.

"We will hold an auction in the public square on Saturday
night, in El Barrio Chino," Norberta spoke up. "Juan and Fang

will be in charge of spreading the word. Everybody for miles around needs to know that a bride is up for sale. Minimum bid will start at 250 pesos."

"Why not five hundred?" questioned Fang. "I need to get my money back!"

"Too high!" Norberta countered. "It will scare off potential bidders."

"I think 250 is high!" Juan got into the fray. "Who can afford that?"

Norberta paused. There was a moment of silence. "Maybe nobody. But that means Fang is out five hundred pesos if you do nothing. You need to make it work. You have to regain your honor." Norberta thought, *they don't care about their names, they just want to recuperate the money.*

"Any objections to conducting the auction?" Norberta put out the question. Neither Juan nor Fang said no.

"Okay, then I get hire the auctioneer," Norberta had in mind either Pedro or Ramón. The former being preferable because he was older.

"How much money will I get?" Fang continued.

"Fifty percent, up to 500 pesos," Norberta asserted.

"That's not fair. It's my wife," Fang complained.

"Fine, if she's your wife, let's all walk away and this matter is closed."

"All right! All right. But it's not fair," Fang was unhappy.
"Who gets the remaining fifty percent?"

"Juan is getting 10%," Norberta needed to keep him happy.
"And we are taking forty percent."

"Why Juan?" Fang blurted as if Juan was not even present.
"He brought you here, didn't he?" Norberta raised her
voice. "You would have no hope if not for him."

This ingrate pendejo! thought Norberta. Her blood was
starting to boil. She wanted to walk away but she had to help
Juan. If she didn't, he would lose face.

Five minutes later everybody finally agreed. Juan was
surprised but was grateful for Norberta's advocacy.

Herculana and Ramón had observed the entire process.
They were impressed by Norberta. She was tenacious and
smart. The two were inspired.

Two days later in the late afternoon, Ramón brought his
pull cart up to Señor Caraballo's firewood loading area.
Customers were requesting more firewood with the onset of the
colder weather.

"Good afternoon, Señor Caraballo." Ramón tipped his hat.

"Hello, Ramón," the older man smiled. "How were your
deliveries?"

Ramón saw an opening. "Señor, more and more people want more and more firewood. The deliveries are getting harder."

"I understand," Caraballo nodded his head. "That's good for business!"

"I'll need more money if I'm going to continue." Ramón was relying on Caraballo's fear of losing a few weeks of income if he left.

"I see," the older man said slowly, rubbing his chin. "How about another five pesos per day?"

"That sounds like a good start," Ramón was trying to emulate Norberta's and Herculana's negotiating skills and tactics. "Plus, five free bundles of firework per week." He knew that his mother and godmother needed more for the upcoming winter months and their large baking needs."

"Five? I'll give you two," Caraballo fired back.

"Two? You already give me two!"

"Okay, four then," Caraballo started to settle down.

"Deal!" They both shook hands.

"But I'm giving you twenty extra houses."

"No problem," replied Ramón. He was elated. He had made a good deal. Norberta and Herculana would be proud of him.

***

Finally, Saturday arrived. The families of Norberta and Lupe, accompanied by Pedro, trudged over to El Barrio Chino.

The auction had been the talk of the valley all week. It was rumored that some residents of Teocaltiche would even attend, and maybe even bid! This was an unusual and unique event. Maybe once in a lifetime! It really didn't matter since no one had ever been to an auction before. Pedro was designated as the official auctioneer. He had seen many horse auctions during his tenure at the mining camp.

Pedro stood in front of a communal building. He thought it might be some type of Buddhist church. He had rehearsed the rules of the auction. Herculana had read them over and over to him a thousand times. Lupe made him a special black eye patch which he loved.

The auction was supposed to begin at seven o'clock. The blue sky was still light. At about a quarter to the designated hour, Fang led a short, chubby woman with black bangs and long hair, to the side of the auction platform. She wore crimson red lipstick. She did not speak. Many onlookers came over to inspect her. Comments were made.

"She's ugly!"

"This thing could keep me warm at night!"

"The poor thing!"

The hour of seven o'clock finally arrived. More and more people were still gathering around the platform.

"Shouldn't we be starting," Fang was nervously fidgeting.

Chinese food and Mexican tamale vendors had set up their posts. They drew a lot of local patrons.

I should have brought my churros, Lupe criticized herself.

At around 7:20, Norberta gave the signal for the auction to begin. Pedro started to talk, but no one could hear him over the noise of the crowd. He tried to shout without success. Finally, a tall gringo wearing a cowboy hat came forward and pulled out a pistol from his holster. He fired it twice into the air. Everybody fell silent. A few had actually dropped to the ground fearing for their lives.

Then Pedro was able to proceed. He started in Spanish.

"Thank you all for coming. Tonight, we will be having a new and wonderful experience . . ."

CHAPTER 39 – GOING TWICE

September 1910
El Barrio Chino

Norberta had scripted out Pedro's entire presentation. There was no room for mistakes. Maya would translate the Spanish to her father. Then Juan would give a Cantonese interpretation between Pedro's speech segments.

"We will start the bidding at 250 pesos. This is cash only. If you don't have the money, don't bid! There is no credit! All deals are final! No refunds!" Pedro had begun.

Maya and Juan repeated this in Cantonese.

"The bidding is now open at 250 pesos. Who will be the first to bid?" Pedro had started the ball rolling.

Nobody raised a hand. Nobody yelled out. *¡Demonios!* thought Norberta. She started to panic.

"250!" shouted the man wearing a cowboy hat. He said this in Spanish with an Anglo accent.

"We have 250!" Pedro shouted. "Do I hear 260?'

There was another long pause.

"260!" called out a rotund Chinese man with protruding front teeth.

A few seconds later came "270!"

Fang was fidgeting. Herculana was squirming with excitement.

The bidding increased in small increments until it reached 320. This last tender had been submitted by a tall, skinny Chinese man who wore a braided queue. People were ogling and standing on their toes to see who was bidding.

"We're at 320," Pedro hollered. "Come on, folks. Who's going to go to 330!"

He didn't receive a response.

"Are you going to let this prize go so cheaply? The nights are getting colder."

This brought a blush to Maya as she translated. There were a few chuckles from the crowd.

"Do I hear 350!" Pedro changed tactics.

"350!" roared the cowboy.

If the bidding stopped here, Norberta thought that Fang had at least made a few pesos. It was better than nothing. *¡Así es la vida!*

"400!" bellowed a short, dark-skinned Mexican with a huge drooping moustache.

I think this paisano is a poker player making his move, Norberta surmised. She scanned the crowd and nodded to herself. *Were there any other potential bidders waiting in the wings?*

"450!" yelled the cowboy who gave the Mexican bidder a dirty look.

"We have 450," Pedro's throat was getting dry. He motioned for someone to bring him some water. "Who will make it 500?'

Herculana ran up to Pedro and gave him a tin cup of water.

"500!" called out the tall Chinese man. He looked unsure of his bid.

We're halfway there! thought Norberta. *Everybody should be happy!*

Tension seemed to be building within the crowd. People were pushing forward and bunching up in the front. The bidding was sporadic, jumping up slowly in twenty-five-peso increments. At 700, the tall Chinaman dropped out. People started to clap and shout after each new bid. There was electricity in the air.

Now it was a three-horse contest. Norberta asked Ramón who the trio were. Because of his work, he knew almost everyone in the valley.

"The fat chino is the butcher. The cowboy owns a cattle ranch about ten miles east of here. And I think the Mexican is from one of the mining camps."

Norberta had a twinge of conscience. *I hope someone will marry "La Fea" and not use her as a piece of meat. ¡Así es la vida!*

"800!" snarled the Mexican as if to challenge the other two competitors to a duel.

"850!" the fat Chinaman threw out nonchalantly.

Pedro was getting exhausted. He was not used to this type of exertion. And he had the urge to pee.

"900!" threw out the cowboy.

A feverous pitch was emerging from the spectators.

"Higher! Higher!" roared the crowd in both Spanish and Cantonese.

"950!" the Mexican exclaimed boldly.

The cowboy nodded his head no. No more for him. He took off his cowboy hat and wiped his brow. He had quit.

The Chinese butcher turned to his right and stared at the Mexican. "1000!" The crowd went wild.

"¡A la chingada!" the Mexican cursed.

"We have a bid of 1000 pesos. Do I hear any more bids?" There was a long pause. "Going once!" Pedro really had to pee. "Going twice!" Pedro was ready to jump off the platform.

"Going three times! Sold to the gentleman over there. Please step forward."

The Chinaman was met by Norberta, Juan, Fang, and Maya. Pedro instantly disappeared. Norberta said a few things which were translated to the successful bidder. The Chinaman took out a big sack of coins and slowly counted the money. It took almost ten minutes. Norberta had Fang put his "X" on the bill of sale and she countersigned it as a witness along with Juan's "X." Norberta signaled Ramón to retrieve the newly purchased bride. The butcher introduced himself as Tsu Sung. He was thrilled and the woman seemed relieved.

"Let's give everyone a hand," Pedro had reappeared. He hadn't finished before everyone started to disperse.

Then Norberta's small group met in a corner far from the platform. Fang was given his 500 pesos. He was so happy! Norberta gave Juan 200 pesos.

"But Señora Pérez, we agreed to ten percent," Juan's face was quizzically contorted. "You paid me too much!"

"You deserved it," Norberta retorted.

Juan then huddled with his daughter Maya. They talked for a minute and then he came back toward Norberta.

"I accept the extra money, but only if we can treat you to a little dinner. We had a stressful evening and I know that we're all hungry. It wouldn't be too much," Juan explained. "It'll be Chinese food."

"As long as there is rice, we're good," Norberta acceded.

She then turned around to look for Pedro. He wasn't to be seen. Then suddenly he reappeared from behind a tree, pulling up his pants.

Norberta was elated. They had just earned three hundred pesos! The extra 100 pesos to Juan was insurance for a time when they might need his assistance. Since he owned a grocery store, he could be very helpful.

The group went to a small and simple Chinese dining spot. Maya had run ahead to gather her mother.

As they all sat down, a couple rushed up to the table. It was the Toys.

"We should get part of the money! She was ours!" Señor Toy barked.

Norberta closed her eyes and then opened them. She stood up and pointed, "Get out! Or you're going to jail!"

The Toys may not have understood, but they left in a hurry.

CHAPTER 40 – SPECIAL DELIVERY

September 1910

Everybody was exhausted from the Chinese feast. There must have been at least a dozen dishes, including egg drop soup, pig knuckles, chow mein noodles, and broccoli with beef. This was a new experience for Norberta and company. They ate and ate until they were gasping for air. Herculana had an effortless time eating with chopsticks with Maya's instructions.

Norberta had the opportunity to converse with Gabriela Soto, the wife of Juan aka Wang. The latter welcomed the conversation in her native Spanish. She was from the State of Sonora. She was much younger than her 38-year-old husband.

Norberta knew she had no time to rest on her laurels after the successful auction. She had to take advantage of her good fortune. Norberta knew that the Chinese in El Barrio Chino had given Juan credit for setting up a gainful endeavor. Everybody bowed as they passed him. Moreover, Juan had assured

Norberta that Señor Tsu Sung, the butcher, would treat his new wife correctly and according to Chinese customs.

Juan sat facing Norberta. They talked, smiling at each other. She hinted that she (and Lupe) wanted to have a business relationship with him. She knew that the prices at his grocery store were a little higher, but his store was only ten minutes away. Norberta and Lupe were deeply concerned about the supply chain in Teocaltiche, especially with the threat of the revolution. They talked a little more. The only problem areas for the two women were the baking soda and wheat flour. Lupe had to rely on Cano's in Teocaltiche. Then Juan offered to order more wheat flour to satisfy Lupe's baking requirements. Life was good!

Norberta was full and wanted to leave, but she knew it would be rude. She scanned the room and saw Pedro fading. She knew that Pedro had been a key to the triumph. She had offered fifty pesos to Pedro for his work as the auctioneer. He tried to decline it, but eventually accepted the money.

However, Pedro, in turn, gave the money to Ramón after they returned to the casita and swore him to secrecy against his mother and godmother. There was a mutual understanding that the pesos were to be used for household needs. The two had a growing friendship and there was a solid trust between the two young men. Ramón planned to hide the money in a secret hiding place in his mom's casita. Pedro was feeling better now and didn't know how much longer he would be staying with Señora Lupe and Ramón in their casita.

***

The Sunday sunrise was spoiled by a light mist of rain as Norberta, Lupe, and Ramón struggled on the road to the plaza.

Later that morning, a two-horse carriage pulled up in front of Lupe's casita. Pedro was outside observing the hummingbird who was defending its territory.

"I missed you, pendejo!" Rico gave his cousin a loud shout and a broad white smile.

"What's new, primo?" Pedro returned the grin. "You're here early."

"Yeah. I brought your stuff like you wanted." Rico pointed to the back of the wagon. Pedro stared in amazement. It was full of stuff, that included a saddle and several full flour sacks. "We need to unload this before I get the supplies in town."

"You want some hot chocolate? I have some left," Pedro felt bad about offering his cousin the dregs of his breakfast. "Sorry, don't have any churros. They took them to the market."

"Don't worry," Rico smiled again and handed Pedro something wrapped in green paper. "These are just as good."

Pedro quickly unwrapped the packet and found three pretzel shaped cookies.

"These are from Rodolfo. He misses you." Rodolfo was the mining camp cook. One of the cook's tasks was to make non-perishable foods that the miners could carry into the mines and eat during the day while they were underground. One of Pedro's duties at the camp, besides taking care of the horses and buying supplies, had been making these "rosquetes." Some were salted. These were the ones the miners carried with them inside the mine. Others were rubbed in sugar and cinnamon. They were the breakfast staple of the camp. The advantage of the rosquetes over churros was that they did not have to be fried. This meant that they had a longer shelf life. Pedro had made thousands of them under Rodolfo's tutelage. He knew the recipe like the back of his hand.

Rico ate an entire sweet one, but Pedro only ate a few bites of the other two. He had already finished breakfast. He wrapped the remains in the original paper.

Although Pedro knew that he wasn't supposed to lift anything heavy, he helped pull the saddle from the back of the wagon. It was hefty and cumbersome. Then there were a few items of clothing in one sack, some flour, salt, and a few canned goods, and cooking utensils in the other two bags. He found a mixing bowl, baking pans, and other kitchenware.

"The cook is trying to get rid of his extra stuff," Rico was talking quickly. "Just in case the mine shuts down and we have to leave."

"I don't understand," Pedro had a bewildered look on his face. "Why would the mine have to shut down?'

"The owners are saying that the revolutionaries have been attacking our tin shipments. They think that it is too dangerous and expensive to continue the operation."

Pedro shook his head. "What does this mean for the workers if the mine shuts down? Where will they go? What will you do?"

"I don't know." But then he threw it back on to Pedro. "So how long will you stay here? The boss says you can have your job back if you come back. I have been doing your pinche work."

Pedro threw up his hands. "I don't know."

"Well, gotta go," Rico hugged his cousin and departed.

Lupe is going to be pleasantly surprised, Pedro thought. Seeing Rico leaving, Herculana and Julia raced over to Pedro who was toting stuff into Lupe's casita. "Who was that?" Herculana inquired.

"Ricardo. He's my cousin."

"Didn't he come to my mom's booth at the plaza one time?"

"Look what Pedro's cousin brought us!" Herculana's smile went from ear to ear. She pointed to the pots and pans. "We could cook them for the entire village!" Everybody was exhilarated.

Norberta was circumspect. She wondered why this stuff was given to them. Some of the items looked old and used, but some looked brand new.

"Comadre," Lupe put her hand on Norberta's shoulder. "Take whatever you want. This is too much stuff."

"I can't," Norberta protested as she seriously examined the merchandise. "I don't need anything." Five minutes later she was packing a metal ladle, a wooden mixing spoon, and some terra cotta cups into an empty flour sack to take home with her.

"Señoras," Pedro interrupted Norberta and Lupe. "I need you all to try these," He broke off pieces of the leftover rosquetes for Norberta, Lupe, and Ramón to sample.

"These are really good," Lupe exclaimed.

"We could make some and sell them," Ramón suggested.

"But we don't have the recipe!" Lupe retorted.

"I know how to make these," Pedro interjected. "I could teach you."

"Teach me too!" popped up a young voice.

¡Ay, Herculana!

CHAPTER 41 – SADDLE UP

September 1910

As a trial experiment, Norberta and Pedro decided to make small batches of rosquete dough. They began by boiling them as the first step. Their major obstacle was that they did not have an oven. The frying pan caused them to burn because of the high heat when the rosquetes were transferred over. Attempts at stove top baking made the rosquetes cook unevenly.

Pedro also demonstrated to Herculana how to shape the rosquetes. Not too big. Not too small.

"It's like saddling a horse," he told her.

"But I've never ridden a horse!" she answered.

"Well, let's make a rope," Pedro cut off a piece of kneaded dough and rolled it into a long tube.

Herculana emulated him.

"Good job!" he said. She smiled with pride. "Now let's both take our ropes and make a stirrup." They picked up both ends of the dough rope and crossed them.

"That was easy!" Herculana said smugly.

"Now we're going to make a bridle."

They twisted the dough rope and folded it over. It was now pretzel shaped.

"We did it!" shouted Herculana.

"Okay, now smash the dough and let's do it again." Pedro instructed.

They combined the old dough with the new. They practiced this technique over and over again. They were having fun and laughing all the time. After lunch, Herculana continued to teach Pedro the alphabet. She always requested that he whistle a song after their lesson was over.

***

A week later, Pedro as he began his cooking demonstration, had a big grin on his face. Herculana looked at him quizzically.

"Herculana, I'm going to tell you a secret about making rosquetes."

Her dark brown eyes got big.

"You can make these in any shape you want. Any shape! You can make a horse collar by pinching the two ends of the rope. You can make a doll, a dog, anything!"

Herculana was eager to learn, and Pedro was energized by teaching her. She was a model student. After their lesson,

Herculana asked Pedro if she could take the old dough back to her casita and practice.

The next day Ramón and Pedro went out together and made firewood deliveries. They were now close friends. Almost like brothers. With Pedro's assistance, they could cover more casitas faster and scavenge firewood from pine copses. As they were talking about this and that, they decided that they should sell Pedro's saddle. It was of very little use to them, and they could use the money before the winter came.

On Friday, Herculana got permission to go to the plaza with Ramón and their mothers. Julia was stuck with doing everybody's laundry. She didn't like doing it, but she didn't complain. At least she didn't have to make that long trek into town.

At the plaza Ramón unloaded Lupe's and Norberta's goods and helped them set up. Ramón and Herculana then rolled the cart over to Loera's Horse Supply and Stables, about a half mile north of the plaza.

Herculana strutted up to the open-air counter where a heavy, unshaven Mexican man wearing a cowboy hat greeted her.

"Buenas días, señorita," the cowboy bowed and tipped his hat. *What could this jovencita possibly want?* he thought.

"How can I help you today?" The cowboy, Álvaro had ae left
ear that was noticeably larger than his right,

"Do you have saddles?"

"Yes, we do. What kind are you looking for?"

"None. I'm looking to sell one."

The cowboy gave a little cough and laugh at the same time.
"Well, normally I'm not in the business of buying saddles. Just
usually sell them. But for you, I could give it a look. Where is
it?"

"Over there," Herculana pointed to the cart that Ramón was
standing next to.

"Benjamín, come on over here!" yelled Álvaro to the room
close to the counter. A wiry man with a big moustache came
out and approached Herculana.

"This little lady wants to show us a saddle," Álvaro pointed
out the young girl to his partner.

The two owners walked over to the cart and peered into it.
Their hands stroked the saddle. They gave a strong tug on the
horn and pulled the stirrup out.

Finally, Álvaro spoke with an unctuous grin, "I'm feeling
generous today. I'll you a hundred pesos for it."

"A thousand!" Herculana shot back before the cowboy
could utter another word.

"It's old and used. I'll give you 150."

"1100!"

"What!" Álvaro's and Benjamín's mouths fell open. They were in shock at the impudence of this girl.

"Señorita, you just increased your price. You should be lowering it," the cowboy said condescendingly.

"1200!"

"¡Que caray! ¡No entiendo!"

"This saddle was made by a master saddle maker. The stuff you sell here is poor quality. The rich customers don't buy from you."

"Then why don't you sell it to them?" Álvaro was getting testy, and his tone showed it. Herculana was getting under his skin.

"I would if I could. We've had two persons interested so far."

"Then why don't you sell to one of them?" Álvaro was calling her bluff.

"We would, but we don't know where they live," Herculana replied nonplussed. "If you're not interested, no problem." She paused for a moment. "But I know that you could sell this saddle for at least double the price you will pay for it. Probably triple. That's a nice profit for very little effort."

Álvaro looked over to Benjamín. He wasn't sure what to say or do. He turned around and whispered something into

Benjamin's ear. For two minutes the partners engaged in an animated discussion.

Herculana made a hand signal to Ramón. Ramón picked up the handles to the cart and started to leave.

All of a sudden Álvaro noticed that the two youngsters were ready to leave. "Okay! Okay! We'll give you your thousand pesos."

Herculana and Ramón continued to walk away. "It's now 1500."

Neither of the youngsters stopped to engage. When the pair had gone about fifty yards, they heard desperate shouts behind them.

Twenty minutes later Herculana and Ramón returned to their mothers' stand with 1500 pesos.

"What two people were interested in the saddle? Were you fibbing?" Norberta had listened to the rendition of the sale at Loera's.

"Well, Ramón and me, of course," she said glibly.

¡Ay, Herculana!

CHAPTER 42 – CLOSURE

September 1910
El Pueblito del Valle

Norberta gave Pedro the entire 1500 pesos from the sale of
the saddle. Pedro tried to give her half back. She refused. He
tried to convince her to take 100 pesos each for Ramón and
Herculana. She still refused. Later that night Pedro and Ramón
discussed the dilemna.

"How do you live with such women" Pedro was
exasperated.

"Well, you nod your head yes and then do whatever you
want," Ramón smiled. It felt good to share his personal
frustration with someone.

Afterwards, Ramón showed Pedro his secret hiding place in
the corner of the casita. It was a small hole underneath a piece
of tile that had a wooden crate of his clothes on top. They
buried the money there in a small tin.

On Saturday afternoon Herculana brought Pedro a baking
tray full of little rosquetes. They had been cooked and had been
hardened. They were in the shape of the letters of the alphabet.

Half of them were burnt. There also seemed to be duplicates of some. Pedro was overjoyed.

Herculana made him arrange the letters in alphabetical order and pronounce them, one-by-one. They both giggled and afterwards he whistled three songs for her. *Life was good!* Pedro thought.

On Sunday morning, Rico arrived in the two-horse supply wagon, two weeks after his last visit. His face looked somber.

"What's up, primo?" Pedro called out. He had noticed that Ricardo's perpetual smile was not present today.

"They're closing the mine!" Rico kicked at the ground. "Everybody has started to move out and look for work elsewhere."

"Come on in, primo. There's some hot chocolate with one of Lupe's churros just waiting for you."

The two sat on the floor and talked. The mining company was caught between the revolutionaries and the Mexican President Díaz. The rebels were attacking the supply chains throughout the country. As a result, the federales raided small villages looking for the insurgents. There was danger and uncertainty everywhere in Mexico. The United States even threatened to get involved. The consortium of the mine owners decided to pull out and cut their losses. After the bloodshed subsided and the government stabilized, their ore would still be there and could be mined again.

"What will you do, Rico?"

"I don't know. The cook and I have been talking. He plans to go to Guadalajara. He has family there. I'm thinking about the Arizona Territory. There are a lot of mines there and I am sure I can get work."

What am I going to do now? Pedro thought to himself. *I can't stay here forever. But now I don't have a job at the camp either. I can't work in town.*

"You should come with me, Pito. The boss is willing to give me a horse cheap. They can't take them. They're leaving everything!"

Ricardo was about to elaborate when a head popped into the doorway. It was Herculana.

"I know who you are," she approached Rico with complete disregard. "You're his cousin. You both came to our chocolate stand before."

"Yes, I'm Ricardo," he gave her a big smile. "You have a very nice family. Thank you for taking good care of my cousin."

"It's nothing. I'm Herculana. I'm teaching Pito how to read."

Rico gave his cousin a surprised look.

"Are you the one who brought all the stuff?" Herculana was being inquisitive.

Rico nodded apprehensively.

"Thank you very much. It's really valuable stuff. All we need now is an oven to make Pedro's rosquetes."

They all talked and talked. Herculana didn't want to stop. She had fresh meat.

"Herculana, Rico has to go to town now to get his supplies," Pedro wanted to get rid of Herculana.

"Actually, I'm not buying any more goods. I'm going to settle up at Los Olivos," Rico clarified. "I also have a few more items for Señora Lupe."

Pedro exhaled deeply. *Oh, well!*

They all fell into a pensive mood. The three of them went out to the wagon since Rico was about to depart.

"I wish I could ride with you," Herculana gave Rico a plaintive look. Pedro gave her a stern stare. She knew that was not permitted.

"Rico, wait a moment," Pedro ran back into Lupita's casita and opened the secret treasure trove tin. He counted out one hundred pesos before putting the tin back into its secret place.

Pedro returned to the wagon and covertly handed the money to Rico as he gave him a goodbye hug and whispered something in his ear. Rico departed without incident.

"Pito, what do you want to do now?" Herculana was trying to avoid assisting her sister in washing clothes.

Several hours later the two-horse wagon returned with Rico and Lupe. Pedro noticed that Lupe was quiet which was unusual for her. Rico brought her goods into her casita. On the second trip to the wagon, Pedro assisted. Lupe was sullen.

"Rico, would you like something to eat?" Lupe asked, although it really wasn't a question. She was going to fix him a little meal anyway.

"No, thank you."

Lupe started to cook something ignoring Rico's response.

Rico and Pedro fell into a deep conversation. Lupe served them both hot quesadillas with a side of beans. They graciously accepted and inhaled them.

"You should really come with me, primo," Rico said within earshot of the others. "We could start a new life someplace else."

Pedro knew that his cousin was right. He had been a burden for Norberta and Lupe long enough. He was an extra mouth that had to be fed. He was not carrying his own weight. And he couldn't get a job around there,

Five minutes later Lupe brought them a second batch of quesadillas. Neither one of the two declined them.

Finally, Pedro made a decision, "Señora Lupe," he called out to her. "I'm going to be gone for a few days. I'll be going with my cousin back to the mining camp. There is some business I have to take care of. After that, we might be traveling to Arizona."

Lupe was not surprised. She had assumed as much when Rico told her of his plans to go to Arizona. She couldn't blame Pedro, but she had grown to like both boys. They were now young men. She also knew that her son Ramón was Pedro's good friend and would miss him also.

"Please let Señora Norberta and Ramón know that I will be back. Probably in a few days," Pedro's voice was shaky.

"Be safe, my son!" Lupe shouted after him as the pair departed.

Pedro had not dared to tell Herculana or Julia that he would be leaving.

Herculana observed Pito and Rico leaving from the door of the casita.

An hour later Norberta and Ramón returned from the plaza. They found Herculana in tears.

CHAPTER 43 – THE OVEN

September 1910

Atepoca Mining

"I think that you are making the right decision, primo," Rico said as he held the reins of the horses. They were riding back to the camp.

Pedro could not think of a reason to dispute his cousin. He had felt that he was a parasite on not just one family, but two. That wasn't right. Besides, they could survive without him. They had done so before.

"We could get jobs at another mining camp or in a town. You could become a blacksmith. I could work at a supply and feed store."

I can't train horses very well with one bad eye. I can cook a little, but no one wants someone who only makes rosquetes. Maybe I can learn to make pan dulce or do bacon and egg breakfasts, Pedro contemplated.

An hour or so later they reached their destination. The mining camp was half-deserted. The foreman Rodolfo, the cook, and a dozen scruffy miners came out to greet Pedro. All had smiles on their faces as they patted Pedro on the back. It was a friendly welcome back. Most of them were even semi-clean with the mine dust cleaned off of them.

"We missed you . . . pendejo!"

"If it isn't Mundaca the pirate!"

"What was her name?"

Next, the foreman invited Pedro, Rico, and Rodolfo over to his private quarters and retrieved a bottle of tequila. He passed around three dirty shot glasses and filled them. They all toasted with the foreman drinking from the bottle.

***

"Mamá, why did he leave us?" Herculana was curled in her mother's embrace, "He was my friend."

"I know, mija," Norberta stroked her daughter's hair trying to sooth her. "He has things to do. He couldn't stay with us forever."

"But I was teaching him to read," Herculana had tears in her little dark brown eyes. "And he was teaching me how to make rosquetes."

"Well, mija, all this means is that you have to teach Julia to make rosquetes. We need to help your madrina." Norberta was trying to deflect the conversation.

Meanwhile, at Lupe's casita, Ramón was whittling a small branch. He was stoic about Pedro's departure, but the sadness was evident on his face. His mother noticed it.

"Yes, mijo, I know you miss him. I do too. He was like a brother to you." She was tempted to add, "and another son to me."

"Mamá, I'm not supposed to tell anyone," Ramón moved over closer to his mother. "But Pedro left us some money for emergencies."

The remainder of the week moved slowly. There seemed to be a lack of energy and happiness without Pedro and his constant whistling.

To make matters worse, torrential rains blew in on Wednesday and Thursday. The roofs of both Norberta's and Lupe's shacks leaked. There were puddles pockmarking their floors. Pots and pans collected the dripping water.

Norberta and Lupe talked and decided not to go to the market. The inclement weather would mean very few customers and Ramón would get soaking wet hauling their goods to the plaza. Instead, Ramón went out and made more firewood deliveries knowing that people needed even more firewood during the dreary weather.

On Friday it cleared up, and by afternoon most things were drying. Herculana started teaching her older sister, Julia, how to make rosquetes. They both enjoyed doing this together, even if they were covered with flour by the end of the day. This was more of a bonding exercise than washing clothes.

Norberta and Lupe discussed Pedro all week. *What if he doesn't come back? Or what if he does come back? What could he do? He couldn't go to work in town with Sergeant Montez and El Piojo ready to harm him again.*

"Comadre, whether or not Pedro returns, I think we should start thinking about some changes." Lupe was worried about the strife between the Mexican government and the revolutionaries. She did not want Ramón caught in the middle. The two women needed him in order to survive. *Could they do it alone?*

"Ramón is fifteen. In a few years he will get married," Norberta was trying to be realistic. "He will need a full-time job. We can't hold him back."

"You're right, comadre," Lupe said glumly. "And the same goes for your girls. They'll soon get married and have kids."

"I guess we two old ladies are stuck with each other, comadre," They both laughed. "I think I can see more grey hairs."

***

Saturday arrived and the month of October had officially arrived. Most of the leaves had fallen from the deciduous trees.

Norberta and the entourage had gone to the plaza. The weather was a bit gusty.

Herculana and Julia were just finishing their hot chocolate breakfast when they heard the sound of clopping horses. Pedro was riding El Brujo. He wore jeans and a big cowboy hat. The two-horse supply wagon was being driven by Ricardo. Sitting next to him was a short, middle-age dark skinned man.

Herculana dropped everything and ran up to hug Pedro as soon as he dismounted. *Her friend was back!*

"Herculana, this is my friend, Rodolfo Zamora. Do you have any hot chocolate to give him? And any churros, if there are some left?"

Minutes later the overjoyed Herculana and her sister Julia were serving the recent arrivals. The three men were discussing the dozens and dozens of bricks stacked up in the back of the supply wagon.

"It needs to be sheltered well. We can move some of the tin siding sheets over here. It should be some space away from the window," advised Rodolfo, the former mining camp cook. "We need to reinforce the roof next to the house too."

Following the camp cook's instructions, Pedro and Ricardo unloaded the bricks and started to form a foundation by the side of Lupe's casita.

"Should we make it square or round?" asked Ricardo.

"Probably round," Zamora answered. "It will keep the heat more even. Things should cook better."

The trio piled the bricks in several configurations. Fortunately, they were not going to use mortar.

"Will they want to bake stacked or spread out?" The young men discussed the advantages and disadvantages of both. Less firewood. More evenly spread heat. Uneven cooking. Finally, they arrived at a compromise that looked like a short, fat chimenea.

"We'll need some sort of stove pipe to let the smoke out."

They placed loose bricks at the bottom of the chimenea that had clearance of almost a foot. This is where the firewood would be lit. The loose bricks were arranged so that three baking sheets could be easily laid next to each other.

By the time Norberta and Lupe returned home that afternoon, the project was about halfway completed. The two women were astonished at the outdoor oven.

When Pedro saw Ramón, he called out. He threw him a bundle. "These are for you." Pedro had given him a pair of jeans. Ramón had never owned a pair.

"Thanks," Ramón's eyes were as big as saucers.

Pedro formally introduced Rodolfo to Norberta and Lupe. "Mucho gusto" was freely exchanged among all. Pedro thought he detected a longer than usual stare by Rodolfo toward Lupe.

Then everybody got back to work. It was dark when the project was finished. Rico wanted to leave, but Norberta insisted that they all stay for dinner and depart in the morning. Nobody dared argue with Señora Norberta.

Rico, Rodolfo, and Pedro had their own bedding and found a place to sleep next to Ramón in Lupe's casita. It was a tight squeeze. Lupe stayed with Norberta.

Before going to bed, Pedro traipsed over to Norberta's place and called out.

"Come on in, mijo," Norberta was expecting something like this.

"Señora, I want to thank you and Señora Lupe for taking care of me. I would still like to give you some money."

Norberta shook her head no. Julia had fallen asleep, but Herculana was listening carefully with her eyes closed.

"I have to leave. Me and Rico will probably go to the Arizona Territories. There are mines there where we can find work."

Norberta was aware that the local mines had been closing. Dozens of unemployed miners were wandering the streets of Teocaltiche. *Did she want him to go or not?* Norberta really didn't know.

They talked for a while and then Pedro wandered back to Lupe's casita. His companions were all fast asleep.

CHAPTER 44 – THE ABDUCTION

Sunday, October 2, 1910

The horizon was beginning to brighten. It was just before dawn when Norberta, Lupe, and Ramón set out for the plaza. Norberta felt bad that she could not fix a decent breakfast for Pedro, Rico, and Rodolfo before their exodus.

Actually, Rodolfo already had a line on a job at the Mi Ranchito eating establishment in Teocaltiche. It was connected to a residence hotel and a cantina. Rodolfo was planning to go there that morning. Pedro had served him and Rico some bean burritos for their breakfasts, washed down by hot chocolate. It looked like they were now ready to depart.

"Primo, I have something to tell you," Pedro looked seriously at Ricardo. "I'm changing my mind. I think they need me here. I have to stay. I don't know for how long." He slipped his cousin some pesos.

"Oye, pendejo, I'm sure Ramón can take care of things. Something told me that you weren't coming," Rico gave his cousin an embrace.

"This is from la Señora Norberta," Pedro handed his cousin a bag of chocolates. "Don't eat them all at once. And El Brujo is now yours."

Rodolfo had saddled up the second pack horse, leaving the other one tied to a tree, eating grass. Rico repacked his belongings onto El Brujo.

"What do I do with the wagon and the other horse?" Pedro asked Rico.

"I don't know. They're yours now."

Rico and Rodolfo started in the direction of town.

"¡Vayan con Dios!" Pedro cried out behind them.

An hour later Rico and Rodolfo arrived at the plaza. They found Norberta and Lupe at their booth and thanked the ladies for their hospitality. The women in turn voiced their gratitude once more for the kitchenware and the oven. Nobody mentioned the fact that Pedro had not accompanied the two guys.

"Hope to see you again," Rodolfo mumbled in Lupe's direction. She was surprised but acted nonchalant.

Rico and Rodolfo made their way to the restaurant, Mi Ranchito. As luck would have it, Rodolfo was immediately hired. He was given a room at the hotel as part of his compensation. He was elated. Rico followed Rodolfo to his new room. It had a real bed versus the hard mat that he had been sleeping on for months. There was even a real pillow and a chest of drawers. But the best thing of all was that he was entitled to a hot bath once a week.

Now that Pedro had decided to stay, Rico was ambivalent about leaving the Teocaltiche. Maybe he could stay and find a job. He decided to tempt fate. He went out looking for a job. He went to the Los Olivos supply company where he had regularly purchased goods for the mine. They weren't hiring. He visited a few other places and was met with very little enthusiasm. One place did have an opening, but the pay was really low. During his tour around town one thing became evident. There were scores of miners and other men loitering around the plaza Too many people unemployed! He even recognized his assistant foreman Rafael from the mines. Rico decided that he would keep to his original plan and leave for the Arizona Territories in the morning.

***

Norberta, Lupe, and Ramón returned home in the afternoon. They observed Pedro instructing Herculana and Julia on how to properly make rosquetes. Nobody said anything out of the ordinary. It was business as usual.

The girls got the hang of how to make a fire for the brick oven. They then attempted to bake several batches of rosquetes. Some turned out burnt. Others came out undercooked. What was wrong?

"How long are we supposed to bake them?" Herculana was already frustrated.

"Say a hundred Ave Marias," Pedro stated.

"But I didn't do anything!" Herculana protested.

"The baking time must always be the same," Pedro responded.

"How do you do it, Pedro?" Herculana was turning it back on him.

"I whistle four songs."

"But we don't know how to whistle," Julia piped up.

"Rodolfo taught me to wait for the smell," Pedro shared. "That's the secret to when they are done."

Three batches later they were having success. The plain ones tasted good.

"That's enough for now. You both did excellent work," Pedro was heaping praise on them. "Tomorrow we'll do sweet and salty ones."

The girls beamed, "Yay!"

After that night's dinner, as Pedro was about to get up from the little table, Lupe called out, "Glad you stayed, mijo."

"Me, too," whispered Ramón.

***

The next week was busy. Julia had taken quite an interest in making rosquetes. It seemed that she had the natural talent for it. The sweet and salty ones turned out perfectly. Pedro praised her.

Herculana was relegated to washing more clothes. Her reward was to be able to go back to the plaza on the weekends. She was happy about this arrangement.

Pedro was assisting Ramón with the firewood and was teaching him how to take care of horses. Ramón named the old wagon horse "El Negro" because of its jet-black color. The horse fed on the fresh grass by the casitas. El Negro was tied by a rope that was staked to the ground.

Ramón had decided to use El Negro and the supply wagon to transport everyone to town on market days. Norberta and Lupe were grateful. The two women sat in the back of the wagon chatting and enjoying the ride.

On Friday Norberta and Lupe decided to take the new product, the rosquetes, to the market. Alfredo and his friends loved dunking them in their hot chocolate. They purchased some salty ones to go.

The next day, Maya Chou was in town with her father Juan doing some business. Juan greeted Norberta and Lupe.

"How are Señor Sung and Jade?" Norberta politely inquired.

"He and Jade very happy!" Juan was renowned as the unofficial lord of El Barrio Chino. The joke around the neighborhood was that Sung was a very wealthy man because he had "lots of jade." Norberta didn't think it was humorous.

Herculana and Maya ran off to the side. They were dunking a sweet rosquete into their shared cup of hot chocolate. Herculana told Maya about getting new kitchen gadgets. Similarly, Maya shared about being given more responsibilities at her father's grocery store.

Norberta took notice that more and more unemployed miners were trickling into town. Haggard. Unshaven. Smelly. They were all looking for jobs.

The mayor and his cronies, Sergeant Montez and El Piojo, took advantage of this. They ran a brothel outside of town. The trio were only too happy to take the last of miners' pesos. The problem was that recently there were more customers; this meant they needed more girls.

El Piojo was excellent at leading young girls astray.

"You are so pretty. You should work for me."

"I know a place where you can be a caregiver."

And if such lines did not work, El Piojo was not above kidnapping innocent girls. During this last week Sergeant Montez had abducted two young girls while their parents were working in town. El Piojo had scouted the two girls for weeks, knowing all the details about them and their families.

On this Saturday morning El Piojo had paid a quick visit to Norberta and Lupe at their booth. He had memorized their routines. He knew that Ramón and Herculana were with their mothers. That meant that the other daughter was home alone.

El Piojo saw Sergeant Montez and waved him over.

"Geraldo, it's safe," El Piojo gave him an evil grin.

"Okay, Jorge, I'll be on my way."

As Sergeant Geraldo Montez made his way out of town, grey clouds were forming in the skies. Foreboding winds started to pick up.

¡Demonios! he muttered.

About an hour later, Montez found himself in the middle of El Pueblito del Valle. Nobody was around. He trotted from casita to casita trying to find Norberta's place. In the distance he thought he could see a short and heavy girl with long black hair gathering up clothes from shrubs and small trees in anticipation of rain.

Montez rode closer and closer toward her. She was folding some of the clothes and did not notice him until his horse snorted.

"Your mother told me to fetch you," Montez shouted in an authoritarian tone. "There has been an accident at the plaza."

Julia's heart raced, "Just let me put these clothes inside before they get wet." As she entered the casita, an uneasy feeling entered her mind. *Wasn't he one of the men harassing my mother?* She tried to think. Then she remembered that she had overheard that this guy had beat up Pedro. *What does this mean? Why is this happening to me?* Her mind and heart told her that something was not right.

She poked her head out of the doorway. "Señor, I need to stay here. I'm not permitted to leave."

"But this an emergency!" Montez gave her a snarling grimace.

"I still can't go."

Montez was now irritated. He slowly got off his mount and walked toward Julia. She did not move. He reached out suddenly and grabbed her wrist forcefully, pulling her toward him. She cried out in pain.

"You are coming with me, cabróna! Who do you think you are!" Montez yanked her forward again.

"You're hurting me!" Julia's body was twisting. She was in pain.

Montez wrapped his bulky arm around her body. He tried to lift her onto the saddle, but she was heavy. The first attempt failed miserably. Now Julia was desperately trying to slip out of his ironclad grasp.

Filled with outrage, he lifted her off the ground and then she slipped out of his grasp and fell to the ground. She shrieked in pain. He mercilessly snatched her wrist again. She screamed loudly. "Help me!"

Montez backhanded her across the mouth. She rolled over on the ground. Julia couldn't move.

He pulled her up from ground and tried a third time to lift her onto his mount. She couldn't resist him any longer.

"Help me!" she weakly cried out again.

Montez successfully pushed her up onto the saddle although it was with great difficulty. She became motionless. He climbed up on the saddle behind her. As he reached for the saddle horn, she lurched forward and bit his right hand. He yelled and then punched her in the head with his left hand.

Julia was dazed.

"That was just a love pat." Montez smirked. "One of many to come your way."

CHAPTER 45 – BLAME

Sunday, October 9, 1910
El Pueblito del Valle

Pedro was tending to the newly-acquired horse and wagon.
He was trimming the harness to make it possible for a single
horse to pull the wagon, rather than two. He had cared for this
particular horse up at the mine and knew it was a hard worker.

Then he went over to Lupe's new oven. They had done a
good job installing it, but Pedro needed to level the baking
grills in the new brick oven. There was a slight tilt. He wanted
to make sure that the flames from the burning firewood would
not lick the rosquetes and burn them. The rosquetes needed to
bake evenly.

There was a noise. Pedro looked around. A scream? Hmm?
Some of the bricks were difficult to maneuver. He needed to
use a boning knife to create a space between some bricks. He
then positioned a tray of raw rosquetes on the grill to test his
work. He was in a deep state of concentration. He wanted to
finish this project today.

A human cry sounded again. Pedro's attention immediately turned to Lupita's casita. There was nothing there! Then out of the corner of his good eye he saw movement at Norberta's house. With the use of only one eye, he had a difficult time focusing. He leaned his head forward and made out a horse. And the two figures. One looked like a big man. The other one was . . . Julia! He started to run toward the shuffling shapes. As he got closer, he perceived there was a struggle. *What was happening?* Pedro was stunned. Then he realized that the sergeant was trying to overpower Julia.

"Stop!" Pedro cried out, but no one seemed to heed him. He was now only about fifty paces from the struggling pair.

"Stop!" he repeated.

Pedro was getting winded. Montez then started to leave with Julia seated in front of him on the horse. She began struggling again. Montez was moving very slowly trying to balance Julia on his lap.

Pedro was closing the distance. He was out of breath. 25 paces left! Then 10 paces. "Stop, I said," Pedro shouted inaudibly.

Montez turned his head in Pedro's direction. As Pedro approached, Montez let out a swift kick that sent the young man sprawling. The sergeant crowed.

"You, again!" Montez smirked. "I thought you learned your lesson!" He started to pull the reins with his injured right hand as he tightened his grip around Julia's middle with his left hand.

Julia gave out one last "Help me!" before she went limp.

Pedro tried to regain his balance and got up from the ground. Then with an extraordinary effort he raced up to Montez on the horse. The sergeant tried to kick him again, but this time Pedro had anticipated the move. He jumped toward the haunches of the horse while at the same time swinging his boning knife in a downward motion toward Montez.

A blood curdling scream erupted from the kidnapper. Montez turned and saw a big gash on his right leg. He lost his grip on Julia who slid out of his arms falling onto the ground with a loud thud.

"You, little bastard!" Montez was slobbering. "You are dead now!"

Montez reached for his holster and pulled out his revolver. He swung his right arm and tried to take aim at Pedro. Suddenly there was a severed right hand and a pistol flying through the air. Montez's eyes were wide open with shock. He started to falter and his body fall onto the horse's mane.

Pedro stared hard at his victim. *This is the pig who attacked me and messed up my eye! I should mutilate this son of a whore! He tried to kidnap poor Julia. I should cut him up into little pieces!*

He felt a drop of moisture on his sleeve. And then another. It had started to rain. He regained his composure.

I need to know if Julia is all right! He pulled her up. He tried to lift her, but she was too heavy for him. Finally, he helped her to her feet. She was groggy. They started to walk slowly toward her casita. She was mumbling something unintelligible.

"Julia, just a few more steps," Pedro couldn't hold her up much longer. "You can do it. Come on!"

A few minutes later he had placed her on a mat in Lupe's casita. She had fallen asleep instantly. He left the casita and went to find Montez.

He walked at a slow pace following the trail of watered-down blood. Pedro finally found Montez hunched over on his horse. It was difficult to tell if the big man was breathing. Then the rain started to come down in buckets.

What should I do now? I would love to chop his head off, the son of a whore! Or cut out his heart if he even had one! I don't know if he came alone or if people knew where Montez was going.

Pedro glowered at Montez. He was fairly certain that the sergeant was dead, but he didn't know what to do with the corpse. *In any event, I have to get rid of the body.* He took the reins of Montez's horse and led if off the road about three hundred paces.

"Okay, you, son of a whore!" Pedro used all of his strength to push Montez off the saddle. It was difficult because of the sergeant's size. There was a mushy sound as the sergeant fell into the wet shrubbery.

They'll be looking for him soon! What can I do? Will they harass El Pueblito del Valle? Who will be blamed? The revolutionaries? Some innocent souls? Maybe I can make it look like a robbery! Pedro rummaged through Montez's clothes. He found an old leather wallet. Not much in it. Pedro took the few pesos and threw the wallet further into the woods.

He started to leave on foot but decided to take Montez's horse. Now Pedro really had to leave Teocaltiche. If they found him, he would be killed.

The horse was a noble beast. Pedro weighed half as much as Montez and the horse breezed along easily. As Pedro headed back to check on Julia, he kept trying to wipe away the blood on the roan horse's mane.

At Norberta's casita, Julia was still asleep. Pedro wanted to tell her not to worry but he didn't want to wake her up. He was sorry that he could not say his goodbyes to Norberta, Herculana, and the others.

Pedro left Norberta's place and went to Lupe's casita. He took a piece of paper that Herculana and he had been using to practice his reading and writing lessons. He found a pencil and wrote:

Ramón, have to go. You know what to do. Use it smart. Trouble if I stay. Thanks to all. Pedro

Pedro grabbed half the money that had been stashed away in the tin in Ramón's special hiding place. He threw a few clothes into an old flour sack and then added a few rosquetes in another.

It was drizzling as Pedro put on his cowboy hat and saddled up. At the main road, he turned eastward, the opposite way from Teocaltiche. He didn't know how far Aguascalientes was, but he knew that he had to put distance between himself any and all potential pursuers.

I guess I may be going to Arizona after all!

CHAPTER 46 – THE AWAKENING

Sunday, October 9, 1910

Norberta, Herculana, and Lupe were soaked by the time
they returned home. Lupe had had a very successful day at the
plaza. People liked the rosquetes, and even took some home.
Luckily, their party was riding back in the wagon in the terrible
weather. At least their feet were staying dry and warm.

But Norberta experienced an eerie silence as she entered
her casita, while Herculana unloaded the wagon. She noticed
drops of blood splattered on the floor. The trail led to Julia who
was lying in a fetal position on a mat with a sarape wrapped
around her. *Is it her time? Her moon? Too much blood! Did
something happen?*

As she looked more closely, she saw the cuts and bruises
on Julia's body. Then she saw more blood. Her heart skipped a
beat. She assumed the worst *My poor baby! Who could have
done this to her? I wasn't here to protect her!*

Her mind was racing. Throughout her life she had seen
women and girls violated by drunken men or angry soldiers.

But this time, it was her own daughter. *Life is so unfair!* Norberta put her hand on Julia's head. It felt warm.

The girl started to moan but did not open her eyes. Norberta got up and started to make some tea of cacao. She would add her special chocolate to it. She took out a leather pouch that she had hidden in a box of clothing. She poured a little of the brown powder into the boiling water and stirred it. There was a nutty bouquet that filled the room.

Norberta went back and stroked Julia's long black hair. It was wet and was encrusted with sand and mud. She got a few dry rags and started to clean her up. She chanted special mystical songs to help heal her daughter. She heard a slight noise by the door. It was only then that Norberta noticed that Herculana had been watching her.

"Mija, help me clean up your sister."

"What happened, mamá? Is she all right?"

"I don't know," the mother was unwilling to share her thoughts. They were just too gruesome for a young child.

"Should I go get my nina?" Herculana asked.

As if on cue, Lupe entered Norberta's place totally unaware of what was going on with Julia.

"Pedro is gone!" Lupe shrieked.

Norberta felt hot flashes exploding in her. Her spirit was being torn to shreds! Her daughter had been violated! Pedro gone! God strike him dead. Her mouth started to foam with anger. "That ingrate! After all we've done for him! To hurt my little girl!" Norberta started to sob. Lupe came over and embraced her.

Ramón had been trailing his mother and started to poke his head into the doorway. But he was stopped by his mother.

"Mijo, you need to go away for now," Lupe lamented.

That night Norberta did not sleep well. Her being had been sent to hell and back. She curled herself around Julia, trying to protect her. *I have failed my family!*

Lupe slept with Herculana, close to Norberta. The only one that slept well was Julia who was still in a stupor.

As the sun arose on Monday morning, Herculana saw that her mother was awake, rocking Julia in her arms. Whispering sweet words and cooing melodies.

"How is she, mamá?" Herculana inquired.

Later, that morning Norberta concocted her special salve from ground cacao, chiles, and cloves. She rubbed the special chocolate salve all over Julia's body.

Lupe had returned to her own casita. She and Herculana spent their time making rosquetes for the next market day.

Meanwhile, Norberta spooned the hot tea of cacao into Julia's semiconscious form. Just after noon, Norberta leaned the child forward and fed Julia pieces of her specially-concocted chocolate. The bits slowly melted in Julia's mouth. Norberta closed her eyes. She was exhausted both mentally and physically. Her hands felt Julia's body getting warm. She opened her eyes and saw Julia's skin starting to redden. That accented her bruises. Her girl's body was emitting heat and sweat. Julia was getting redder and redder. Hotter and hotter. A purple mist of sparks flowed from her skin. The scent of fresh lavender permeated the room. Then Julia's body convulsed. Her color changed to a cobalt shade of blue. The sweat disappeared. The girl started to shiver. Her skin paled into white. Julia convulsed again. After several minutes, her skin tone came back to normal. The good news was that Norberta didn't observe any discoloration around the girl's genital area.

Norberta was distraught. *What happened? What can I do?* She felt helpless, yet she knew that she had to be strong.

"Señora Virgen, please save my daughter! She is so young and innocent. She needs your protection!" Norberta prayed to La Virgen and promised a million things for her daughter's salvation.

Maybe I am being punished for my relationship with Reverend Lucero?! That was so long ago. This is all my fault!

It was getting time for the midday meal when Herculana came into the casita to deliver a meal that Lupe had prepared. Herculana gathered up clothes to be washed.

In the afternoon, Herculana came back and asked her mom, "Mamá, would you like me to make the chocolate pieces? I know how, you know."

Norberta gave a faint smile. "No, I need to do it, mija. Thank you for offering. You are a little angel." The mother got up and started to make preparations. *Be strong!*

Herculana hand washed her sister and changed her clothes that were moist. Julia remained catatonic during this cleansing.

Norberta finished making the chocolate just before twilight and started rubbing the chocolate salve on Julia again. Suddenly, there was a movement under her hand. Norberta was startled and pulled herself back from her daughter.

"Mamá, I brought all the clothes in," Julia said groggily as she raised her head suddenly. "So, they wouldn't get wet in the rain."

Norberta's black eyes widened. She grabbed and hugged Julia. Tears overwhelmed her. She stroked her daughter's hair.

"Mi amor, you're all right!" Norberta's voice cracked with joy and gratitude. *¡Gracias a La Virgen!*

"Mamá, why are you crying?"

"Mija, do you remember what happened to you?" Norberta cringed as she asked. *Do I really want to know?*

Before Julia could answer, Herculana came in accompanied by Lupe and Ramón. Lupe had made some of her special tacos that were a rare treat.

"Julia, you're awake!" Lupe rushed over to hug the child. Herculana followed her lead.

Meanwhile, Ramón snuck a taco.

CHAPTER 47 – EXONERATON

Monday-Wednesday, October 10-12, 1910

"Ramón told me that the rosquetes were all burnt," Lupe was attempting to say something to her comadre. "It took him a long time to scrape those pans clean."

So? thought Norberta. Then suddenly she jumped out of her stupor. She thought she understood what her comadre was trying to say. *How could Pedro have been making rosquetes and at the same time assaulting my daughter? It didn't make sense. But do crimes of passion ever make sense? But why did he run away without a word. That is very suspicious. It's really a sign of guilt. Oh, I don't know what to believe! My mind tells me one thing, but my heart tells me something else. Am I fooling myself?*

"Mamá," Julia interrupted the adults. "I think I remember. I was washing clothes. It started to rain. I gathered the clothes and brought them inside . . ."

Maybe it would be better if Julia didn't remember anything! Norberta thought.

"It was raining. And this big fat soldier wanted me to come with him. I said I couldn't. Did I do the right thing, mamá?"

"Of course, mija! ¡Sí!" Norberta grabbed her daughter and rocked her in her arms.

"But Pedro saved me!"

"How, mija?"

"I think Pedro stabbed the soldier!"

"Who?"

"The fat man who tried to get me!"

It was then that Norberta realized what had happened. She took a deep breath and blew it out. *I accused the wrong person!* A tear flowed from her left eye. *Pedro was the hero who saved my little girl!*

Norberta wanted to celebrate. The next day Ramón and Herculana took the wagon to El Barrio Chino. They went to Señor Sung's butcher shop and got some choice chicken parts. He had graciously remembered them from the auction and sent heartfelt greetings to their families. Jade was there, dressed in Mexican type garb and looking very presentable. The two youngsters swung by Juan's grocery store and bought some noodles. Herculana was able to spend a few minutes with Maya who was now a clerk for her father.

On Wednesday Ramón drove the wagon to town. Norberta's two daughters sat on the buggy seat next to Ramón.

Julia had rarely come to town. Norberta no longer wanted to leave Julia alone at home. She wished that Pedro was still with them.

After they set up the booth, Norberta took leave of the group and walked into the church. She went to the small chapel for the Lady of Guadalupe. She knelt and gave her thanks for the salvation of her daughter. When the confessional was open, she told Padre Santiago how she had blamed an innocent person for a most egregious act. For her penance she had to pray one rosary.

In mid-morning, Norberta returned to her market stall. She was at peace. A giant burden had been lifted from her shoulders. Half of the rosquetes were already gone! Everything went well the rest of the morning. A cold wind from the north started to pick up. Bad weather was on the horizon.

As an afterthought, Norberta asked Ramón to track down Rodolfo who was working at El Ranchito restaurant. She wanted a special meal to give thanks for Julians's return to good health. Rodolfo was overjoyed to be of assistance. He cooked them a mole dinner using the chicken from Señor Sung's butcher shop which Norberta and company took home with them.

The food was delicious. Everybody was licking their fingers.

"I ate too much!" Lupe complained. "I'm going to be a fat old lady."

They talked. They laughed. They teased.

"How did you like the market today, Julia?" Lupe asked conversationally.

"Fine! I can start making rosquetes again," Julia was being assertive. "I really like making them."

"What about me?" Herculana gave a little pout.

Norberta saw the problem and she was caught in the middle.

"Julia, you're the older sister, do you want to cook or wash clothes. You choose."

Her middle daughter thought about it for a moment and said, "I will do the wash if I can make the rosquetes."

Then everyone looked at Herculana expecting an argument. The youngest said, "Fine, I'll cook but that means I make the chocolate with mom."

"This sounds great. I'm glad I have two sensible daughters," Norberta smiled, having just dodged a bullet.

"But nina, I think we should be putting the rosquetes in packages of three or six. People can take some home. We can sell more this way. Maybe give add an extra pilón if somebody buys a dozen," Ramón suggested.

These entrepreneurs discussed the chocolate, churro, and rosquete business for the next hour coming up with some innovative ideas. The new ideas meant that everyone had to work harder on non-market days.

Everybody was exhausted and ready to call it a night when Ramón spoke up. "What are we going to do with El Negro?"

"He helps us get to the market in a shorter time," Lupe replied. "I don't get so tired from walking."

"My bones are getting stiff from not walking," Norberta added. "And speaking of not gaining weight." They all laughed, and the discussion went on for another half hour.

"What do you think, mijo?" Lupe prodded. "You raised the question."

"El Negro was catching a cold, but he is all right now. We have a few problems. First, I don't know anything about horses. Don't know what to do if he gets sick or throws a shoe," Ramón was exhibiting good business sense. "We can't afford taking him to the stables. Second, we don't have a safe shelter for him. He won't survive the winter," Ramón paused as everyone was yawning, wanting to go to bed. "And lastly, you ladies need the exercise."

"¡Ramón!" Lupe took a swipe at her son but missed. Everybody started to laugh.

"Mamá, you said you didn't want to get fat."

"Maybe you should sell the horse," Julia piped in. And then as an afterthought she added, "and the wagon too."

Norberta thought about this latest proposal. They could use the money. However, they had business assets: a horse and a supply wagon. *Why should we sell them? We could use them as leverage for an investment.*

Although tired, they brainstormed for a while more before everyone gave up and went to retire for the night.

Blessed Virgen, thank you! Forgive me for thinking bad thoughts. Help me be better. Protect my children. Norberta prayed before going to sleep

CHAPTER 48 – EL NEGRO

Thursday, October 13, 1910
Teocaltiche

On Thursday some transients heard a dog barking from a grove of trees off the main road to Teocaltiche. They were curious and went to look. They found a bloated body with flies swarming from open wounds caused by carnivorous predators. They reported it to the local police who questioned them for a few hours.

Two policemen and ten soldiers were dispatched to the scene to retrieve the body and comb through the area. There was a putrid smell emanating from the body as the soldiers lifted it off the ground. A corporal examined the body and noted a missing limb and several jagged bite marks. He noted the pockets of the deceased had been turned inside out. His gun was missing and presumably a horse. They assumed it was the missing Sergeant Montez.

The military wagon carried the body back to town, escorted by six soldiers. The other military men broke up into three pairs and canvassed the area where the body was found.

The police pair also explored the grounds. "There's a lot of horse tracks in the mud. We don't know exactly what we're looking for," said one member of the police duo.

"Most of the people around here don't have horses. If they do, the horses are not shoed," said his companion. "We should be looking for tracks like our horses."

This first pair followed several sets of tracks that turned into false leads. But then they found a promising set that led to El Pueblito del Valle. These soldiers went to explore the area.

That afternoon Ramón was rubbing down El Negro in front of his casita. The last few days the horse had been wheezing. El Negro basically slept outside with very little protection from the elements. Being out in the rain could not be good for the horse. Ramón was concerned. He didn't know what to do. He threw an old sarape over the poor beast.

A few hundred paces away the two policemen spotted Ramón grooming his horse. They were suspicious of this mestizo owning a horse. *Could this be Sergeant Montez's horse?* They rode over to him.

"Hey, where did you get that horse?" yelled one of the policemen.

"From the mining camp," Ramón was not frightened of these two.

"Which one?"

"I don't know. The tin one. What do you want?" Ramón decided to engage with them and throw them off balance.

"We're looking for Sergeant Montez," said the second one. "Have you seen him?"

"What does he look like?"

"Big guy. Heavy. Big moustache. Long sideburn," said the first policeman.

"Smelly? Ugly?" taunted Ramón innocently.

"You could say so," one said trying to seem friendly.

"Don't think so."

The two thought the youngster was a smart aleck and was messing with them.

"Your horse is very similar to his," remarked the first policeman.

"Only if he rode a pack horse." The ploy of the two men did not work. They finally gave up and rode away.

At the end of the day, the corporal made his official report to the police capitán.

"Sir, we think it was highway robbery. His clothes were ransacked. His gun and horse were missing. He had no money on his person." He continued to detail the wounds. "The cause of death was indeterminate. Looks like the work of several men."

At the word "several" the captain's attention perked up. "Could it have been the revolutionaries?"

"No, captain."

"Why not!?" the captain barked.

Later that night the police captain met with the municipal president, Don José Sáenz Mejia. He was with Jorge "El Piojo" Contreras. They were discussing their brothel business that still needed more girls.

"Put out a release that Montez was viciously assassinated by the revolutionaries," the mayor dictated. "He put up a brave defense but was overwhelmed by sheer numbers in a cowardly crime. We shall find the perpetrators and bring them to swift justice!"

"El Piojo" was incredulous. He knew that Montez was on his way to kidnap Norberta's middle daughter. *What happened?* He knew for a fact that Ramón had been at the plaza with Norberta and Lupe. *What went wrong?*

¡Así es la vida! They went back to talking business.

***

On Monday morning the air was crisp. Ramón could see snow on the mountain tops. He drove El Negro and the supply wagon over to Señor Caraballo's business which was about five minutes away.

"He's at the house," a young man who knew Ramón pointed to the nearby brick and wood house, about one hundred meters away. "His wife is sick again."

"Thanks, Rogelio," Ramón jumped off the wagon and made his way toward Arturo Caraballo's home.

"Good morning, Ramón," Señor Caraballo greeted him from his door. "You're starting early today."

"Good morning, Señor Caraballo," Ramón reciprocated the greeting.

"Would you like some coffee?" inquired the older man.

The weather was cold, and Ramón knew that business dealings were better with food and beverage.

Ramón nodded affirmatively.

"Silvia, please bring Ramón a cup of coffee with milk and sugar," Caraballo directed his maid. "And find some biscuits."

The old man pointed to a chair on the porch for Ramón to sit down. He seated himself on the other chair. "What's up, my boy? It must be something important for you to come see me this early," Arturo smiled. "You want more money, I presume."

"More than that," Ramón said distinctly. He did not want to be dismissed as a begging employee. "I want to be a business partner with you."

Arturo's forehead furrowed. "What? What are you talking about? Who told you that I was selling my business? I'm not! I have to take care of my wife and myself. I'm not going anywhere!"

"How about me giving you something that would make your business more valuable? Make your business operate more efficiently? That would mean being able to sell more firewood and make more money?" Ramón cast out the bait.

Arturo remained silent. His eyes blinked. His mind was thinking, trying to take all of this in.

"I know how this business works. The workers have to chop down the firewood and then load it onto a pull cart. Small loads take a long time to get to the warehouse area. The workers are exhausted and the second and third cuttings are smaller and take longer. You're losing money!"

The firewood business owner leaned in closer.

"Well, what could you offer me to improve this?" Caraballo's interest was piqued.

"A pack horse and a supply wagon. It could carry at least three times more firewood faster and with less effort."

"What would you get out of this?"

"Half of the net profits."

"No way! That's too much! I have to support my wife and myself."

"Señor Caraballo, come over and look at El Negro and the wagon." The two walked over to where the horse was. Caraballo rubbed his hand over the animal.

"I don't know. You want to take half of my business away. What I really need now is another cutter. You know, Luis just quit. He was with me for four years. I need to replace him before I can think about anything else."

They ended the conversation and then shook hands.

Ramón went to the warehouse and picked up his firewood allotment. He could load much more firewood in the supply wagon than a cart. *Well, at least, he didn't say no,* Ramón thought.

CHAPTER 49 – DAISIES

Wednesday, October 19, 1910

On Wednesday, Norberta and the others braved the cold, and arrived at the plaza half-frozen. Julia came with them. She was now a permanent member of the entourage.

As they unloaded the wagon, they found a tin can with a little bouquet of white daisies in their market stall.

"Mamá! Look at these!" Herculana's had eagle eyes. "Where did they come from?"

Norberta was thinking, *who was pursuing whom? I haven't noticed anyone showing an interest in any of them.*

Per their daily routine, Alberto showed up with two of his bookend friends. They ordered their hot chocolates and sweet rosquetes. They became animated in their latest arguments regarding the government and the revolutionaries. "They say that Madero had fled to San Antonio," Alberto was gesturing with his hands in the air. "He is gathering support. He wants a rebellion!"

"His Plan of San Luis Potosi would favor Mexican enterprises rather than foreign businesses," Mauricio said skeptically. "Is that a good idea? This sounds like too much political liberalism."

"Well, we would have a democracy rather a dictatorship under Díaz," Noe put his hand under his chin. "Which is better? Maybe they are both the same?"

Alberto bought another churro. "I hear the rebels are coming here. They will be here in the spring."

"The pinche mayor is trying to double the fees on all municipal services. I don't see the roads being fixed."

"I saw more soldiers coming into town. They are assisting the local police."

Norberta wanted to catch Alberto's attention but didn't want the others to notice. But she had no luck.

"Comadre, where did these flowers come from?" Norberta pivoted in Lupe's direction.

"Certainly not for two viejas like you and me," The two older women laughed. "Anybody pursuing Julia? She's almost of age."

Norberta wanted to strangle her but kept her self-control. *¡Ay, comadre!*

A new face arrived and drew their attention.

"Buenos días, Señora Norberta. Buenos días, Señora Lupe," beamed a forty-year-old, clean shaven man.

The two women reservedly reciprocated the greeting.

The new guest ordered a hot chocolate and a sweet rosquete. "These are absolutely delicious!" he remarked. "I don't know if you remember me. I'm Rodolfo. Rodolfo Zamora. I worked with Rico and Pedro. I helped build your oven."

"What a pleasant surprise!" Rodolfo looked so different, all dressed up and clean shaven, that at first she didn't recognize him. Norberta did remember his ruddy cheeks and soft smile though. She grabbed an extra rosquete and gave it to him.

Lupe gave a noncommittal grunt.

Rodolfo kept chatting as his body slid along the counter slowly until he was directly in front of Lupe.

"I hope you liked the flowers," he said with his brown puppy dog eyes. "I brought them here the other day but you weren't here."

"We only come here on Wednesdays, Fridays, Saturdays, and Sundays," Lupe spurted out involuntarily.

"I hope it wasn't too presumptuous of me. I've been here just a few weeks and really don't have many friends," he explained.

Rodolfo started barraging Lupe with a lot of questions. Lupe gave him curt answers. Norberta was too busy with customers to pay attention to the exchange between Rodolfo and Lupe. The youngsters were trying not to stare at Lupe. They had never seen her in this kind of situation.

"And when the other day your son, Ramón, ordered the chicken mole, I remembered you," Rodolfo said shyly. "Everybody was so nice to me."

Lupe barely remembered him.

"Maybe one of these days, I could invite you all over to El Ranchito for lunch. That's where I work."

"That would be nice, but we usually go home around one o'clock. We have to get back. We have lots to do," Lupe was trying to cut off the conversation.

"Well, maybe some other time," Rodolfo's tone seemed sad. "I would like to see you again."

Rodolfo left. As he did so, Ramón slipped out from the corner of the booth. He followed Rodolfo at a quick pace. Soon he was directly behind the man.

CHAPTER 50 – LALO

Thursday, October 20, 1910
Atepoca Mine

Ramón woke up before first light that Thursday morning. The luxury of having the wagon to carry the entourage and their goods had made things easier for him. He wasn't as tired or sore as when he was pulling the cart. He could now do things more easily.

He drove the horse and wagon to the firewood depository, where Señor Caraballo was there waiting for him. Next to Ramón sat a tall, slender young man bundled in a sheepskin coat, jeans, and cowboy hat.

***

The day before, Ramón had met with Rodolfo who had been the cook at the Atepoca Mine. It had been Pedro who told Ramón that the mine was closing. Now there were so many men out of work. Ramón had seen it with his own eyes. Miners drifted into the town and left if they did not find work. Ramón knew that Rodolfo would know them all because he had cooked for them at the mine. Maybe Rodolfo would still be in contact with some of them.

"Señor Zamora, do you still have friends that are looking for work?" Ramón had asked without ceremony.

"Sure, but call me Rodolfo," He offered his hand. "I hope that I was not too forward talking to your mother, but I find her interesting." Rodolfo was talking quickly. He didn't want to buy any trouble from Lupe's son. "What kind of work?"

"Chopping firewood. It's a business. It's about an hour from here."

"I think I might know a few."

***

This morning Lalo Vargas and Jaime Bojorquez were supposed to be at Ramón's casita by nine o'clock. Unfortunately, Jaime did not show up. Lalo and Ramón had hot chocolate and rosquetes before they drove over to Señor Caraballo's place.

"Buenos días, Ramón," the old man called out holding a cup of coffee in his hand.

"Buenos días, Señor," Ramón was being cool."I want you to meet Lalo Vargas. He was the assistant foreman at the Atepoca mine until it closed. You said one of your guys quit. Can you use an extra hand?"

Caraballo rubbed his unshaven chin and gave a smug smile.

"Here's the deal," Ramón asserted. "He gets paid the same as the other cutters. And he gets a place to sleep and two meals a day."

"A place to stay is no problem. He can take Remo's old bunk. The bed should still be warm," he chuckled and then became serious. "But if I feed him, I have to feed everyone."

"And what's wrong with that?" Ramón was surprised at Caraballo's cavalier attitude.

"It costs me money!"

"Workers work better if they are fed and are warm," Ramón contended.

Caraballo stopped and rubbed his chin. He was contemplating this suggestion. "Well, I think maybe we can work something out."

Nobody talked for about a minute and then Caraballo shouted, "Angelito, go fetch a horse and take this young man into the forest." A dark-skinned ten-year-old boy rushed off.

Minutes later, Angelito and Lalo were riding horses down a narrow dirt path.

"Let's see how he does," Caraballo remarked as his eyes followed the two riders that had just left. Then the old man spoke in a serious tone, "Ramón, about our conversation the other day. Fifty percent ownership for an old horse and rickety wagon is too much."

What would Herculana do under these circumstances?
Ramón thought. He knew! She would demand sixty percent!
But this situation seemed different. Caraballo has a storage
area, barn, and a bunk house at a minimum. There were other
horses and carts. *Maybe I pushed too hard!* But Ramón could
not admit this. It would show weakness and put him in an
untenable position. *I would be bargaining with myself.*

They both talked a little more with neither of them
budging.

Finally, Ramón left. He went to make his deliveries with
his supply wagon that was at least twice as efficient as the cart.
Today, since the weather was colder, people wanted more
firewood. He could now accommodate them. The customers
were pleased.

***

The following Tuesday, Ramón returned to Caraballo's
place of business. Once again, the old man was expecting him,
holding a cup of coffee in his hand. Next to him was Lalo who
also had a cup of coffee.

Greetings were pleasantly exchanged.

"I hate to admit it, Ramón, but you and Lalo are making my
business more profitable. Lalo says that we need to run this
business like the mine. We can stock up on firewood. We can

use the wagon for regularly scheduled pickups, . . ." Caraballo went on and on about new ideas for the business.

"I'm glad, Señor Caraballo. I was hoping that you would be more successful." Ramón respectfully commented.

"One more thing. I'm making Lalo the foreman of this business. Do you have any reservations about this?"

"Absolutely, not!" *Why is he asking me?*

"Lalo has been a wonderful dinner guest every night with my wife and me. He has some great stories. He's lived an adventurous life."

Ramón forced a smile.

"Ramón, can you drop by the house after your deliveries? We need to talk."

Talk about what? Ramón wondered.

Ramón rushed through his deliveries and arrived at Caraballo's house in the late afternoon. Upon his arrival, the housekeeper Carlota escorted him to a small drawing room where a porcelain coffee pot sat flanked by a plate of cookies with chocolate chip chispas.

"Ramón, you have done me a great favor, but fifty percent is too much. My wife's health is not great, and I must provide medical care for her. It's not cheap. Thank God we have Carlota. She does everything for us. Also, I'm not getting any younger and maybe my ideas are old-fashioned. I have to guarantee that my wife is taken care of if something happens to me. And Carlota's care too."

Ramón now understood. He was in the same predicament with his mother and Norberta's brood.

"I would promise that, Señor Caraballo," Ramón stated solemnly.

"That's reassuring, my boy," the old man padded Ramón knee. "Now let's talk terms."

Two days later Señor Arturo Caraballo signed a partnership agreement with his "X." It was an easy transaction that was facilitated by Norberta who had done bills of sale before. She delivered two copies of the document that Ramón had dictated.

Señor Caraballo was elated. A burden had been lifted from his shoulders. Now he and his wife (plus Carlota) were protected. Ramón would be his guardian angel in case he became incapacitated or even died.

This was equally true for Ramón. His family had something to fall back on. In the end, they had agreed to a thirty percent interest in the business rather half. As a concession, Ramón had the right to use El Negro and the wagon to transport everyone to town on market days.

Additionally, Ramón agreed to pick up supplies for Caraballo from Luis Cano's grocery store on a weekly basis.

Caraballo had to make sure that his household had all the goods that they needed.

Herculana would be proud of me!

CHAPTER 51 – THE FEAST

November 1910

Every Wednesday morning at exactly nine o'clock Rodolfo visited Norberta's and Lupe's booth. Half the vendors in the plaza had left because of the high fees or the cold weather. This situation gave Norberta added incentive to exploit the need for hot chocolate.

Although her comadre Lupe was still making churros, the demand for rosquetes had soared. Packaging them in bundles of three and six was a grand success. It was convenient for the customers and the rosquetes lasted several days. As Norberta found out anecdotally, old men liked to dunk their rosquetes in their hot chocolate or coffee, especially the sweet ones. Women, on the other hand, ate them with their tea.

Rodolfo had bought a dozen of the salted ones to sell in the cantina attached to El Ranchito Restaurant. The entire batch sold out within two hours. It became a daily event at the cantina since the salted rosquetes went really well with the beer.

This accomplishment was repeated over and over.

Lupe was happy that she was finally making some money. She permitted Rodolfo to take her on short walks around the plaza, Heads turned, but she didn't care. She was feeling younger and younger. The edges of her personality were even softening.

In late November, Rodolfo invited Lupe and her entourage for comida at El Ranchito. He promised them a special meal. Lupe tried to say no, but Norberta finally convinced her to accept the invitation.

On the last day of November, Lupe and her group left the plaza early. Ramón transported everyone in the wagon. El Ranchito was less than a ten-minute ride away. No one knew what to expect.

The restaurant looked like a combination of a diner and a cantina. It had at least ten tables. There were a few private rooms off to the side. A young girl with coiled black hair and a colorful-ribboned blouse led the party consisting of Lupe, Norberta, Ramón, Julia, and Herculana to a big table at the back of the diner. The youngsters had never been to a real restaurant. The table was set with green place mats and tin flatware. There were little flower vases strewn around the large room. One reddish Christmas cactus was in full bloom.

Lupe sat at the head of the table with Norberta to her right. There was an empty seat on the other side of Lupe. The youngsters filled in the rest of the seats.

A fragile girl brought over some type of aromatic tea, served in small cups. It was hot cinnamon tea. Great for such a cold day!

"Welcome to El Ranchito, my friends," Rodolfo welcomed them hospitably. "Here is where I work. I really love it here. I wanted to share my passion with you."

Everybody looked in amazement as a tureen of tortilla soup was placed in front of Lupe. The young waitress ladled out bowls for everyone.

"¡Buen provecho!" Rodolfo exclaimed. He had not yet sat down. Everybody nodded and muttered something unintelligible and started to eat. Nobody said a thing.

"This is wonderful!" Lupe finally uttered. "Thank you!" She gave him a big smile.

"¡Ay Dios Mío!" Norberta thought. "Is Lupe falling for this guy?! *Well, she deserves a little happiness. In a short time, Ramón will marry, and he won't be around to keep her company.*

"This is really good!" Herculana said excitedly to her sister and Ramón.

"It must cost a lot of money," replied Julia. "We would never have the money to do something like this."

Ramón remained quiet as he stared at his mother.

The waitress removed the soup bowls and five minutes later the main course arrived.

"I must apologize, dear friends. I wanted to cook carne asada but procuring beef has been difficult lately."

Ramón was aware that supply wagons in the valley were continually being attacked. The mayor blamed the revolutionaries. Others thought it was the displaced miners. Ramón had a cynical suspicion that it was the federal soldiers in disguise.

Moreover, Ramón knew that the inventory at Cano's grocery store was depleted. Ramón now had to make regular runs to Wang "Juan" Chou's grocery in El Barrio Chino. The prices were a bit higher, but the quality was better. Besides it was less than ten minutes away from El Pueblito del Valle. He saved himself potentially an hour or two.

***

Ramón had been going to Juan's store two and three times a week. A few times he took Herculana so she could talk with her friend Maya. But more often, he took Julia with him because she knew exactly what she needed in order to make the rosquetes.

The pair talked business. The two families were pleased when they heard that Ramón had negotiated free firewood for them. Their casitas were so much warmer.

"Ramón, I think we could make more money if we baked more rosquetes and sold them at Juan's grocery store," Julia was not shy around Ramón. "And maybe at Rodolfo's restaurant."

"Hmm! Sounds good," Ramón was a firm believer in "working smarter, not harder."

"But mamá won't let me. She doesn't want me to be home alone."

Neither said anything, but Ramón believed that Pedro had been somehow involved with the death of Sergeant Montez and had to flee. Nothing else made sense.

On their latest foray, Julia unexpectedly remarked, "I think Rodolfo likes your mom. What do you think?"

"I don't really care. She has the right to live her own life. She can't take care of me forever," he got animated. "I need to take care of everyone. I'm the man!"

Julia gave him an "oh, wow!" look.

***

The Yucatan achiote pork dish with camote was juicy and aromatic. The waitress replenished the first batch of corn tortillas with another.

Rodolfo was now seated. He had hardly eaten anything.

Then came the coconut tarts that were to die for.

"Thank you, Rodolfo! Everything tastes like it was made in heaven." Lupe spontaneously turned her head and gave him a little peck on the cheek. His face turned beet red.

On the way home, Norberta commented to Lupe, "that was a great meal. Rodolfo is a kind and gentle man." She didn't want to push it. Or did she?

Everybody started to wrap their shawls and blankets around them. It started to rain.

When they got home, everybody wanted to retire early.

"Mamá, my nina is acting kind of crazy. Are they going to get married?"

"I don't know, mija."

"Adults are so strange. I'm never going to get married!"

¡Ay Herculana!

CHAPTER 52 – THE HOLIDAYS

December 1910

EL Negro snorted as he ambled into town that frigid December morning. Ramón could see the condensed clouds of steam emanating from its nostrils. The horse paused in the middle of the rutted dirt road and gazed to the right. Ramón subconsciously followed the glance. He cracked the thin leather whip and the horse started up again. Ramón inhaled deeply even though it was difficult in the cold. He shook his head in disbelief. He had witnessed two shirtless bodies of skinny men hanging from tree limbs.

Robbers? Revolutionaries? Ramón knew that these days, trouble was just around the corner. He had to protect his extended family.

In town Norberta was busy composing letters and greetings for Christmas and for the Day of the Three Magi.

December 12, 1910

"Oh, Blessed Virgen of Lupe, pray for us. You are our salvation. You never abandon us. You're our mother in Christ who takes care of us and protects us . . .

December 25, 1910
Dear Jesusita,

We hope all is well with you and your family. We wish you a Holy Christmas and a Prosperous New Year. We have missed you and hope you are enjoying living en el otro lado. Thank you for the money. It is very helpful. With God's help we will see you soon . . .

December 31, 1910
Dear Concuño,

We pray that you will visit us when you return to see your granddaughter.

She is so precious. We have seen her, and she is growing every day. We feel so old. We are having a small party to celebrate The Day of the Three Magi. We await your visit . . .

These days, Lupe was staffing a small table at El Ranchito restaurant selling her rosquetes while Julia was experimenting with making different types of pan dulce.

Rodolfo's affection for Lupe was boundless. Norberta saw it. But Lupe was not making any commitments.

Norberta was finally earning some money and trying to make more. She had heard that one of the tortillerias in town went out of business. Lupe and Norberta did not want to buy it because of the small profit margins. *¡No vale la pena!*

Meanwhile, Ramón was being resourceful. He was now one of the best customers at Juan's grocery store in El Barrio Chino. He easily convinced the grocer to sell Julia's rosquetes at the store. They were quickly in demand, especially among the younger population. They wanted to be more Mexican.

A few days before the end of the year, Ramón and Juan Chou struck a deal. Ramón would deliver two wagon loads of firewood to sell to the denizens of El Barrio Chino.

Ramón had discussed the possibility of this arrangement with Señor Caraballo, getting insight first from Lalo. Norberta, Lupe, and Julia were in support of this venture. It could mean more money coming in.

Recently, Señor Caraballo had seemed distraught. His wife's healthy was waning and he was worried. While he liked the increased business, he wanted to spend more time at his wife's side.

Ramón and Señor Caraballo decided that Ramón would have to give up making his personal deliveries. He needed to take on more managerial duties. One of the cutters, Tomás, was more than happy to be switched to a delivery man. The challenge now was to find another supply wagon and at least one new cutter.

The procurement of a supply wagon would be a challenge. Ramón checked around. The stables and other supply businesses were short of wagons because of the raids. Any available ones were prohibitively expensive.

One day when the lechero Abelardo Gutierrez was making his Tuesday delivery, Ramón inquired if the milkman knew anyone who had a wagon to sell. Abelardo said no, but said he had an old one if Ramón was desperate. He could not vouch for its condition, however, he would sell it as is. Ramón and

Abelardo finally came to an agreement for two hundred pesos plus thirty piles of firewood.

With a couple of nails and wooden planks, Ramón had acquired another wagon for his firewood business. Lalo was pleased.

Herculana now rarely saw her mother and sister who were busy composing letters and making rosquetes. She was making twice as much chocolate, both for the hot chocolate drink and as candy bars. Rodolfo had also agreed to sell chocolate bars at El Ranchito, next to the rosquetes.

Lupe was spending Friday mornings at El Ranchito ostensibly selling rosquetes and chocolate. Rodolfo liked her around, out of prying eyes.

However, "El Piojo" had noticed that Lupe was sometimes absent from Norberta's booth at the plaza. With a little investigation and the wagging tongues of the towns people, "El Piojo" discovered the amorous relationship between Rodolfo and Lupe. *Julia is ripe. And Herculana is getting there. Need to pick the fruit soon!*

***

Alberto dipped his rosquete into his hot chocolate. Mauricio was not feeling well and had not been around for a while. Suddenly, Noe arrived out of breath and exclaimed, "the rebels are coming to the plaza next week!"

The streets had been filled with rebellious activity. "¡Viva La Revolución!" was painted on the city hall wall. The rabble-rousers chanted "¡Death to Díaz!" against the current president of Mexico.

Alberto blurted out, "Pinche Taft and the yanquis want to invade Mexico!"

Norberta observed her loyal customers but said nothing. In the late morning, a young postal delivery boy carrying an oversized delivery pouch stopped by Norberta's booth.

"I have a special delivery letter for Doña Norberta and Señora Lupe," he said in a high-pitched voice.

"That's me," Norberta took the letter and handed the boy a small coin. It was a letter that was wrinkled and smudged. She unsealed the letter with Herculana peering over her shoulder.

> Dear Dona Norberta and Senora Lupe,
> How are you? I am fine. I am working in my cousins tabac. He has two of them here in Morenci. We sell supplies and cigarettes to the copper miners.

Thank you for helping me. I had to go. I miss you and my brother Ramon and Julia.

I am learning to read and write English! Thanks to my good teacher Herculana.

God willing, I will see you again one day.

Your servant,
Pedro Campos
c/o Tabac de Campos
Morenci Arizona

Norberta read the letter to Lupe.

"Comadre, what's a tabac?" Lupe shouted over to Norberta.

Before the Norberta could answer, Alberto imposed himself. "It's place like where I buy my newspapers. You can buy cigarettes, stamps, or all anything. It's a good business."

CHAPTER 53 – SURPRISE

1911

Cold winds and dark grey clouds brought in the new year. The Day of the Three Kings was being celebrated. Ramón had bartered with Juan Chou for dresses for Julia and Herculana and sweaters for Norberta and Lupe. He gave an additional load of firewood to Juan as a gesture of generosity.

Rodolfo hosted another feast celebrating the Epiphany at El Ranchito. He invited a few other local denizens. He even baked a rosca de reyes to observe this holy day. The local cantina owner got the baby Jesus doll that was baked into the cake. Because by chance he got the doll, the cantina would have to provide tamales for everyone in attendance on February 2nd according to Mexican tradition.

"I wish Pedro was here," voiced Herculana. Her mother had given her permission to write back to him.

Lupe was now passing more and more time at El Ranchito. Finally, one Wednesday, she informed Norberta that she would be spending Wednesday and Thursday in town to manage the sales of rosquetes and chocolates. Nobody said anything. *She's a good woman!* Norberta thought. *She can do whatever she wants.* Ramón had no problems with this arrangement. He was too busy administering the firewood business. He began spending time with Julia so she could teach him how to read the books and financial statements from Señor Caraballo.

The sad news was that Señora Caraballo was getting worse. It was believed that she had pneumonia. Ramón suggested bringing in the curandera Señora Pacheco but was politely rebuffed. Arturo was a strong believer in the Catholic church.

"We don't need a bruja, son," Arturo Carabllo said somberly. "God will take care of her. I pray to Him every day."

At the plaza Norberta's hot chocolate business started to diminish. The holiday season was over and fewer parishioners came to church.

***

In early March there was a heavy rain and most people stayed at home. Taking advantage of the inclement weather, about fifty revolutionaries attacked the municipal palace where the mayor and the police had their offices. After a three-hour skirmish, the rebels retreated.

This caused several businesses to close their doors. People were afraid to go out on the streets. The mayor ordered soldiers to patrol the plaza area and place guards outside his home, twenty-four hours a day.

These events did not prevent Lupe from visiting Rodolfo, however. In fact, it gave her a better reason to spend more time with her gentleman friend.

Back at El Pueblito del Valle Norberta, decided to have a serious talk with her comadre.

"You say that he wants to get married," Norberta probed.

"Why, yes."

"Why don't you?"

"Because I still need to take care of my Ramón."

"Comadre, Ramón can take care of himself. He's a young man," Norberta said. Ramón was her godson, and she would be responsible for him if need be.

It was getting close to Easter and Norberta thought she might force the issue. She plotted to concoct the same special chocolate love potion that she had prepared for María Antonia and Pedro. She would add extra cinnamon, cloves, and anise seed. She wanted to force Lupe's hand.

The next day was a beautiful morning. Norberta spent it concocting the magical love elixir for Lupe.

"Good morning, comadre," Norberta gave a shining smile. Norberta had walked over to Lupe's casita.

"Good morning," Lupe was more subdued.

"I just made some fresh hot chocolate. Please have some," Norberta handed the steaming cup to Lupe.

"Mamá, I can't find my gloves!" Ramón yelled from outside.

"Oh, mijo, you're always losing them!" Lupe got up from the chair and walked out the door leaving the cup of chocolate on the table.

They were now running late so the entourage had to take off. Herculana and Julia stayed back. Herculana was busy making chocolate disks and pieces while Julia baked rosquetes all day. The demand for their products was overwhelming. Julia felt hot and sticky from slaving over the hot oven. She took a break and quaffed the hot chocolate that had been abandoned by Lupe.

Suddenly, her skin started to glow a reddish-orange tint. Then it morphed into white and then to purple. She was sweating profusely. Julia exuded energy and sparks. Her whole body shivered. The nipples of her breasts felt hard. Her body tingled. Her eyes rolled up in her head. She had trouble breathing.

***

Easter came and a weeping Carlota came running to look for Ramón. There had been a death at the Caraballo home. Ramón and Norberta quickly rode over to Carlota's house. They were shocked to find Señora Caraballo in a wheelchair sobbing over the body of her husband, Arturo.

A week later Señor Caraballo was buried in the local El Pueblito del Valle cemetery. Padre Santiago from the Teocaltiche church performed the interment ceremony. The funeral service was attended by neighbors and the firewood workers.

The following day Ramón convened a meeting with his mother Lupe and Norberta. "Now that Señor Caraballo has gone on to Heaven, what are we going to do?"

"According to the bill of sale contract, I think that Ramón is the new owner of the whole business," Norberta opined.

"How about the house?" Ramón asked.

Nobody knew.

"In any event, I know that Señor Caraballo would want us to take care of his wife," Ramón stated.

They discussed several scenarios. Then Ramón held up his hand.

"Let's take a short break," he left the two women.

Ten minutes later he returned escorted by Julia and Herculana. The two women curiously stared at the girls. *What were they doing here?*

"Julia and I will move into the Caraballo house. We will help take care of Señora Caraballo," Ramón said matter-of-factly.

"I don't understand, mijo!" Lupe's jaw dropped. She was in shock.

"Julia and I are getting married. We were going to tell you both later, but now seems as good a time as any."

Both ladies had their eyes and mouths wide open. They had not seen it coming. However, this was a relationship made in heaven. The two youngsters had known each other since birth and had gotten along well with each other, although it had been more of a sibling relationship. This marriage would bring everybody closer and formalize the family ties. Additionally, it would ensure a mutual economic bond.

Norberta was happy for her daughter. She was also elated that now Lupe was free to be with Rodolfo if she wanted to. *Life is good,* Norberta thought.

CHAPTER 54 – TWO MANY COOKS

1911

That night Julia and Norberta talked as Herculana slept on her little mat.

"Mamá, I'm sorry I didn't tell you sooner. It just happened. One day I felt to an urge to be with Ramón."

"Don't worry, mija. You're old enough," Norberta sighed. She wanted to reassure her daughter. Julia was almost fifteen and had been maturing in front of her own eyes. *Why wasn't I paying attention?* Norberta wished she could keep Julia a child forever. To protect her. But she knew that her daughter would have to leave sooner or later. Julia was ready to fully control the rosquete business and knew how to manage the accounts of the firewood enterprise. She had an acute business sense.

"Mamá, Ramón and I will take care of Señora Caraballo. But I'm not sure how the living arrangements are going to be."

"How so, mija?"

"The best thing would be for Señora Caraballo to remain in the house. This way Carlota could still take care of her."

Norberta nodded in head in agreement.

"You and Herculana would still stay here. When I move out, it would mean one less person in your casita."

Her mother nodded again.

"Now comes the difficult part. Ramón's mom can't stay in her casita alone."

Norberta was slowly seeing the dilemna. Julia and Ramón were concerned about the "older folks."

"I wonder if it would be comfortable for comadre to live in the Caraballo house." Norberta said. She could already see Lupe complaining about how she had to reside with strangers. Lupe would be living apart from her comadre and best friend.

Norberta thought about it and then nodded her head okay.

"Ramón and I would move into the big house and also look after Señora Caraballo."

"Then who would live in Lupe's casita?" Norberta asked with a furrowed brow.

"Rodolfo!" They both started to laugh. A little love nest? But they knew that he had to stay in town to manage El Ranchito.

"How about that nice young man, Lalo, from the firewood business?"

Their discussion was interrupted by a movement in the direction of Herculana's mat.

"What if my madrina's casita could be a real bakery and kitchen for rosquetes, churros, and chocolates," Herculana drowsily blurted out.

Norberta and Julia did a double take in Herculana's direction. She seemed to be eavesdropping the entire time.

That might work! Norberta thought. Julia shook her head in approval. Then they both burst out laughing.

***

The next day they discussed their proposal with Lupe. Lupe said that she wanted to talk it over with Rodolfo first. She said that Rodolfo wanted to buy two new ovens for them to keep up with the high demand for rosquetes. If Lupe's casita was empty, they would have room for them. Previously, Rodolfo had wanted to buy El Ranchito but there were inherent problems of securing essential supplies like flour and sugar. He had said that it was better to make the rosquetes off-site. There were too many problems with the mayor and his cronies.

"Maybe my madrina and Rodolfo should get married," Herculana contributed. "That could solve the problem."

¡Ay Herculana¡ her mother cringed.

In the upcoming days, both Ramón and Rodolfo were brought into the conversations minus Herculana's suggestion of marriage. Ramón believed that a single center for operations worked the most efficiently. He agreed that the bakery should be in El Pueblito del Valle. Fortunately, there were no problems with supplies or the revolutionaries yet in that area.

***

As to be expected, Alberto reported one morning that organized villarista troops under the command of Susano Arango were approaching. He was animated making his report. "They're coming from Chihuahua. Orozco and Pancho Villa!" Alberto almost choked on his rosquete he was talking so fast.

"I hear Emiliano Zapata is leading thousands of campesinos in his fight for land reform under El Plan de Ayala," Mauricio added.

"But they are already here!" Noe spit out. "There are raids to get food and supplies. Their commander is the brother of Doroteo Arango (aka Pancho Villa)!"

Norberta said nothing. She knew that the revolutionaries usually left places like El Pueblito del Valle and El Barrio Chino alone.

However, they made periodic raids on Teocaltiche in broad daylight. They left the plaza vendors alone. Instead, they concentrated on bakeries, butcher shops, and supply stores. One example was the Moreno Panadería. It had been having trouble lately getting its provisions, and when it did, it was completely robbed of its inventories. Old man Moreno was on the brink of abandoning town with another dozen shopkeepers. The police and soldiers were equally as bad. They would order a meal or a food item and not pay for it. Everybody was literally stealing bolillos from poor Señor Moreno.

Rodolfo passed this latest information on to Ramón. On his next trip into town, Ramón made Señor Moreno an offer he couldn't refuse for his four ovens. Señor Moreno left town with a smile on his face and money in his pocket.

The following week Ramón and Lalo transported the ovens to what once was Lupita's casita. A few days later the ovens were functional. Everyone were ecstatic.

Within a month, everything was running smoothly. Lupe complained to Norberta about having to live and interact with Señora Caraballo who was a vegetable. Conversely, she would rant and rave about how well her son's business was doing.

"What are the sleeping arrangements?" Norberta asked innocently.

"The bed over there is not as nice as Rodolfo's," Lupe let slip. Her face reddened. Norberta pretended not to notice. *¡Ay comadre!*

***

May came and the flowers were bright and beautiful. There was a perfumed scent floating through the air. The wedding of

Ramón and Julia was celebrated at the Caraballo home. Padre Santiago came from town and performed the ceremony. Ramón's workers, neighbors, and the Chou clan were guests. Herculana was the bridesmaid and Lalo was the best man. Rodolfo had ordered a pig to roast for the reception. And the dessert, of course, was chocolate cake with white frosting.

For the next several days, the newlywed couple was besieged with presents from the vendors from the plazita. Candles, embroidered towels, and a beaded necklace. Señora Pacheco even sent a cache of special spices and herbs.

Now Lupe and Julia were working hand and glove in the production of rosquetes. Sales had gone up tenfold. Life was good!

Ramón's workers were content. They had decent jobs. They did not trust the government, especially the mayor and his cronies. While the employees may have been philosophically sympathetic with the revolutionaries, they were not willing to join the revolution. *Why should they starve or get killed? For what?*

Ramón's private fear was that the women in his family were in more danger from El Piojo and the federales than from the revolutionaries.

***

The rest of the year passed quickly. Lupe spent half her time in town. Fortunately, there was no longer any trouble with the revolutionaries.

Ramón, as the new owner of the firewood business, gave Lalo a 30% interest in the business. Lalo was now in charge of procuring new forest lands from which they could increase their firewood production. Their enterprise was expanding.

At the plaza, things had begun to settle down. A few vendors were slowly making their way back into town. The mayor and his cronies were so preoccupied with the revolutionaries that they were failing to collect taxes.

One note of sadness was the day, Noe, Alberto's daily coffee companion, passed away form pancreatic cancer. Alberto sponsored a little gathering one morning with Norberta supplying the hot chocolate and rosquetes.

"Noe was a good friend," Alberto started a little eulogy to the guests "I'm anxious to see what Madero is going to do now that he had come to Mexico."

"Díaz is old and sick!" yelled out Martín Figueroa, a semi-retired barber, who replaced Noe at the daily hot chocolate ritual. "He won't put up much of a fight."

CHAPTER 55 – THE PRODIGAL DAUGHTER

1912

Alberto and his colleagues were proven right. The revolutionaries led by Madero, Orozco, and Pancho Villa had attacked Ciudad Juarez on the Rio Grande. The tiny fort there surrendered on May 21. Madero and an envoy from Díaz signed the Treaty of Ciudad Juarez. Díaz resigned and became exiled in France. Madero became the President of Mexico in the elections of 1911.

For Norberta and her clan, life was seemingly precarious. The revolutionaries left them alone, but they were constantly hounded by "El Piojo" and the mayor who wanted to extort more money from them.

To make matters worse, Señora Caraballo had succumbed to her illness and passed away the day after her birthday. Her breast cancer had metastasized and had spread throughout her body.

Norberta had brought tea of cacao to her on a daily basis. She was only a ten-minute walk away. Señora Caraballo was in total agony during her final days, but the widow still refused to see Señora Pacheco, the curandera.

After Señora Caraballo had departed from this world, her caretaker, Carlota, decided to move back to her native Nayarit home, despite Julia's pleas for her to stay on.

"I'm too old to start with a new family," Carlota had said.

Business for Norberta's clan in the plaza was improving. Herculana and Julia had created a new variation of rosquete. They sold rosquetes dipped in chocolate. They were sinfully delicious! They became an overnight success. Alfredo was ordering two at a time. Julia thought they were certainly good in cold months but might be messy during the summer.

When spring finally arrived, so did the villaristas. Moreno's bakery was closed down, so they had to find other targets. Fortunately, Rodolfo and El Ranchito were off limits to them because the chef provided useful intelligence to Susano Arango's group. Alternatively, the revolutionaries went after gun shops, looking for more ammunition, booteries, and hardware stores. They came in groups of ten or twelve and were quick and efficient. They rode away within five minutes. Most of the time the police were caught flat-footed. The mayor's men seemed to lack the courage and commitment to defend against the intruders.

Ramón was Rodolfo's salvation. He was the only one who could deliver supplies with impunity. It was early afternoon when Ramón dropped off Norberta and Herculana at their casita. He continued on to his "new" home, formerly known as the Caraballo house.

As the mother and daughter approached the doorway, they saw movement within. Something small. It moved about in a slightly off-balanced sway. It looked at the astonished Norberta and Herculana with its big dark brown eyes.

"Mamá?" it seemed to eke out.

Norberta frowned and quickly stomped into the house. Inside there was a girl wearing a dark shawl. She stood in the middle of the room. Actually, she was a young woman.

"Hello, mamá," the young mother voiced.

Norberta looked at her. The young woman had aged five years since she had left and her body had filled out. Norberta's mind seemed frozen but her heart knew better. She rushed forward toward Norberta.

"Oh, Panchita!" Norberta threw her arms around her estranged daughter. "How we have missed you!"

"I'm so sorry, mamá," Tears flowed down Francisca's cheeks. She sniffled. "I was such a stupid girl!"

Herculana joined the family hug.

"Mocosa, how you have grown!" Francisca's voice shook as she addressed her little sister.

All three were sobbing.

"Where's that lazy Julia?" Francisca asked trying to smile.

"Oh! She's with her husband," Herculana spoke up. "Ramón."

Francisca was struck dumb. *What!!!*

"They live really close to here with my nina," added Herculana.

Norberta turned her attention to the child that went and wrapped himself around Francisca's leg. He looked at Norberta and Herculana trying to figure out who they were and why his mother had brought him here.

"What's the baby's name?" Norberta asked.

"Lucero," Francisca answered. "His name is Lucero."

"Well, you and the little man must be hungry." Norberta's maternal instincts took over. "Let's feed you!"

Minutes later they were indulging on beans and tortillas.

"Mi amor, this is your abuelita," Francisca pointed to Norberta. "Mamá, he's one and a half."

The child gave a cute little smile. Norberta probed his mouth with her hand trying to see how many teeth that he had.

"Ten," Francisca said.

Lucero walked over and gave Norberta a piece of his tortilla.

"And this is your tía Herculana, mijo," Francisca grinned and turned directly to her sister. "I can't believe you're an aunt!" Because she had been gone so long, Francisca was the only one who could truly discern how Herculana had developed into a graceful young girl. *Where did that little girl go to?*

They talked. They laughed. They cried. All was good.

"Are you staying?" Norberta said in a serious tone to her daughter.

"If you'll have us," Francisca gave a tearful look.

"Of course, mija," Norberta's eyes started to water, and her heart pounded. "We are family!" *And besides I have a grandbaby!*

"But after what I did and everything."

"That's the past. You are with us now."

Later that night, with both Lucero and Herculana asleep, Norberta scooted closer to Francisca on the mat. "So, what happened?"

Francisca narrated that when she fled, Luis and she went to Guadalajara. He found a job at a dairy. He was popular and went drinking with his buddies almost every night. Then she found out she was pregnant. Luis was ambivalent about his son. Sometimes he was loving and other times he was apathetic. He was not happy, and he blamed Francisca for ruining his life. He met an older woman at a cantina and started seeing her. She had two kids. He spent most nights with her.

One night he came home dead drunk and struck Francisca. She was one step from stabbing him with a kitchen knife after he passed out.

The next day after he left for work, she rushed to pack a few things for her and the baby and left him.

Francisca told her mother that she would never go back to Luis. It had been a tragic mistake. She had thought she was in love with him. Her goal now was to raise Lucero.

"We're family. We stick together," Norberta tried to be upbeat. "Ramón has been wonderful. Now he will have another man around the house."

After a few weeks had passed, everyone settled into a routine. Francisca still knew how to make chocolate, so she was now in charge of that. This coincided with Norberta spending most of her days interacting with Lucero. She would tell him stories or read him a book. The two sometimes took little walks around the pueblito.

In the late afternoons, Francisca would take Lucero over to Lupe's to visit with Julia and Ramón, who spoiled him. Life was good!

At the market, Norberta and Herculana managed the booth, mostly out of habit.

Then one day the cloying smell of Seven Roses aftershave permeated the air. It was followed by the unctuous appearance of Jorge, "El Piojo."

"Good morning, ladies," he gave a slimy smile.

The mother and daughter nodded.

"How I miss the beautiful Señora Lupe. I hear she has a proper suitor at El Ranchito. She deserves to be happy."

The smell of rancid cigar smoke emanated from his clothes.

"And little Julia is married to Ramón. What a lovely pair!"

Norberta wanted to poke his eyes out.

"So, there is only one jewel left," he turned to Herculana. "If she needs anything, I'm sure it can be arranged."

"You'll be dead before that happens!" exclaimed Herculana.

¡Ay Herculana!

CHAPTER 56 – THE BATTLES

1912

In the midsummer of 1912, a small squadron of Mexican soldiers led by Lieutenant Colonel Alfonse De Plessey arrived in Teocaltiche. He was the grandson of a French soldier who had fought at the Battle of Puebla for the Emperor of Mexico, Maximilian I of Hapsburg. De Plessey was injured and remained in Mexico at the conclusion of the war. During his recuperation he met a local Mexican girl and married her. Now his grandson was leading the Mexican federal soldiers.

This military unit had winterized in Guadalajara, but for the last few months were pursuing Pancho Villa all over Mexico. New orders arrived, and thirty or so of De Plessey's soldiers were ordered to protect Teocaltiche. Trenches were dug around the plaza displacing several vendors, benches, and garden areas. Mondragón rifles were mounted behind sandbags at the four corners of the plaza. The square itself remained open but had very few pedestrians.

Once a week the mayor would take a short carriage ride through the plaza illustrating that the city was safe.

Near the end of August, Susano Arango, the brother of Pancho Villa, attacked the plaza. About twenty percent of his men were mowed down by the Mondragón semi-automatic rifles. A dozen horses were killed and several of the animals had to be put down. The dead revolutionaries were buried in a mass unmarked grave. Wounded villaristas who had been captured by the federales were hung outside the city walls.

De Plessey's command had only two wounded casualties.

Norberta was told by Lupe who had been warned by Rodolfo of the planned attack by the rebel forces. Rodolfo as a restauranteur had an informal network of ex-miners, teachers, and agricultural workers who supported Pancho Villa and the Revolution. Government officials often ate at El Ranchito and talked loudly about their plans to defeat the villaristas. The revolutionary intelligence network and Rodolfo traded information and favors.

Norberta and her entourage stopped coming to town on Wednesdays and Fridays to minimize their risk of harm. Ramón and Rodolfo had cautioned them of the dangers of getting caught in the crossfire between the federales and the villaristas.

In any event, Julia preferred not leaving her home to travel into town. On the other hand, Lupe always wanted to go and then stay overnight with Rodolfo.

On the day of De Plessey's victory over the revolutionaries, Norberta was whisking her chocolate with her wooden batidor. *Why don't they get married? I could give her one of my special love potions. Hmm! That backfired on me the last time,* Norberta was pondering.

Señor Abelardo Gutierrez came by the casita to make his milk delivery. On Mondays the amount had increased to five liters. He was not normally a curious man, but he did like to know the tastes and needs of his customers. Goat milk here. Butter there. Queso casero, occasionally. But with Norberta's extended family, he knew that she used a lot of milk for her hot chocolate. Then, coincidentally, he noticed two things. Norberta requiring an extra liter of milk and a little boy running around her casita. Sometimes the young boy was tugging at Norberta's skirt or playing with Herculana.

One day Abelardo saw another young woman sitting next to Herculana. They looked very similar. Abelardo's eyes blinked. He frowned. *What was he seeing?* He left his horse and wagon and approached the two females and the child.

"Good morning!" Abelardo greeted them in a jovial manner.

Herculana politely returned the greeting, but Francisca did not.

"Who's the boy?" he asked in a seemingly innocent tone.

"None of your business!" Francisca reacted quicker than a rattlesnake striking.

The man's head jerked back in surprise and fear.

Norberta heard the commotion and came out running from her casita. "What's happening?" she cried out.

"Is that my grandson? Did they come back?" Abelardo moaned woefully.

"No, WE did not come back!" emphasized Francisca. "Your son abandoned us for some puta!"

"Is this my grandson?" Abelardo plaintively asked again. There were tears forming in his eyes as his voice quivered.

"If Luis doesn't treat him as a son, how can he belong to you?" Francisca continued her angry rant.

"But I need to see my grandchild," he lamented. "I don't have anyone left."

"I'm not raising this child for your benefit. Especially since your son is shameless. He cheated on me and abandoned us. Please leave us alone."

Norberta could feel her daughter's hot anger and Abelardo's pain. She had never blamed Abelardo for his son Luis' abduction of Francisca. Her daughter had made a mistake and was now paying for it.

"Girls, you all go inside the house," Norberta ordered. "I have things to talk to Abelardo about."

A minute later Norberta and Abelardo were walking slowly toward the tree with the contentious hummingbirds.

"Your son took advantage of my daughter," Norberta said gently. "He was much older. She was young and innocent."

"I know, Doña Norberta," he pleaded. "I'm very sorry. It wasn't my fault. Without a mother, I did what I could to raise him. You are right. I didn't do a good job." More tears rolled down his cheeks.

"I know that, Abelardo, but now Francisca has to raise a child by herself," Norberta said in an empathetic tone. "I will help her, of course. She is my daughter."

"Can I see the child?" he begged.

"You have to ask Francisca. This is between her and you."

"What if she says no?"

"I don't know. You'll have to give her reasons to say yes.'

"Like what?"

"For starters, free milk and other things."

An hour later Francisca said that Señor Gutierrez could visit the child on Sunday afternoons but only in her presence. The free milk, cheese, and eggs for Norberta's family clinched the deal for Francisca.

"Señor Gutierrez," Francisca addressed him after the trauma. "His name is Lucero."

***

Days after the revolutionaries' defeat, Susano Arango was
still fuming. While his men, and a few women, had courage
and conviction, they could not defeat a well-trained army that
had semi-automatic weapons.

The news of the revolutionaries' debacle spread like
wildfire throughout the valley. Mayor Don José Sáenz Mejia
commended Commander De Plessey and sent a messenger to
President Madero and the Mexico City newspaper describing
Teocaltiche's victory over the villaristas.

Meanwhile, when Ramón dropped off Lupe at El Ranchito,
he also delivered food items that he had purchased for Rodolfo
from Juan Chou's grocery store.

"How bad was it, Rodolfo?" Ramón inquired of his friend.

"Really bad! It was like there was a fort around the plaza
without the walls. The noise of the gunfire was terrible! And
the smell! God have mercy!"

They discussed more things and the current events. Rodolfo
served Ramón some eggs and bacon. This was a rare treat.
Ramón had spent his whole life around Teocaltiche. He knew
every square inch of the town and then some.

"Rodolfo, I have an idea," Ramón said inhaling his third
tortilla.

Three weeks later two dozen villaristas entered the back of
the church during the 6 o'clock morning mass. The few

parishioners paid them little notice as they made their way through the aisles. They stopped at the large wooden doors at the main entrance of the church. Sixteen of the rebels surreptitiously slipped out the front. The remaining eight stood in front of the doors. There were almost no pedestrians in the plaza at this hour. The federales guarding the plaza and municipal palace were inattentive.

Suddenly, there was a warning shot from one of the soldiers. Gun shots rang out and two of the Mondragón rifles were immobilized.

At the far end of the plaza, another gun fight ensued. The soldiers were not able to quickly reposition the semi-automatic weapons. The rifles had been aiming outwards and now the attack was behind them. At the end of twenty minutes, all the soldiers were either dead or wounded.

The villaristas rushed into the municipal palace where the mayor worked. There was nobody around. Susano Arango knew that from a strategical point of view, their victory meant nothing. However, the taste of revenge was sweet!

Arango's triumph was short-lived. The next day, his men were being called back to assist Pancho Villa in Chihuahua.

The fever of the revolution was rising.

CHAPTER 57 – THE STRANGER

1913

Norberta and Lupe kept short hours at the plazita in the beginning of February. Alberto had informed everyone that Victoriano Huerta had arrested and assassinated President Madero and José María Pino Suárez and had installed himself as the dictator president.

"The people are up in arms," Alberto told his colleagues. "They are destroying everything."

Back at El Pueblito del Valle, Francisca was busy extracting the chocolate disks from their molds. Lucero was banging a small tin cup on the ground garbling some unintelligible words.

She saw movement out of one side of her eyes. A form was approaching. Now it was two forms. A man with a big sombrero on a horse. As the rider got closer, she saw that he was young, sported a scraggly moustache, and wore a black eye patch over his left eye.

When he was within twenty-five feet, he halted the horse.

"Is Doña Norberta at home? Does she still live here?"

Visitors and strangers were few and far between. They were mostly people who needed Norberta's services as a scribe.

But this person was different. He wore a bandolero and had a rifle in his saddle. He must be a villarista, Francisca thought. She casually slipped her knife from her left hand to her right one. Lucero was oblivious to the stranger. She was all alone with this man. *What should she do about her son?*

"She should be home soon," Francisca gave a little smile, trying to buy time until someone came by.

"If you don't mind, I will wait by the tree over there," he tipped his hat. "Is Señora Lupe with her?"

"I don't know," she spoke the truth. Nobody knew where Lupe was these days. She was floating between Ramón's house and Rodolfo's place in the center of town.

He dismounted and walked over to the child and patted its head. Then he sauntered slowly to the tree whistling. Lucero perked up and started walking toward the stranger before Francisca noticed. She started to panic but a minute later the stranger was making Lucero laugh with his whistling.

A little later a supply wagon stopped in front of Norberta's casita. As Norberta was about to get out, everyone saw the stranger as he ran toward them.

"Doña Norberta! How I missed you!" he yelled, throwing his arms around her.

"Pedro! Is it you!? Oh, how we have missed you, too!" Norberta felt tears of joy flowing down her cheeks. "You're a grown man now!"

And the two were jarred by another body. "Pito, you're back!" Herculana had her skinny arms around both of them.

Lupe had gotten out of the wagon and joined the group hug.

Lucero ran over confused. He was curious about the commotion. Francisca picked him up into her arms.

"Mamá, who is this?" Francisca asked without grace.

"He's our friend," Norberta said proudly. "He's like a son."

Then Ramón drew closer and embraced Pedro and whispered something into Pedro's ear. "Thank you. We know what you did."

Two hours later everyone was at Ramón and Julia's house. Pedro was surprised that Ramón and Julia were married but was happy for the couple. Señora Lupe started to tell stories about how they took care of Pedro after he was beat up by Sergeant Montez and Jorge Contreras. She used a few choice words in describing the culprits.

Francisca listened in amazement with Lucero fidgeting on her lap.

Lupe had roasted a chicken which they ate accompanied by beans and rice. Pedro was starving and ate with reckless abandon.

After dinner, everyone sat in a small living room. Pedro explained that after he left El Pueblito del Valle, he traveled east and then north, eventually making it to Arizona. He vaguely knew where his cousin Ricardo was and eventually tracked him down. He did not mention that he was always looking over his shoulder, fearful of being pursued by the police because of Montez's death.

Pedro got a job managing one of his cousin's tabacs in Morenci. He then pulled out a cloth bag that had little boxes in it. He handed one each to Norberta and Lupe. They opened up the packages and found terra cotta cups with the word "Morenci" etched on them. Then he gave Ramón a tiny gift wrapped in paper. It was a twisted copper wire bracelet. Ramón was ecstatic! Then he pulled out a bag of coconut candies that he gave to Norberta's daughters.

"I never heard about you," remarked Francisca with an air of suspicion. "What do you plan to do around here?" *Was she protecting her family or herself? One more mouth to feed?*

"Well, I heard about you," Pedro slapped his leg and his face beamed. "You were the wild one!" The room went silent.

Francisca's jaw dropped. She was speechless. Then they all started laughing.

"But why are you really here?" Francisca persisted to Norberta's dismay. She was not going to be made a fool.

"To support the revolution and to get rid of corrupt government!"

"You think you can really make a difference," pressed Francisca.

"He has already made a difference," the normally reserved Julia spoke up. "He saved my life. That pig Montez was trying to kidnap me."

"Montez was going to take her to a brothel and make her work as a puta," Pedro interjected softly.

There was gasping in the room. Nobody had heard this part of the story before. Norberta felt pangs of guilt for misjudging Pedro. *May God forgive me!*

"There's a whorehouse in town?" Lupe asked incredulously. "I've never heard of it!"

"Owned by the mayor and that slimy dude who bothers you at the plaza," Ramón answered. "And I also heard that Montez and 'El Piojo' beat you up at the mayor's orders," he turned and said to Pedro.

There was a pall of silence engulfing the room.

"Well, like I said," Pedro broke the silence. "I'm here to support the revolution."

An hour later everybody was ready to disperse. Pedro pulled Norberta and Lupe aside and handed them little black cloth pouches. In each were five gold coins.

"This is partial payment for what I owe you." They tried to decline the offer, but he insisted and eventually prevailed.

Afterwards, Ramón insisted that Pedro spend the night. He did. The two talked past midnight. Ramón asked Pedro if he wanted his secret tin back.

"I forgot about," Pedro laughed. "You keep it."

The next morning, after they said their goodbyes, Pedro could be heard whistling as he rode away.

A week later, a group of federales were ambushed while leaving the brothel. The rumors flew about how a one-eyed captain of the villaristas had liberated the girls enslaved at the whore house. The sex slaves were delivered to a nunnery several hours away.

The remainder of the summer was uneventful around Teocaltiche. Most of the fighting was in central Mexico. Pedro was nowhere to be found.

One evening when there was a nice breeze, Norberta and Lupe were reminiscing. Norberta was grateful that her life had been successful in spite of all her tragedies. Her circle of friends was also doing well. "Comadre, what does the future hold for us?"

"It's not important. We just need to count our blessings."

And Norberta did. Life was good!

Señor Gutierrez insisted on paying for the entire christening of Lucero. Ramón and Julia were selected to be the godparents. The reception took place at El Ranchito. Rodolfo served a roasted pig.

Norberta delegated the writing of December holiday cards to Francisca. She wanted her daughter to succeed her as the town escribana and to be self-sufficient.

Ramón and Julia had been given the dairy business by Gutierrez. No one expected his son Luis to ever return.

Herculana took over the bakery operations when Julia announced that she was pregnant. Norberta was beside herself with the news. However, Norberta discussed the situation with Ramón, Julia, and Herculana. They decided to hire two bakers. Ramón later talked to Rodolfo who found two women to fill these positions.

"Mamá, why doesn't my nina get married?" Herculana asked judgmentally. "She's not getting any younger."

¡Ay Herculana!

CHAPTER 58 – PLANNING

April - July 1914

It was early April, a week before Easter, when the baby arrived. Julia and Ramón were the happiest of parents. Norberta and Lupe had their hands full making clothes. The cinnamon-skinned Gabriela was born with a smile.

Everyone made a fuss over her, and she was the princess of the Pérez and Nava clans. Things seemed to be good. Ramón talked about Gabriela's christening. He wanted it done as soon as possible. The revolutionaries had been quiet for a while, and he wanted to take advantage of the peace. The festive event occurred in early June. Francisca was the madrina and Lalo the padrino. Once again Rodolfo cooked a mighty feast of cabrito on skewers with black beans and corn tamales. The guests thoroughly gorged themselves on the delicious fare.

Norberta would wonder if Lupe and Rodolfo were ever going to get married. Everybody was getting older and now she could enjoy her granddaughter. *Should I concoct a special love potion for Lupe? I'm so tempted. But I better not! Last time it ended up bringing Julia and Ramón together.*

***

Norberta's loyal customer, Alberto, was getting long in the tooth but was still rabble rousing in front of her booth as he dipped his sweet rosquete into the hot chocolate. He began exulting the constitutionalists victories. In early June, he exclaimed, "Good riddance to bad rubbish! Huerta has crawled into exile."

Martín, one of his two hot chocolate partners, asked, "Now that Carranza has declared himself president, what is Pancho Villa going to do? He is not very happy with Carranza's closure of the trains to the north."

"He better be worried about the pinche yanquis. They have invaded Vera Cruz!" Mauricio ranted, spilling part of his drink. "They are trying to steal our oil. Between President Carranza and the yanquis, we are screwed!"

"The yanquis just want an excuse to make war and take over our lands!" Alberto railed. "Just like the Spanish-American War."

The short, wiry Candelario interrupted the trio of old geezers. He was a low-level governmental clerk. He stopped in front of Alfredo and Mauricio. "They let him go!" he yelled in a mournful tone.

"Who?" asked Alfredo in bewilderment.

"El Piojo!"

Recently, Jorge "El Piojo" Contreras had been arrested for murder. He had knifed a woman's husband who had caught them in an act of intimacy. The police investigated the situation and determined that since the victim had been stabbed in the back, it was murder. The magistrate agreed and "El Piojo" was sentenced to three years in jail.

However, the mayor interceded and ruled it was self-defense. Jorge Contreras was released and now resided in the mayor's casona.

"Another miscarriage of justice!" screamed Alberto.

Mauricio joined in the debate. He noted that although there were problems with the United States and rumblings of a war in Europe, the Mexican Revolution was still going on.

***

Mayor Don José Sáenz Mejia was smoking a cigar in his office with his police captain, Juan Contreras, and Jorge "El Piojo" Contreras. Juan and Jorge were cousins.

"How did they know about the brothel!" the mayor was fuming with expletives. "Our cash flow has been disrupted."

"And they ambushed our soldiers," bemoaned the police captain. "We don't know how the revolutionaries found out about our place."

El Piojo lit up a cigarette. The smoke mingled with his Seven Roses aftershave. He knew that there were loose lips within the military ranks. The soldiers were young and immature. On the other hand, the revolutionaries were not stupid and had their spies.

"The problem now is not whom to blame," he said with authority. "The problem is how to restart the business."

"Where?" asked the mayor. "What about the old place?"

The police captain and El Piojo rolled their eyes and silently sighed.

"Señor mayor, probably not a good idea," the police captain could on occasion press the mayor who was not known for his intellect. "The revolutionaries would find it without any difficulties."

"But we lost our business!" the mayor vigorously countered. "I'm looking like a damn fool! And weak!"

The trio began to brainstorm on some options and discussed the advantages and disadvantages of each.

"There is an old army barracks east of town," suggested police captain Juan Contreras. "It was abandoned several years ago."

Neither the mayor nor his cousin knew about it. It sounded like a possibility.

"What's it being used for now?" asked his cousin Jorge. "Anything?"

"Nothing much," answered Juan. "Some chronic troublemakers, a few revolutionaries, . . . a few native girls."

El Piojo had a history of kidnapping young girls, especially mestizas. Either by stealth or actual force.

"Speaking of girls," the mayor was back to business, "How many do we need?"

"Probably between eight and ten," El Piojo answered.

"Well, how soon can we get them?" the mayor pressed. "We are losing money every day!"

"Maybe a week or so," Jorge surmised. "Maybe sooner."

"Well, let's do it!" the mayor raised his fist. "Let's get it done!"

"It's not that easy, mayor," Jorge said. "We need to give the men choices. They all don't want pinche mestiza meat. They want chinas, negras, and even güeras."

"They can't have any white girls!" the mayor yelled angrily. "That's un-Christian!"

"We could always arrest more girls," the police captain suggested. "but that is going to be difficult. Their mothers are always around."

"How about raiding a school?" the mayor threw out.

"That's a tricky one, mayor," Jorge answered. "Some of the students may be daughters of your supporters."

The threesome thought and thought. The mayor brought out some tequila. They took shots. "Maybe we should have a party and invite everyone,"

They all laughed.

"That's it," "El Piojo" shouted out. "We need to have a spectacle. A town gathering! Instead of trying to track girls down, they will come to us. Is there a holiday coming up soon?"

"No," the mayor responded, "but I want to show off my new Daimler limousine, Well, almost new. I can show that the revolutionaries are gone and we are all safe."

Everybody liked the idea and thought it could work. Police captain Juan Contreras and his cousin Jorge "El Piojo" Contreras would work out the details. The mayor's minion, Arias, would be in charge of publicity."

"We could give a prize to the prettiest girls!" the mayor was getting excited about this idea.

"What prize?"

"A ride in my car," the mayor was seeing possibilities. "Afterwards, we could grab them!"

"And we could blame the revolutionaries," the police captain suggested.

"Not a good idea," Jorge argued. "We're trying to show that the revolutionaries have gone away."

"Well, dammit!" the mayor was feeling frustrated. "Who are we going to blame?"

"Not important," the police captain jumped in. "We'll just say that our police force will investigate and bring the guilty parties to justice."

There was a silence and then they started to laugh.

CHAPTER 59 – THE PASEO

July 1914

A week after the mayor's meeting with the Contreras cousins., the spectacle was scheduled to take place at the plazita of Teocaltiche. The days leading up to the mayor's event were filled with activity that hadn't be seen in years.

. The news of the mayor's public spectacle that centered around the mayor's car, spread like wildfire throughout Teocaltiche and some of the neighboring pueblos. The people had longed for a diversion. The Mexican Revolution had thrown them into disarray. Some supported the federalists. Others liked the villaristas. However, most of them kept their political opinions to themselves.

***

The days leading up to the mayor's public spectacle were filled with activity that hadn't been seen in years. The news of the parade spread like wildfire throughout Teocaltiche and the neighboring pueblos. The people wanted a diversion. And the mayor was giving them one. The Mexican Revolution had thrown the city into disarray. Some supported the villaristas;

others the federalists. However, most kept their opinions to themselves.

Alberto was the exception. "Does the mayor think we're estupidos?" He dunked his rosquete into his hot chocolate spilling liquid all over the table. "This is all smoke and mirrors. His amigo Diaz is going down!"

Norberta didn't know what to make of it. She talked to Ramón, and they discussed ways to take advantage of the public event. Lupe was only coming to town once a week. Rodolfo understood that she wanted to spend time with her new granddaughter. Likewise, Ramón was also minimizing his travel into town. Ramón was doing well and was supporting his mother. Norberta had to pick up the slack. She didn't want to broach the possibility of not selling churros any longer in favor of more rosquetes.

The unintended consequence of these changes was that Norberta could no longer rely on Ramón carting her goods to the plazita. Ramón didn't want to leave his nina stranded, so he furnished her with a small pack wagon and a horse. He taught Herculana how to drive the cart. She was a fast learner but gave her mother a heart attack when she went too fast.

Norberta and Ramón came up with a plan. He was getting better at developing his business skills. They knew that there

would be at least a hundred vendors and hawkers at the event.
They were ready to make some money.

Their proposal was to sell rosquetes and chocolates at the
parade. They reasoned that people would be hungry or simply
craving something sweet. The scheme was that Ramón and
Herculana would walk around the plazita peddling their treats,
starting from the south end of the plazita. Herculana would go
clockwise; and Ramón would circle counterclockwise. They
would do one circuit and meet up at the south end. They would
then resume their walks after making contact.

On the day of the event, Norberta and Lupe insisted that
Ramón and Herculana spend the night at Rodolfo's downtown
place because it would be too late and dark to return to the
pueblito.

***

The last rays of the sun glistened off the surrounding hills.
A few gun metal gray and pink clouds sat on the sunset. The
scheduled time had arrived, and the band played a few marches
at the gazebo in the park. Then they filed out to be at the head
of the parade. Behind them, twelve well-groomed horses were
pressed in military formation. They acted as the color guard.
Their riders wore shiny light armor with plumed helmets. Each
soldier had a long, curved sword posed in front of him. The

mayor's limousine waited behind them. An additional dozen soldiers were positioned behind the mayor.

The parade began to move. Several members of the onlookers left their places and joined the procession.

"¡Viva, mayor Sáenz!"

"¡Down with Villa!"

The shills were in the audience were trying to stir up the people.

The mayor was in good spirits and wore a big smile. His limousine would stop every once in a while. He would reach out the window and shake everyone's hand. The participants were happy. Ramón and Herculana started to make their rounds. Ramón took about twenty minute to circumnavigate the plazita and return to their southern starting point. Herculana arrived about five minutes later. Each had sold about a third of their goods.

"Herculana, be careful around that pinche dog next to the flower shop," Ramón warned her. "He looks like he's going to bite."

"I will," Herculana nodded.

The second round went a little quicker and resulted in approximately the same amount of sales. The crowd seemed to ebb and flow. The noise level was still high. It was now dark, and the vendors were a little more aggressively trying to sell their goods before the night was over.

Suddenly, there were red, green, and white sparkles in the eastern part of the park. Dogs howled. The fireworks had begun.

Flash! Boom! Flash! Boom! Flash! Boom! Repeated countless times.

Ramón and Herculana met again.

"This is so much fun!" Herculana blurted out to him in passing.

"See you soon!" Ramón shouted out over the din.

Moments later, the mayor's limousine stopped in front of the church. The soldiers disbanded and the band retreated back to the gazebo. The musicians started to play more marches. Then they stopped. A 21-gun salute came from the east side of the plazita. The crowd went wild, jumping up and down,

Ramón was back at the prearranged meeting spot after twenty minutes. He had sold most of the chocolates and rosquetes. What a successful night!

Ten more minutes passed and no sign of Herculana. *Why is she late! I want to go home! She's usually so responsible.*

People started to scatter and go home. *Maybe she ran into a friend?!*

Another fifteen minutes passed. No Herculana. Ramón's feelings went from anger to fear. He couldn't go to El Ranchito to meet up with his mother and Rodolfo without Herculana. How could he explain to them that he had lost Herculana.

Ramón decided to retrace their routes. He started off counterclockwise. He started off slowly, looked to the right and then to the left. Every once in a while, he would see someone he knew.

"Have you seen Herculana?"

The heads always nodded no.

He walked by the gazebo and where the fireworks had occurred. Nothing. The band and the soldiers were gone.

Finally, at the northwest portion of the plazita, he saw a twig basket on the ground. A few rosquetes and pieces of chocolate were being pecked at by black grackles.

Herculana, where are you?

CHAPTER 60 – THE INTRUDER

July 1914

Ramón's first thought was to go to the police, but he knew
how corrupt they were. They were the mayor's lackeys.
Instead, he jogged over to El Ranchito. He was mentally and
physically exhausted. *This is my fault! I failed everyone!* At the
restaurant he ran into Rodolfo who was happily schmoozing
with his customers. Ramón did not see his mom.

He tried to catch Rodolfo's eye; and when he did, he
pointed with his head to the back corner. His mother's novio
excused himself from his guests and slid into the back.

"Herculana is missing!" Ramón uttered nervously.

"What?" Rodolfo was in shock. "Calm down. Tell me what
happened."

Ramón related the whole incident. Tears were rolling down
his cheeks. His voice was breaking. Afterwards, the two men
went next door to Rodolfo's city lodging. There they found
Lupe resting on the bed.

Her son repeated the story to her. "I'm sorry, mamá. It's all
my fault!"

Lupe wrapped her arms around him. "No, mijo, you are not to blame. I know that there have been some evil doings going on."

"What are we going to do?" Ramón was frazzled.

Rodolfo had taken a few candles and was walking out the door. "I'm going to the plazita and look around," he announced.

"Mijo, tomorrow we will do the same," Lupe sighed. "Then we have to tell your madrina."

Rodolfo returned a few hours later with no success.

The next morning, after another futile endeavor, Lupe and Ramón rode over to Norberta's casita.

The bad news was met with cries and anger.

"Who could have done this to my daughter?!" This brought up repressed emotions of the attempted abduction of her other child, Julia.

Everybody stayed home that day.

"Where's Tia Herculana?" asked the toddler, Lucero.

***

Reluctantly, Norberta and Lupe were at their stand the following morning. Ramón had a heavy heart. He felt that he had let everyone down. His wife, Julia, had tried to comfort him but he was despondent.

By the end of the morning, thanks to Lupe blabbing and Alberto pontificating, half of Teocaltiche knew that Herculana was missing.

People stopped by Norberta's stand and gave condolences. A few bought rosquetes and chocolates out of respect and sympathy.

"I'll pray for her safe return."

"She'll be back."

"Maybe she's with a friend."

Norberta nodded and gave a fake smile. *What do these people know? It's not their daughter!*

A few people had even suggested that she should see the priest and asked for guidance. Maybe even purchase a mass. Norberta was religious in her own way. She did not have to go to church to ask for the Virgen's help. *If God is on my side, why is my mija missing in the first place!* Norberta was angry. She was afraid. She was responsible for her family. Now she was paying for her sins.

The day ended the way it started. No good news. Normally, Lupe would stay the night with Rodolfo, but she knew that her comadre needed her emotional support. Rodolfo was supportive of Lupe going home with Norberta.

The night was long. Nobody slept well. Francisca tried to console her mother. Lucero kept her company.

On the following day, Norberta and Lupe were greeted by Rodolfo at their stand. He handed them warm tortillas filled with scrambled eggs and chorizo. They gave him hot chocolate.

This type of visit by Rodolfo was unexpected, especially since he was still running his restaurant.

"Señora Norberta, I may have found a clue as to your daughter's disappearance," Rodolfo whispered.

Norberta made sure that she was out of earshot of Lupe.

"Some of the soldier boys were whooping it up last night at the cantina. They were in good spirits. One of them said that the brothel was opening up again. And that there was new merchandise."

Norberta's face tightened. Her brows knitted. Her veins hardened. *Of course, this all makes sense now! "El Piojo" and the mayor are up to their dirty tricks again!*

"Thank you, Rodolfo," Norberta gently patted his hand. "Do you know where the brothel is?"

"No," he replied. "But one of the soldiers is a regular customer at the restaurant. He loves the chile rellenos."

Norberta frowned. *How can I retrieve Herculana? Ramón would be no match with a soldier. Alberto and his friends are too old.*

"Rodolfo, is Pedro around?" she was reaching. "Is there any way you can get a hold of Pedro?"

"I don't know," Rodolfo was nervous. He didn't want to disappoint her. "I can try. I can put the word out."

How much time do I have? She knew that bastard "El Piojo" was somehow involved. What could she do? Jorge was protected by the mayor and his cousin, the police captain. She knew that talking to "El Piojo" would be worthless. He could not be trusted.

The next few days were hell for Norberta. She bounced between depression and fury.

Alberto was coughing as he dunked his rosquete into this hot chocolate. "Death to Diaz! Down with the federalists! Support the people!" he choked out his words.

His two friends stopped drinking when a dark figure approached Alberto from behind. He put his hands on Alberto's shoulders.

"If you were a younger man, you might be arrested for treason," threatened El Piojo. The smell of his cloying aftershave identified the intruder. "But you're just a crazy old man that no one takes seriously. So, no problem. However, your colleagues could be negatively affected by being associated with a pro-revolutionary supporter."

Alberto was livid, but he dared not say anything.

Norberta had seen the whole thing. She had one hand on a sharp knife. She wanted to make "El Piojo" pay.

"El Piojo" gave a small laugh and went over to Norberta's counter. "A hot chocolate and one of your wonderful rosquetes," he ordered. "I need to satisfy my cravings."

Norberta wanted to throw the hot liquid in his face.

"Where's the little one" he asked seemingly innocent.

Norberta was savvy. She knew he was pushing her, trying to get her to react. She refused to respond. She wasn't going to play his game. She wasn't going to fall into his trap.

After a silent impasse of about a minute, he added, "If you need any assistance, I can make things happen.

Norberta remained mute. He drained his hot chocolate and took one bite of the rosquete before throwing the remainder away.

Lupe firmly held Norberta's arm.

Norberta was rattled all day. When she returned home, she went straight to bed.

She was awakened when someone was shaking her leg.

CHAPTER 61 – FREE

July 1914

"Mamá!" Francisca shouted. "There is someone here to see you!"

"¡Como friega!" Norberta moaned. "It's late! Can't it wait until morning?'

"Señora Norberta, it's me," a strong male voice interrupted.

At first she was confused as to who the speaker was. But a moment later, she exclaimed, "Pedro, my prayers have been answered." She pulled her blanket up to modestly cover up.

"Mija, get us something to drink please," she directed Francisca.

Norberta got up and moved over to sit on an old tree stump that served as a chair. "How have you been?"

Pedro ignored the question. "I heard what happened. Rodolfo told me. I will try to find her. I have a few of my best men with me. We will track down the cabrones and make them pay.!"

***

It was almost eleven thirty when Pedro and his three compatriots rode into town with Ramón. Ramón entered El Ranchito cantina and talked to Rodolfo who was working late.

Five minutes later, Ramón came back out and told Pedro, "he's wearing a black shirt, black pants, and military boots. He's the one that has been shooting off his mouth. Place closes at midnight.

"Thanks, brother, go home now," Pedro squeezed the other's wrist. "You can't be part of this."

Ramón abandoned the group. At a few minutes past midnight, the young soldier, clad all in black, staggered out of the cantina. He began working his way toward the town garrison a few blocks away. He was half-drunk and did not hear Pedro and his men sneak up behind him.

The rifle butt to the knee brought him down in an instant. He didn't even have time to cry out. He was shoved into an abandoned alleyway, a gun pointing at his face.

"Where is the girl? If you tell us everything, you will be able to keep most of your body parts," a heavy voice said.

"I don't know anything," the young soldier with the pencil moustache screamed out.

Pedro nodded to his men who grabbed the soldier from behind and pushed him hard, headfirst into a wall. He felt sorry the young man. The teenager was uneducated and had had to choose among slaving on a finca, starving as a revolutionary, or being conscripted. No good choices. Pedro could have been in this pobrecito's place. But ¡así es la vida! He was not here to argue the politics of war and poverty. He was here to rescue Herculana. He owed Norberta and the family his life. He would do whatever it would take to repay his benefactress.

Slash! A sharp blade came down and sliced off the soldier's baby finger.

The soldier roared in pain. "I don't know anything!"

Pedro then said, "Okay, let's don't waste any more time. Let's do the whole hand."

The soldier squirmed furiously as they grabbed his bloodied hand again. A rifle butt into his solar plexus stopped the struggle.

"Okay! Okay! I'll tell you whatever you want to know!" the soldier was coughing up blood. "Please, just don't hurt me anymore!"

He sobbed and sniffled as he recounted that the police captain had recruited his cavalry unit to lead the mayor' limousine a few days earlier.

"After the parade, we were supposed to grab young girls from the crowd. We would get rewarded if we did. It sounded easy. We were told that nobody would even notice or even care with all the people and noise. It sounded like fun."

"How many did you take?" Pedro asked sternly.

"Three or four. I don't remember."

"Take the hand," Pedro ordered loudly.

"Four! Four! Please don't hurt me!"

Pedro waved off his men.

"Where are they now?"

"We took them to an abandoned army barracks. The police captain runs it."

"Where is it?"

"About three miles from here."

"You're going to take us there."

Minutes later, Pedro, the prisoner, and his men were riding in the dark, out of town.

As they approached an old adobe building on top of the hill, Pedro could make out a lone guardsman outlined by a lantern on the large front wooden gate.

Pedro pointed to the sentry and whispered to his prisoner, "what's his name?"

"I don't know his real name. They call him Chato."

"If you do exactly as I say, you and Chato will live to see another day. If you don't, you're going to suffer in Hell."

Minutes later, the soldier approached the guard.

"¡Oye, Chato! It me. Léon. Don't shoot!"

"¡Oye, pendejo, what are you doing here in the middle of the night? You could have been shot!"

"I am here to save your life," replied León, the injured soldier.

"What?"

Chato felt the cold tip of a gun next to his ear.

"Drop the gun!" a voice commanded.

Chato complied.

"How many of you are there?"

"Three, including me."

"Where are the other two?'

"They should be asleep in the dormitory. Nothing else to do here."

"How many girls are there?"

"Four."

"Where are they?"

"In the jail."

"Have they been touched?"

"No, señor, I promise no!" Chato said in a panic. There was an odor of fear emanating from his body. "No, I swear. Captain Contreras said he would castrate us if we molested the merchandise."

"Who has the key?'

"Not me. Probably Nardo."

"Okay, you lead us to the dormitory. Tell Nardo that we have the place surrounded. If he does anything stupid, you all will die. You have to be very convincing."

The dormitory was easy to access. The other two soldiers were snoring loudly and were easily disarmed.

Five minutes later the four girls were found in a jail cell. The floor had straw and there was a wooden bucket in the corner. The miasma was overwhelming. None of the bedraggled girls had a blanket or warm clothes.

All four soldiers, including Léon and Chato, were handcuffed to the jail cell bars.

The party of eight left the barracks. Each of Pedro's men had a girl seated in front of him. As they approached the city of Teocaltiche, Pedro directed his three men to deliver their three rescued girls to their respective homes. Waiting until morning would not serve any useful purpose. The inconvenience of being awakened in la madrugada would be worth it to the parents.

Pedro detoured toward El Pueblito del Valle.

"I knew that you would rescue me!"

¡Ay, Herculana! Pedro thought.

CHAPTER 62 – REVENGE

July 1914

The pueblito came to life when Pedro delivered Herculana back to her mother and family. Both were smothered in hugs and kisses.

Pedro wanted to leave and rejoin his men, but Norberta wouldn't hear of it. He spent the night in Lupe's casita. He was exhausted and did not wake up until almost ten o'clock. Nobody had gone to work.

Over breakfast, Herculana, ever the storyteller, told of being grabbed at the parade. At least two men had thrown a flour sack over her head and threw her into the back of a wagon. She could hear conversations. She thought that she had recognized the mayor's voice, but for sure she smelled Seven Roses aftershave.

They were taken to the abandoned barracks and put in the jail cell. They were guarded by soldiers who were never around. Herculana met the two sisters and the other girls. They were scared to death.

"I kept them calm and stopped their crying. I knew we were going to be rescued," she kept going on. "I was also trying to teach them the alphabet. To keep their minds off those bad men."

Norberta nodded. She was so grateful for her daughter. She was maturing. She was much more an adult than a fourteen-year-old.

***

Later that afternoon Pedro and Ramón walked out into the woods. Pedro would be staying with him for a few days before he made his next move.

"I heard the police captain was shot in the head as he was leaving the mayor's office this morning! Do you know anything about this?"

"I would say Fate intervened. By the way, Ramón, when you were a boy, you delivered my letters to the mayor's casona, didn't you?" Pedro pivoted around the question.

His friend laughed. "I've done a lot of favors for you."

"Beside the main road, was there another way to get there?" Pedro's tone was serious.

They continued talking until sunset.

For the next few days, Pedro's scouts watched soldiers traveling to and from the mayor's palatial residence. It seemed that the guard was rotated every twenty-four hours from the town's central garrison. A supply wagon always accompanied the troops.

On the fourth day, there was a bright dawn and a dozen soldiers were returning from guard duty at the mayor's place. The men were tired and ready for a period of repose.

Twelve shots were simultaneously fired. Ten soldiers were thrown from their horses. The other two tried to fight back but within seconds they too were dead.

Meanwhile, a mile up the road near the mayor's house, Pedro's men were assembled into three groups.

"Compañero Rios, in exactly thirty minutes you will begin shooting at the entrance of the house and walls. Do not advance. Do not let anyone leave. Understood?"

"Sí, mi capitán!"

"Compañero Alanez, you will stay here at this location. You are our reserve. The signal for reinforcements will be two short coronet blasts. Understood?"

"Sí, mi capitán!"

"The rest of you come with me. May God be with us."

Pedro led a group of villaristas to the west. They were surrounding the mayor's house and moving toward the family cemetery grounds. They did not observe any guards on that side of the property. They slowly advanced, hiding behind headstones, one by one. Pedro could see a small wooden door on the outside wall of the house. His men stopped and waited about fifty feet from the door.

From two hundred yards away, they heard two blasts from the coronet. Gunfire from Rios' men began. Cloudy smoke and the acrid smell of sulphur permeated the air.

There were shouts from the mayor's guard detachment as they tried to form a single line of resistance. They started to return fire. Pedro's advance guard was prepared to break down the door, but it had been left unlocked.

The men rushed in. Four men covered the thick double doors. The other six of Pedro's team laid down and positioned themselves behind the line of the mayoral security. They did not want to get shot by friendly fire.

Pedro raised his gun and shot into the air. "Surrender now and you will live!"

The guardsmen looked behind them. They were in confusion. They ceased firing. Rios' men also stopped firing. The mayor's men were caught in a pincer move and had no hope of surviving the ordeal. Two of them had already been wounded, but nobody was dead yet.

There was dead silence. Finally, a soldier threw down his rifle and raised his hands. This was followed by another and then another until all eight men had yielded. They were separated from their weapons and led to a wall. There were frightened looks in their eyes. They were afraid that they were going to be executed.

Rios' men joined Pedro's men. They took charge of the prisoners.

"Who is in charge?" barked Pedro. His right eye was watering from the gun smoke.

"Corporal Jimenez, at your service!" a diminutive soldier with a pencil moustache, wearing two red chevrons on his sleeve stepped forward.

"Corporal, you will enter the front door and order the guards to drop their weapons and surrender. If they do, they will live." Pedro pointed his pistol at him. *"If they don't, you'll probably die."*

"Yes, sir!" Jimenez saluted as he started to march up to the double doors. Beads of sweat seem to be sprouting on his forehead. He approached and pounded on the brass knockers.

"Give up, men! We have surrendered!" shouted the corporal. "They will let us live. Throw down your weapons!

He was met by a loud silence. His armpits were soaking wet.

"Open up, men! I'm coming in. Don't shoot!"

Still there was not sound from the other side of the doors.

Jimenez turned around and looked at Pedro. He gave out a look of despair. He had the greatest urge to urinate.

Pedro, trying to stifle a cough, motioned him forward with his pistol.

Jimenez tried the front door. It was open. He pushed it free. There was a line of domestic servants lined up in the foyer.

"Come out!" Pedro yelled to the domestics. "Let them through!" he said to the soldiers.

One of his men led them to another section of the outside wall, far from the enemies that had already surrendered.

Jimenez started to move forward in the foyer. Then four soldiers appeared in front of him. He looked at them and they stared back. No one moved. Then the soldiers threw down their arms.

"Any more soldiers inside?" Pedro barked.

The men nodded no.

"Anybody else here?"

Nobody said anything but one of the men pointed upstairs with his right hand,

The guards were led out by some of Pedro's men.

Pedro and the remainder of his men followed the corporal. Four of them conducted a search of the first floor and found no one.

"Clear, capitán!"

Then they all slowly climbed up the stairs. The men systematically went down the long hall, inspecting room by room. Nobody.

Finally, they reached a big wooden door at the end of the hall.

Pedro motioned the corporal to open the door. He obeyed. They found a man with reddish grey hair sporting a moustache, long sideburns, and a goatee sitting casually in an elegant leather chair behind a beautiful black walnut desk. A gold watch fob could be seen on his vest. He looked up at the intruders.

"What is the meaning of this? How dare you ruffians invade my home. You shall pay for this intrusion!"

Pedro advanced with his pistol aimed at the mayor. "Please look outside the window."

The mayor hesitated but finally got up and went over to the window. He could see his soldiers lined up against the wall.

"So, what do you want!" Sáenz screamed irately.

"Well, a few years ago I wanted your daughter, but you took her away from me. I would have treated her well."

"She couldn't be with animal scum like you!"

Pedro approached the mayor. His men were totally absorbed in the drama between this pair. Pedro subconsciously detected a faint sweet smell. He was too absorbed to think about it.

"Then you had your thugs try to kill me! Or at least, beat me," Pedro said in a deliberate tone. "What a coward you are!"

Then, suddenly he felt the stab of molten metal enter the back of his left shoulder. He cried out in excruciating pain. Instinctively, he pulled the trigger and the mayor's face was suddenly splattered with blood. The bullet had entered the mayor's left eye socket.

Pedro's body twisted as he fell to the floor with a knife sticking out of his back. His eyes blinked and he felt like he was going to faint.

Then he saw the face of "El Piojo" staring at him with an evil grin.

"You're going to die!" "El Piojo" stepped forward. Pedro smelled the cloying Seven Roses aftershave. Pedro felt nauseous.

"Painfully!" The traitor Jorge made a motion as if to kick Pedro with his steel-tipped boots. Pedro's men were in shock and did not move.

By his survival instinct, Pedro's body curled to the left and he deflected part of the strike with his right shoulder. At the same time, Pedro automatically kicked out and connected solidly with the groin of "El Piojo." He crumbled to the floor holding his genital area, howling like a hyena.

Pedro turned his head back and spotted his pistol. Braving the agonizing pain, he crawled over and picked it up. Then he lifted himself up and pointed the pistol at "El Piojo."

"One day you will go to hell," Pedro said, gasping for breath as blood dripped out of his mouth. "And today is that day.

Pedro fired six bullets into "El Piojo's" genital area.

"Capitán, shall we bring these two prisoners with us?"

"No, if they are not dead now, they will be in fifteen minutes." The bodies of the mayor and "El Piojo" were soaked in blood.

CHAPTER 63– THE WEDDING

1914

El Pueblito del Valle

The tea of cacao was going down smoothly as Pedro sipped the hot beverage. Francisca was taking care of Pedro on those days when Herculana went to the plaza. Norberta had prepared a special magical chocolate blend for him.

It had been just over six weeks since the death of the mayor. Pedro's injury had put him in critical condition. His men had brought him to their doctor who really was a barber. The stabbing wound had been deep and just missed a major artery. He had lost a lot of blood. He required 34 stitches with thick black thread. Several days later the area around Pedro's left shoulder was red and so was his left arm. An infection had set in. Tequila was rubbed on the tainted area a dozen times a day.

Susano Arango reassembled his troops, and everyone left the Teocaltiche area except Pedro. A message was sent to Rodolfo. who made arrangements to transport Pedro to Lupe's casita in El Pueblito del Valle. The curandera Señora Pacheco was called in. She rubbed her special salve of ground chile peppers, aloe vera, and garlic gloves over the infections. Señora Pacheco chanted over him. Fumes emitted from the wound. The stench was unbearable. After a week the infection subsided. Juan Chou sent over some special Chinese spices and ginger root to clear up some of Pedro's intestinal issues. And now, Norberta had prepared her own magical tea of cacao. As he drank it, his skin color changed from dark to bright red. It became very hot and steamy and then very cold and frosty. Pedro groaned the entire time.

When she was home, Herculana would bring him soup and fresh tortillas.

At the plazita, Norberta's routine remained the same. She and Lupe were still running their business with great success. The increased production was profitable for them both.

Alfredo was still arguing politics with Martin and Mauricio and their new silver-haired paisano Manuel.

"I hear the yanquis are still occupying Veracruz. That pinche yanqui president Wilson is trying to meddle in our government!" warned Alfredo.

"At least we won't be involved with that pinche European war," Mauricio commented. "The German cousin doesn't like his Russian cousin and the English cousin doesn't like the

Russian one either. Family fighting family. Can you believe it? How ignorant is that? That wouldn't happen in Mexico."

"I hear that President Huerta is trying to get military assistance from Germany," Manuel added. "I would settle for just their beer." They all laughed.

"Those pinche yanquis! Why are they interfering in Mexican affairs?" Alfredo restarted the conversation.

Observing their customers, Lupe said to Norberta, "those old farts can talk for hours. And men say that we women are the gossips!"

The two ladies chitchatted for a bit. Then Lupe asked uncharacteristically, "How do you think Pedro is doing?"

"Good," Norberta replies. She thought that her comadre had asked a loaded question.

"I see that Francisca and Herculana have been nursing him back to health. He would be a good addition to our families. Lucero likes him."

¡Oh, Blessed Virgen! Listen to her. She's crazy. She won't get married to Rodolfo who loves her. But instead, she now wants to be a matchmaker! Norberta shook her head in exasperation. She took a deep breath. Actually, it is not a bad idea. Pedro is a decent man, and we all love him.

That night Norberta and her two daughters were making light conversation as they washed and dried the dinner dishes and put away the food.

"Francisca, do you ever think that you will get married?" Norberta probed innocently.

"I don't know, mamá," her oldest daughter looked a little forlorn. "I have Lucero to look after."

Later that night Norberta made a special chocolate-rosemary salve to ease the pain in Pedro's shoulder. She became very pensive. *Well, I promised that I wouldn't make a love potion for Lupe, even though she needs it. I've kept that pledge.*

Norberta subconsciously grabbed her special chocolate ingredients stash. Maybe a little elixir for Francisca would loosen her up a little. She is too young to give up hope. She stirred in the magical spices for the love brew and set it aside on the counter. Norberta was getting tired. But she didn't have to get up early the next day to go to the plaza. *Francisca, I want you to be happy!*

The next morning Norberta called her daughter over. "Herculana, please take this to Pedro!" She handed her daughter a cup of tea of cacao and warm tortillas with beans." The smell was overwhelming. Herculana left to go to the other casita where she found Pedro sitting up.

"How are you feeling, Pito?" she gave him a nice smile as she asked. Herculana showed genuine concern and caring for Pedro. She was no longer a child.

"Better, thanks."

"How's the pain?"

"Almost gone!"

Later that day, Norberta wandered over to see Pedro. It was time for her to rub him down. She pressed her fingers into the salve and rubbed Pedro's left shoulder. He groaned. *There's going to be an ugly scar there.*

Pedro spontaneously asked her to write to his cousin Ricardo and inform him that everything was fine. And that he was considering going back to Arizona in a few months. There was no mention of his injury.

Herculana appeared in the doorway with the magical tea of cacao.

"Mija, finish rubbing the ointment to his shoulder and back. Be gentle." Norberta walked back to her casita. "I have to do something."

Sunset was approaching and Norberta saw her daughter Herculana approaching, whirling and twirling. The girl's skin was turning different colors as sparks exploded from her body. It was almost as if she was levitating. Norberta stepped quickly toward Herculana. Norberta tried to grab her. Herculana's skin burned her hands. Herculana's eyes fluttered. Her mouth opened. Norberta tried to seize her again. *What have I done!* Norberta muttered to herself.

***

Two months later the marriage took place in the home of Ramón and Julia. Ramón was Pedro's best man and his wife, Julia, was the bride's matron of honor.

Norberta was crying. Lupe was holding her tight.

"Comadre, they make such a nice couple," Lupe said.

Norberta nodded.

"More grandchildren for you. More children for us both," Lupe laughed. "They will keep us on our toes or make us old."

Norberta gave a smile. She had done the best that she could with her life.

CHAPTER 64 – PUMPKIN

1915

Something happened to Herculana when she had been assisting in Pedro's recovery from his stab wound. Rubbing his body with salve had stimulated sensual feelings within her. She knew it was natural, but she did not share her sentiments with her mother or sisters.

The third time that she treated Pito she heard him moan. It was more than that. It was a sound from deep within his being. He turned over and gazed into her eyes. It was as though he was seeing her for the first time. He was enchanted by her.

As for Herculana, she realized that she had always been captivated by Pedro's mesmerizing whistling. He had given her life meaning.

What started off as medical treatments soon became an expression of love and passion. They wanted each other. They needed each other.

***

Back at the plazita, Alfredo was having his hot chocolate. "¡Ay diablos! I've lost two more teeth," he complained. "And my hemorrhoids are killing me! They say that Carranza is going to become a provisional president. So much for Pancho Villa!"

"Amigo, you were right about the yanquis leaving Veracruz," Mauricio admitted. "And now the pinches are asking for our help to fight Germany! The United States has changed its attitude toward Mexico. Now that the yanquis have entered the war, they have to make nice with Mexico and focus their resources in Europe. I guess we will send petroleum to England even though, so far, we're neutral.

Martín yelled out, "Maybe we'll be eating sauerkraut tacos soon!" They all laughed.

Norberta and Lupe were rearranging their goods on the counter. A postal carrier came by. He dropped off a very fancy envelope.

Norberta examined the exterior. "It's from them," she remarked excitedly. She had not heard from her daughter in months.

"Well, open it, comadre! Don't keep us waiting! Open it!" Lupe was also growing excited. "What does it say?"

Norberta was anxious.

September 15, 1915
Morenci, Arizona Territories

Dear Mamá,

How are you? I miss you so much! How is my nina Lupe? We are fine, gracias a Dios.

Pedro bought his own tabac from cousin Rico. Business is good. There are lots of families here in Arizona. Lots of Mexicans with wives and kids. We'll be part of them soon.

Pedro now calls me his pumpkin. My panza is huge and so are my chichis.

I am craving your hot chocolate. We finished the bags of cacao beans we brought with us. We made chocolate pieces from them, but they didn't taste as good as yours. But Pedro did plant some beans in the ground. Maybe one day we will have some trees.

Pedro is also getting good at reading and writing.

I'm thinking about becoming a schoolteacher. They could use one for all the kids around here.

I miss my sisters and babies Gabriela and Lucero, too. Please give everyone un abrazo from us.

May the Virgen protect you.

Love you.

Your daughter
Herculana Campos Pérez

p.d. By the way, we are going to name the baby, Rosquete.

Norberta gave a deep sigh.

¡Ay Herculana!

CHAPTER 65 - EPILOGUE

1920

Teocaltiche

Alberto died from the long-term effects of diabetes. Mauricio took over as the city's political town crier. Norberta's hair had turned silver grey. She continued to attend her booth even when Lupe had passed from breast cancer two years prior. The good news was that Lupe and Rodolfo had gotten married four years prior (without the intervention of Norberta's magical chocolate love elixir). Francisca accompanied her mother to the plazita.

Ramón's businesses were very successful. He turned over the firewood business to Lalo when the latter married Francisca. Lucero was joined by two siblings thereafter.

***

"That pinche Huerta is back in power!" Mauricio shouted in his shaky old voice. Carranza's presidential term had ended leading to the start of revolutionary generals running the country. The good news was that the size of the armies was reduced, and reforms were being institutionalized. Huerta even pardoned Pancho Villa (who would later be assassinated),

***

Julia was now running the food and beverage business. She had expanded their product line and her mother had a more-relaxed role to play. But Norberta's stature as the pillar of the pueblo increased with the recent arrivals from the southern parts of Mexico who sought her advice and escribana services.

Norberta was a strong matriarchal leader of her family. Her major worry was about Herculana and Pedro in the United States. Herculana had had four more children: Lupe, Alberta, Rigoberta, and Roberta. She and Pedro had been forced to learn English in Arizona in order to survive. They became quite proficient, and their children were bilingual.

Last year Pedro sold the tabac business and moved the family to Los Angeles for greater opportunities. He found a job managing a warehouse where most of the workers were Mexican. Herculana worked as a part-time librarian.

Life was good! That was until Rosquete thought he could fly and jumped off the roof of their little house. Nothing too serious. Just a broken leg.

¡Ay, Rosquete!

NORBERTA'S LETTERS TO HERCULANA "MARIA"

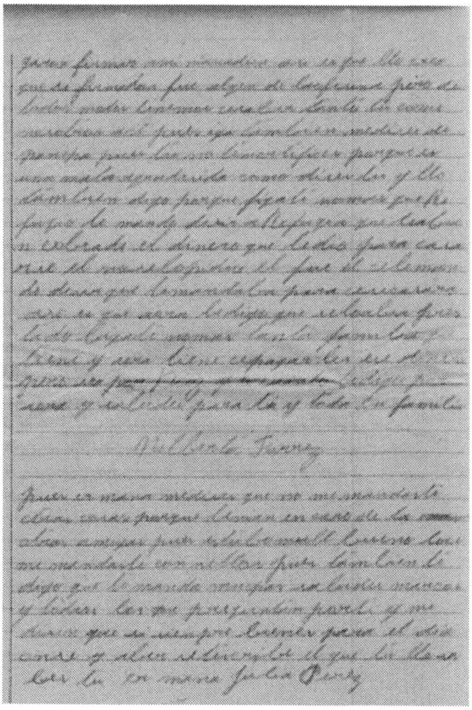

ABOUT THE AUTHOR

Rocky Barilla lives in the San Francisco Bay Area with his wife, Dolores, and the dozens of avian friends who visit their back yard daily, ranging from hummingbirds (one is named Taquito) to red-tailed hawks. The couple spend part of the year in the paradise of Zihuatanejo, Mexico.

He was formally educated at the University of Southern California and Stanford University. He also spent two academic quarters in Vienna, Austria. His passions are 19th century French literary fiction, Mexican history, global traveling, studying foreign languages, ceramic painting, and cooking.

Rocky has been actively involved in human rights, social justice, immigration, and multicultural issues, especially those involving Latinos and other people of color. As a state legislator, he was heavily involved in the Oregon State Sanctuary movement in the 1980's.

His books have won several International Latino Book Awards (ILBA) and Latino Books into Movies Awards.

Rocky's mantras are "Life is Good," "Do Good Deeds," and "Be Grateful."

Made in the USA
Columbia, SC
26 October 2023

24915619R00248